HEAVY VINYL

Y2K-O!

BOOM! BOX™

BOOM! BOX™

HEAVY VINYL: Y2K-O!, March 2020. Published by BOOM! Box,
a division of Boom Entertainment, Inc. Heavy Vinyl is ™ and
© 2020 Scheme Machine Studios, LLC. All rights reserved.
BOOM! Box™ and the BOOM! Box logo are trademarks of Boom
Entertainment, Inc., registered in various countries and
categories. All characters, events and institutions depicted
herein are fictional. Any similarity between the names,
characters, persons, events and/or institutions in this
publication to actual names, characters, and persons whether
living or dead, events, and/or institutions is unintentional
and purely coincidental BOOM! Box does not read or accept
unsolicited submissions of ideas, stories, or artwork.

For information regarding the CPSIA on this printed material,
call: (203) 595-3636 and provide reference #RICH – 879548.

BOOM! Studios, 5670 Wilshire Boulevard, Suite 400,
Los Angeles, CA 90036-5679. Printed in USA. First printing.

ISBN: 978-1-68415-495-1, eISBN: 978-1-64144-653-2

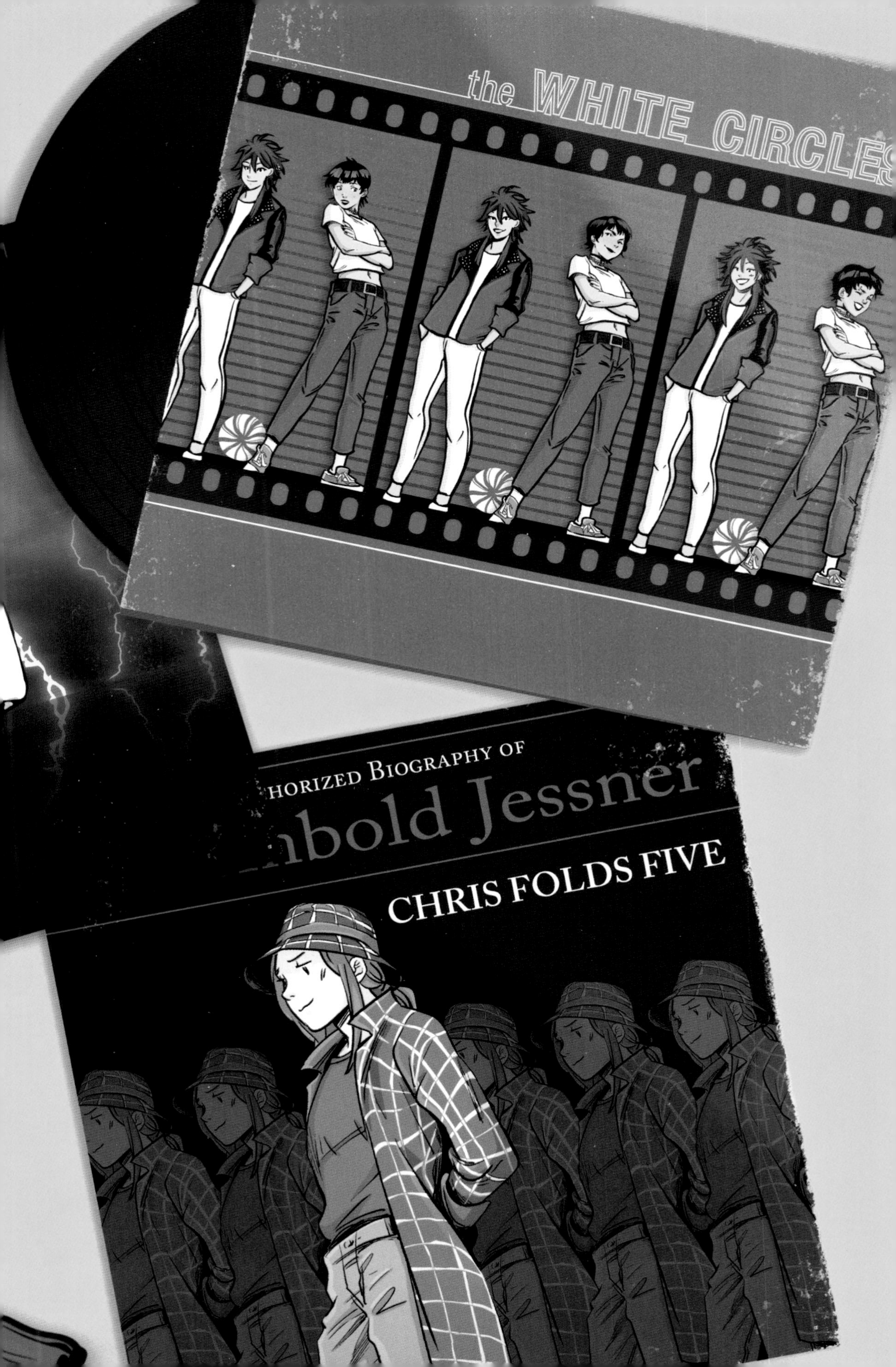
the WHITE CIRCLES
HORIZED BIOGRAPHY OF
nbold Jessner
CHRIS FOLDS FIVE

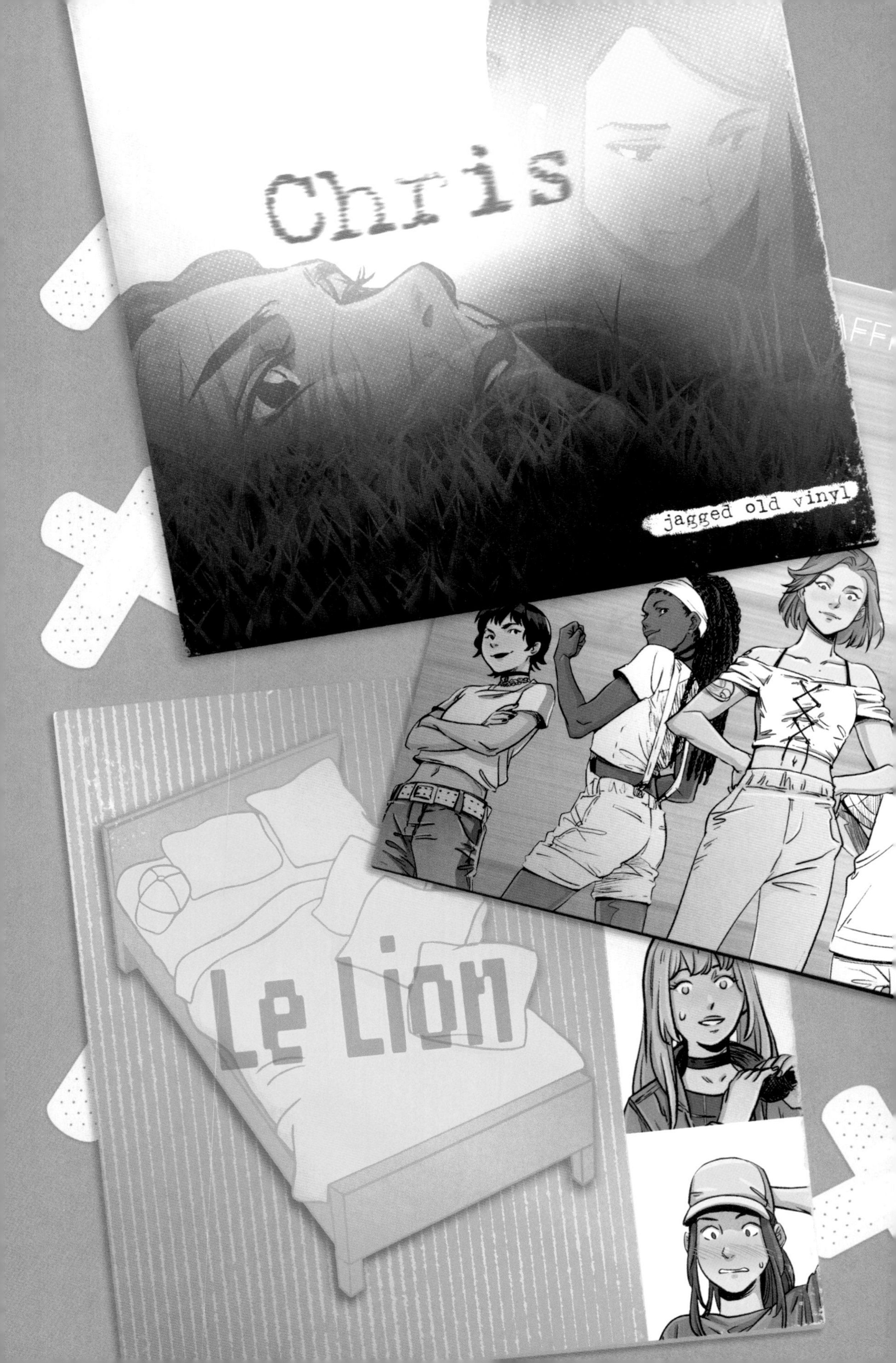
Chris
jagged old vinyl
Le Lion

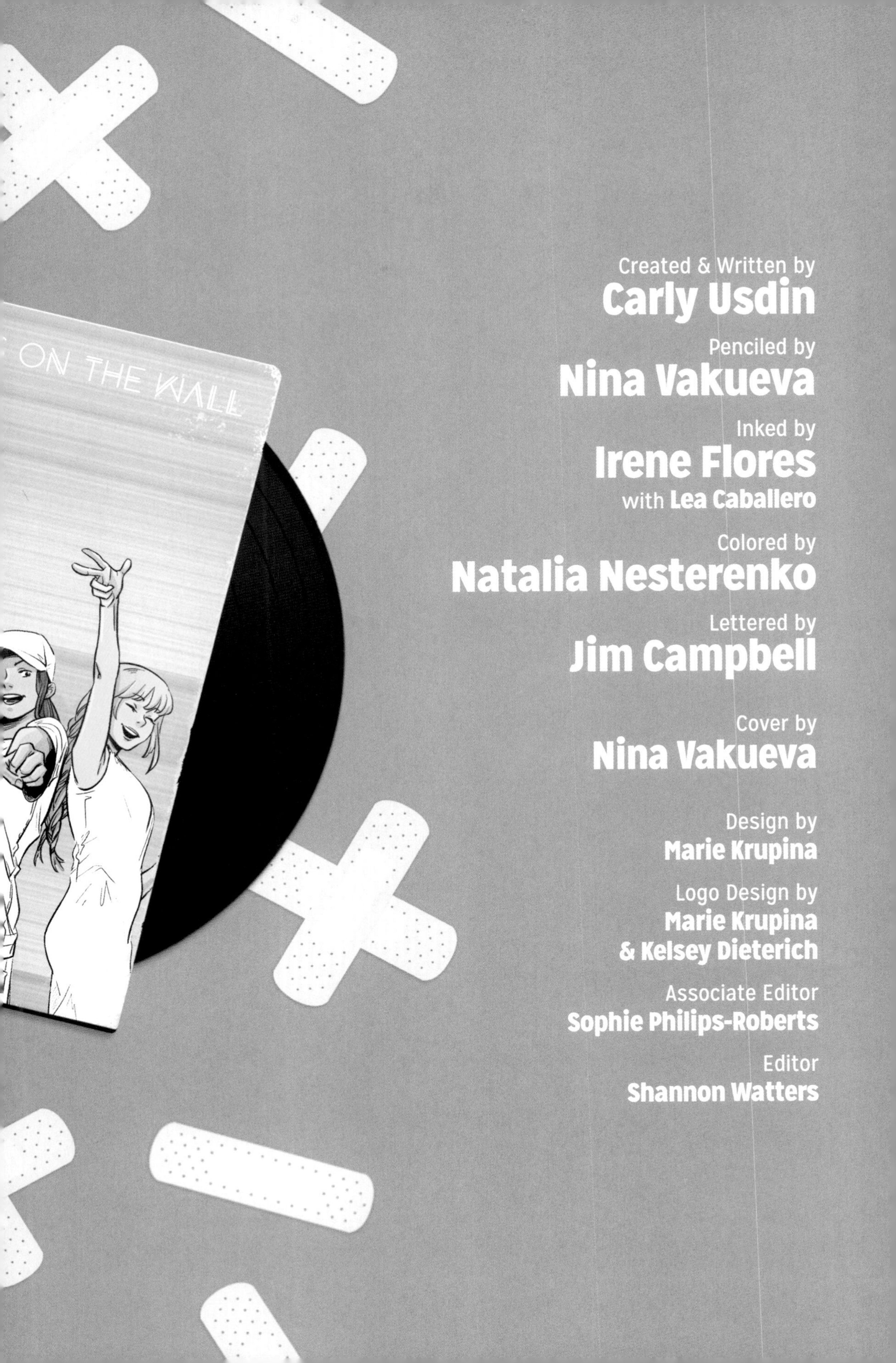
ON THE WALL

Created & Written by
Carly Usdin

Penciled by
Nina Vakueva

Inked by
Irene Flores
with **Lea Caballero**

Colored by
Natalia Nesterenko

Lettered by
Jim Campbell

Cover by
Nina Vakueva

Design by
Marie Krupina

Logo Design by
Marie Krupina
& Kelsey Dieterich

Associate Editor
Sophie Philips-Roberts

Editor
Shannon Watters

STEGOSOUR

CHAPTER FIVE

VOLCANO G...
STEGOSOUR · STE...
SHELL OR HIGH WATER · PHANTOM MAID...
COADY AND THE CREEPIES · TURTLE TOWER
NUMERICAL MERITOCRACY · THE EMPTY NESTS
CHARLOTTE LIGHT AND THE HUMMINGBIRDS
DAHLIA DIAMOND · ELECTRIC MOUSTACHE
CRIMSON TSUNAMI · THE PEANUT BUTTER BOYS
JASPER & JUNE · THE MOD POD · KNIFE BONES
IGUANA PARTY · FULL BLOWN MAYHEM
FEMALE TROUBLES · POISON NEBULA
FRIDAY 7PM

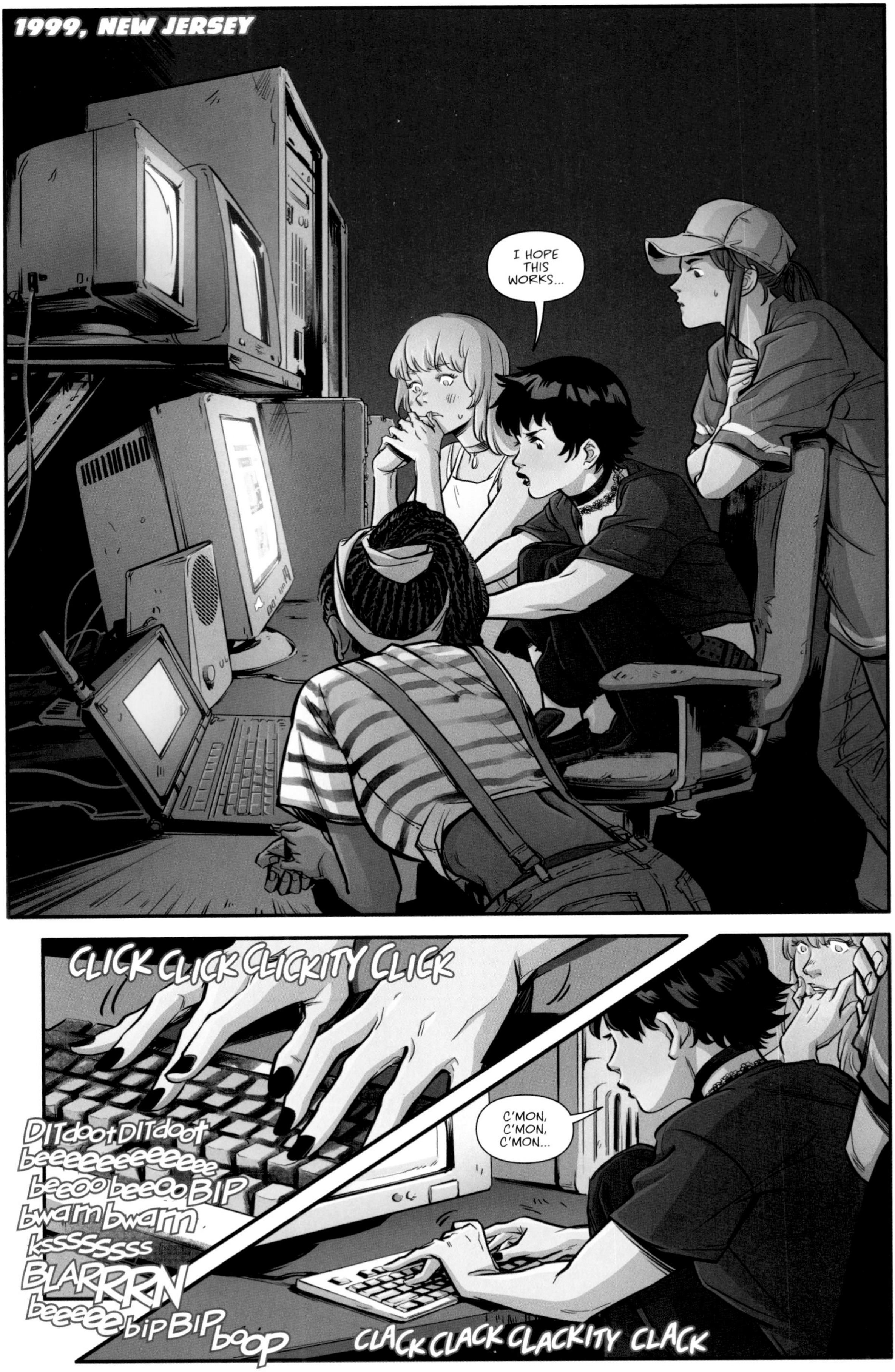
1999, NEW JERSEY
I HOPE THIS WORKS...
CLICK CLICK CLICKITY CLICK
DITdoot DITdoot
beeeeeeeeeeeee
beeoo beeoo BIP
bwarn bwarn
ksssssss
BLARRRN
beeeee bip BIP boop
C'MON, C'MON, C'MON...
CLACK CLACK CLACKITY CLACK

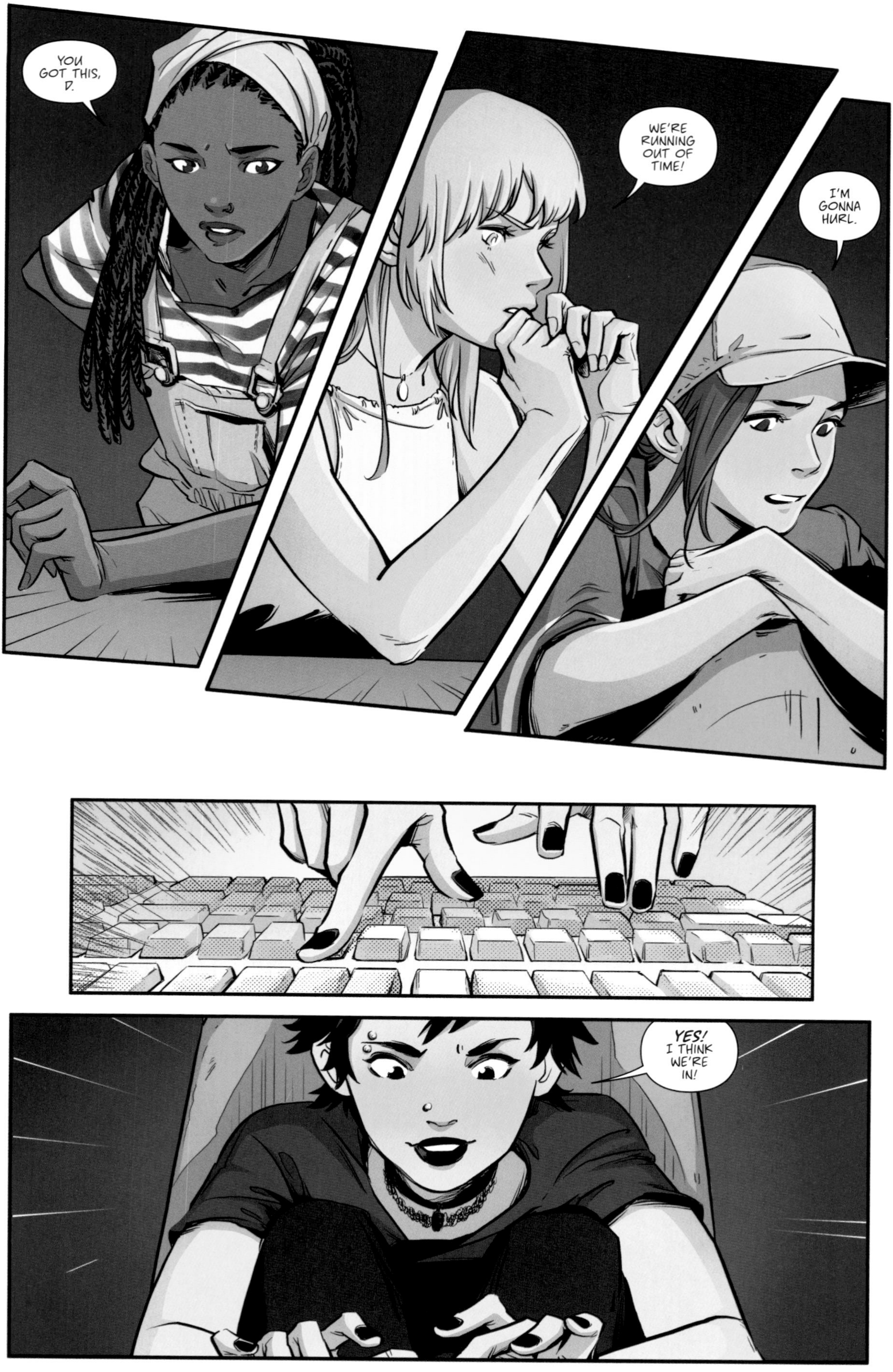
YOU GOT THIS, D.
WE'RE RUNNING OUT OF TIME!
I'M GONNA HURL.
YES! I THINK WE'RE IN!

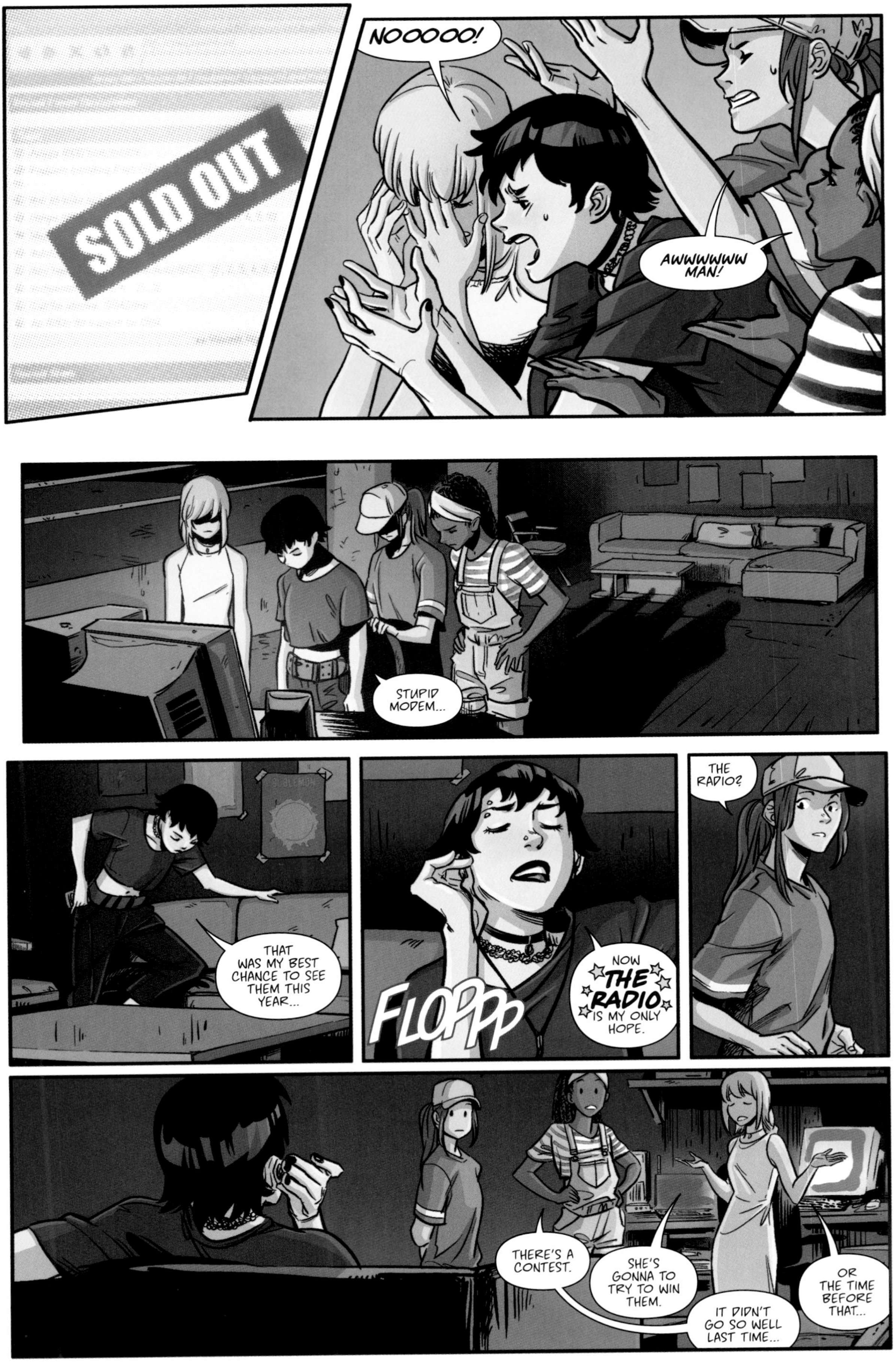
SOLD OUT
NOOOOO!
AWWWWWW MAN!
STUPID MODEM...
THAT WAS MY BEST CHANCE TO SEE THEM THIS YEAR...
FLOPPp
NOW THE RADIO IS MY ONLY HOPE.
THE RADIO?
THERE'S A CONTEST.
SHE'S GONNA TO TRY TO WIN THEM.
IT DIDN'T GO SO WELL LAST TIME...
OR THE TIME BEFORE THAT...

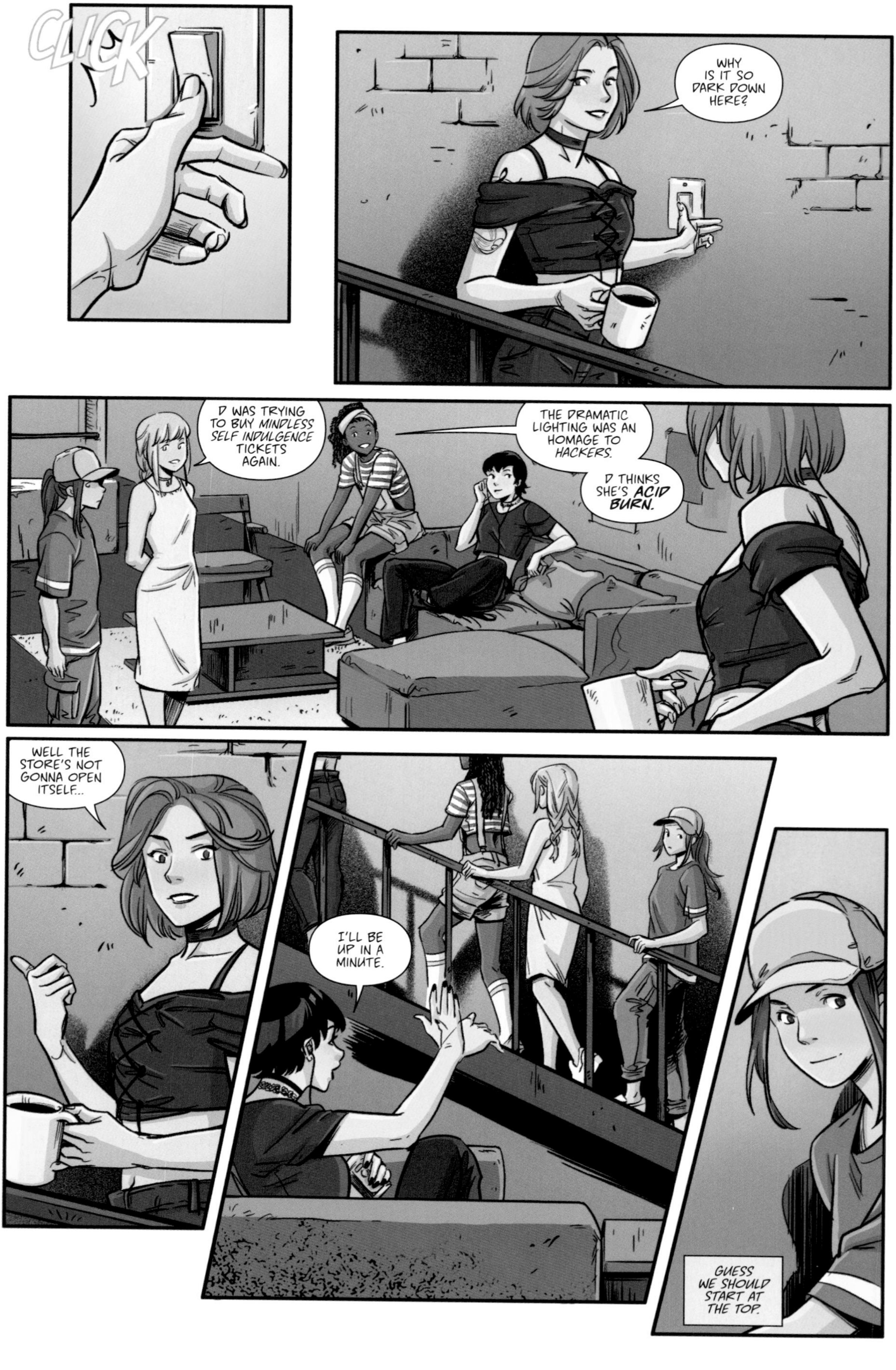
CLICK
WHY IS IT SO DARK DOWN HERE?
D WAS TRYING TO BUY MINDLESS SELF INDULGENCE TICKETS AGAIN.
THE DRAMATIC LIGHTING WAS AN HOMAGE TO HACKERS.
D THINKS SHE'S ACID BURN.
WELL THE STORE'S NOT GONNA OPEN ITSELF...
I'LL BE UP IN A MINUTE.
GUESS WE SHOULD START AT THE TOP.

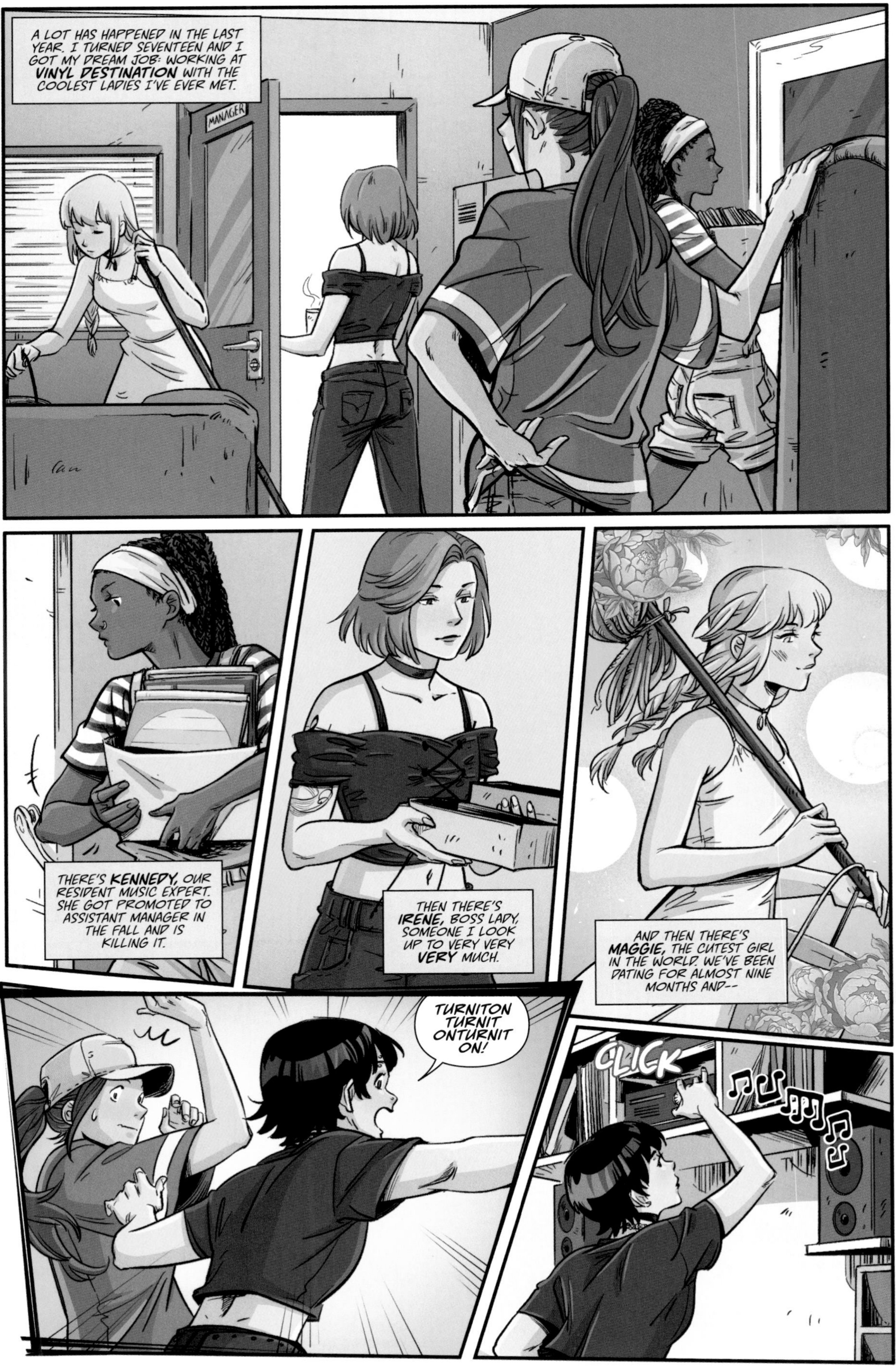
A LOT HAS HAPPENED IN THE LAST YEAR. I TURNED SEVENTEEN AND I GOT MY DREAM JOB: WORKING AT **VINYL DESTINATION** WITH THE COOLEST LADIES I'VE EVER MET.
MANAGER
THERE'S **KENNEDY,** OUR RESIDENT MUSIC EXPERT. SHE GOT PROMOTED TO ASSISTANT MANAGER IN THE FALL AND IS KILLING IT.
THEN THERE'S **IRENE,** BOSS LADY, SOMEONE I LOOK UP TO VERY VERY **VERY** MUCH.
AND THEN THERE'S **MAGGIE,** THE CUTEST GIRL IN THE WORLD. WE'VE BEEN DATING FOR ALMOST NINE MONTHS AND--
TURNITON TURNIT ONTURNIT ON!
CLICK

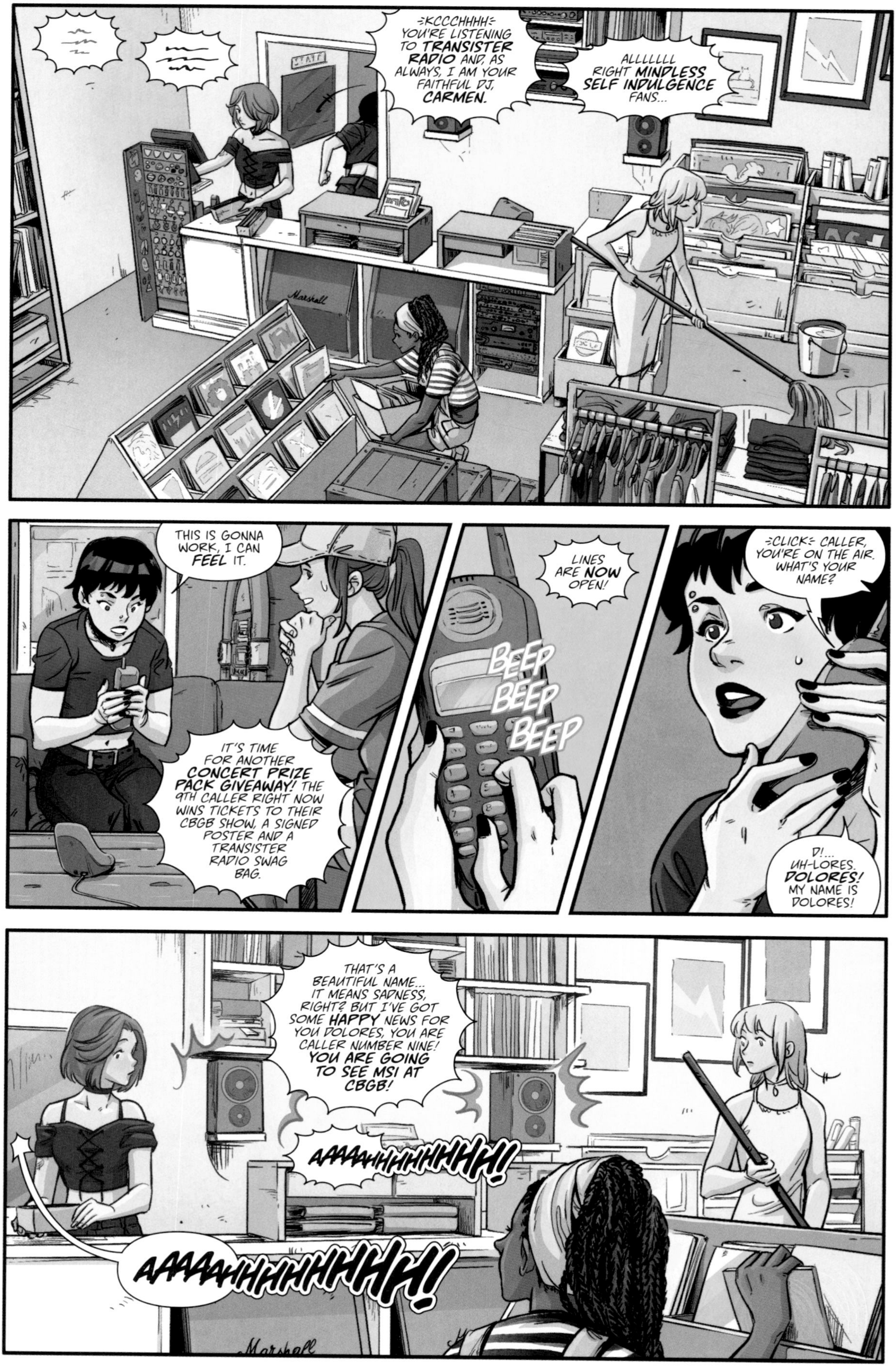

=KCCCHHHH= YOU'RE LISTENING TO TRANSISTER RADIO AND, AS ALWAYS, I AM YOUR FAITHFUL DJ, CARMEN.
ALLLLLLL RIGHT MINDLESS SELF INDULGENCE FANS...
THIS IS GONNA WORK, I CAN FEEL IT.
IT'S TIME FOR ANOTHER CONCERT PRIZE PACK GIVEAWAY! THE 9TH CALLER RIGHT NOW WINS TICKETS TO THEIR CBGB SHOW, A SIGNED POSTER AND A TRANSISTER RADIO SWAG BAG.
LINES ARE NOW OPEN!
BEEP BEEP BEEP
=CLICK= CALLER, YOU'RE ON THE AIR. WHAT'S YOUR NAME?
D!... UH-LORES. DOLORES! MY NAME IS DOLORES!
THAT'S A BEAUTIFUL NAME... IT MEANS SADNESS, RIGHT? BUT I'VE GOT SOME HAPPY NEWS FOR YOU DOLORES, YOU ARE CALLER NUMBER NINE! YOU ARE GOING TO SEE MSI AT CBGB!
AAAAAHHHHHHHHH!
AAAAAHHHHHHHHHH!

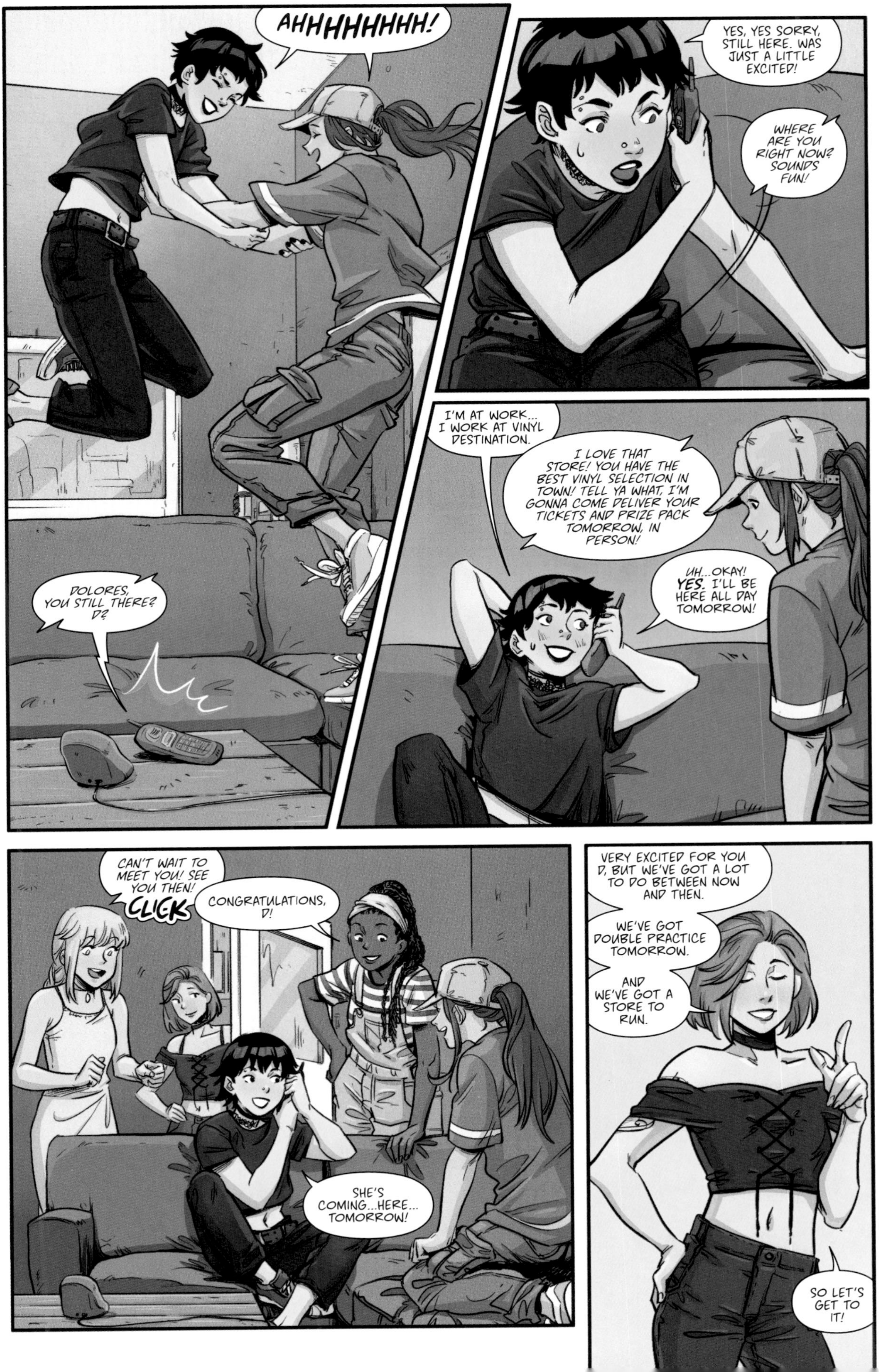
AHHHHHHHH!
DOLORES, YOU STILL THERE? D?
YES, YES SORRY, STILL HERE. WAS JUST A LITTLE EXCITED!
WHERE ARE YOU RIGHT NOW? SOUNDS FUN!
I'M AT WORK... I WORK AT VINYL DESTINATION.
I LOVE THAT STORE! YOU HAVE THE BEST VINYL SELECTION IN TOWN! TELL YA WHAT, I'M GONNA COME DELIVER YOUR TICKETS AND PRIZE PACK TOMORROW, IN PERSON!
UH...OKAY! YES. I'LL BE HERE ALL DAY TOMORROW!
CAN'T WAIT TO MEET YOU! SEE YOU THEN!
CLICK
CONGRATULATIONS, D!
SHE'S COMING...HERE... TOMORROW!
VERY EXCITED FOR YOU D, BUT WE'VE GOT A LOT TO DO BETWEEN NOW AND THEN.
WE'VE GOT DOUBLE PRACTICE TOMORROW.
AND WE'VE GOT A STORE TO RUN.
SO LET'S GET TO IT!

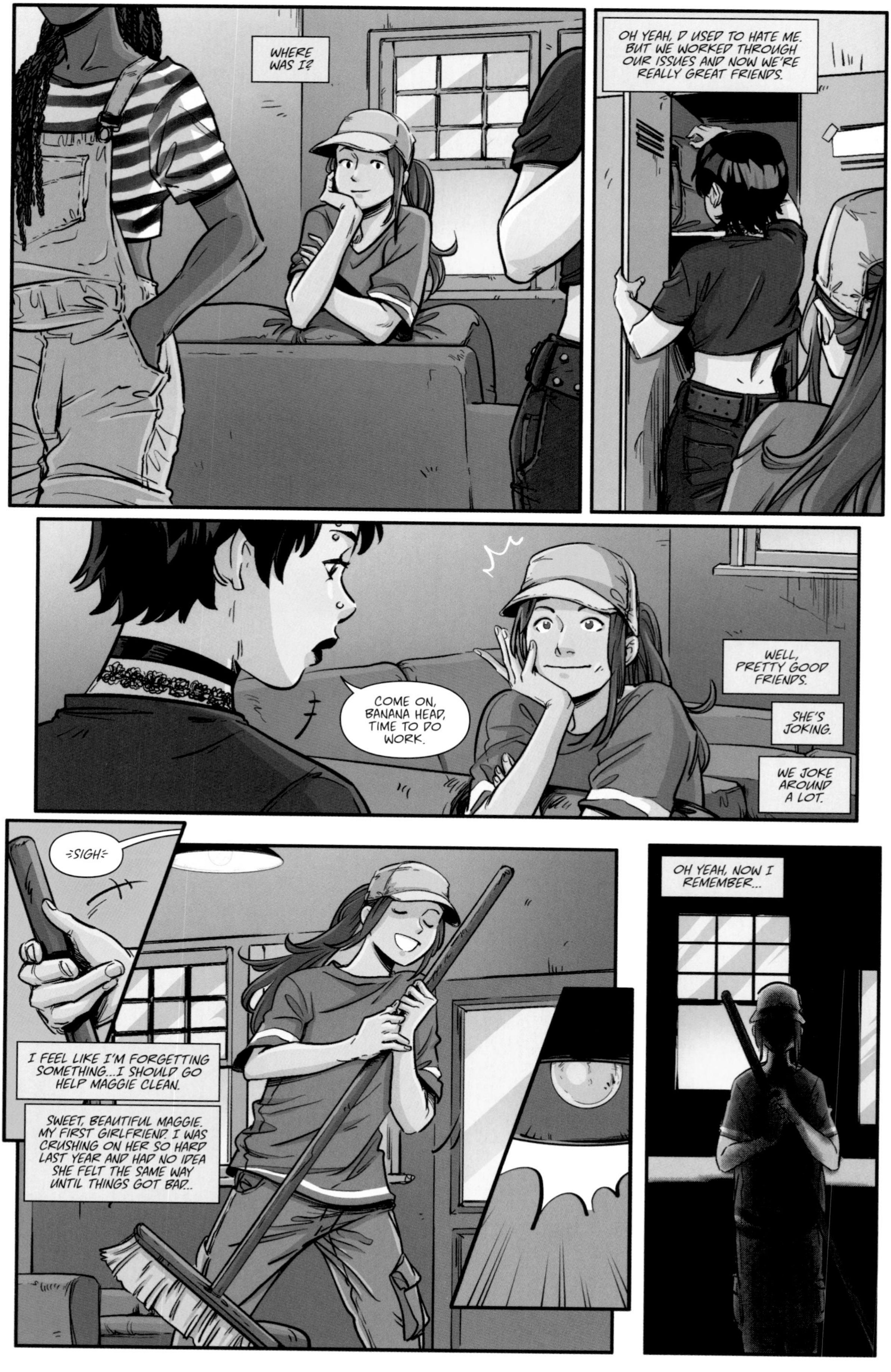
WHERE WAS I?
OH YEAH, D USED TO HATE ME. BUT WE WORKED THROUGH OUR ISSUES AND NOW WE'RE REALLY GREAT FRIENDS.
COME ON, BANANA HEAD, TIME TO DO WORK.
WELL, PRETTY GOOD FRIENDS.
SHE'S JOKING.
WE JOKE AROUND A LOT.
=SIGH=
I FEEL LIKE I'M FORGETTING SOMETHING...I SHOULD GO HELP MAGGIE CLEAN.
SWEET, BEAUTIFUL MAGGIE. MY FIRST GIRLFRIEND. I WAS CRUSHING ON HER SO HARD LAST YEAR AND HAD NO IDEA SHE FELT THE SAME WAY UNTIL THINGS GOT BAD...
OH YEAH, NOW I REMEMBER...

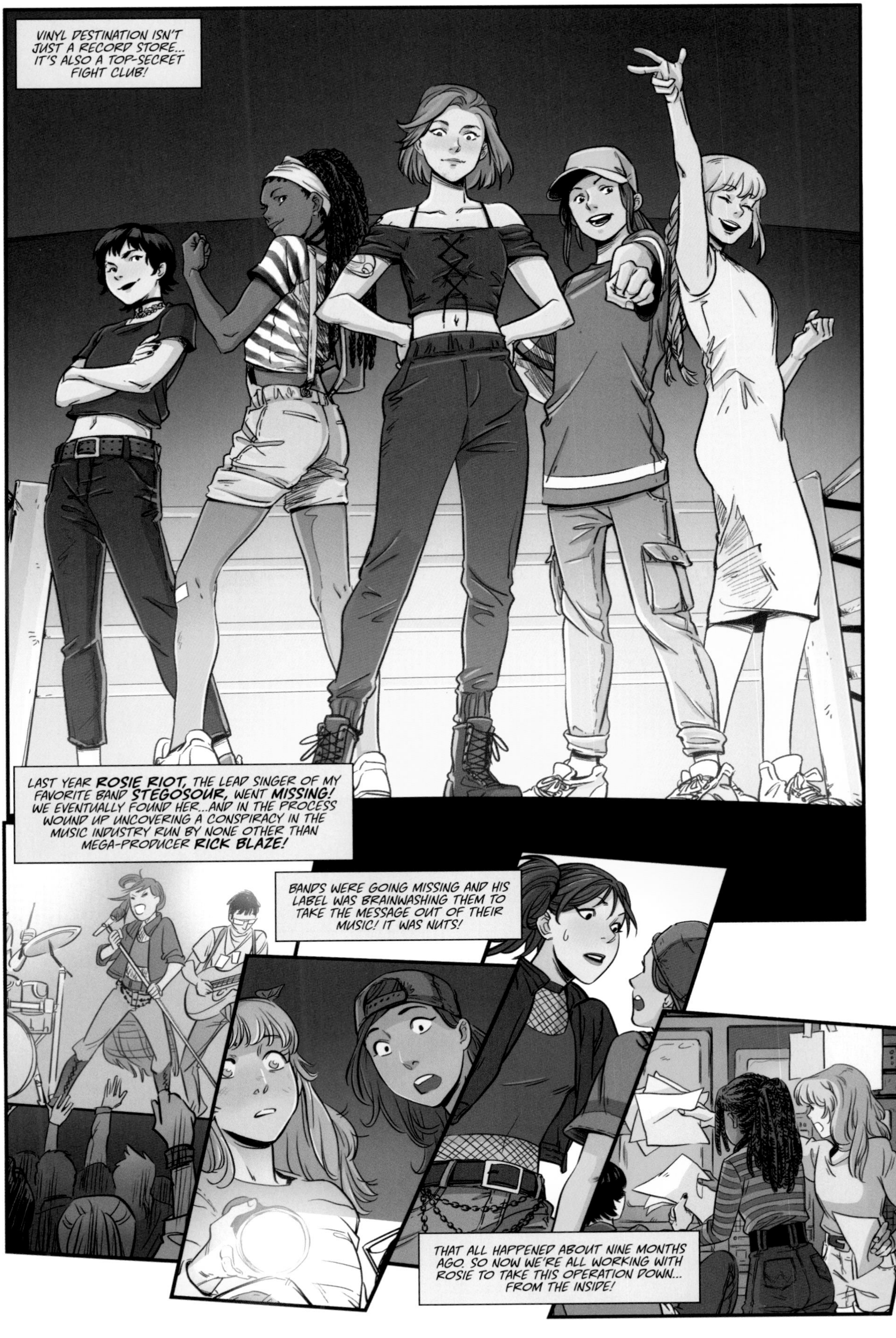
VINYL DESTINATION ISN'T JUST A RECORD STORE... IT'S ALSO A TOP-SECRET FIGHT CLUB!
LAST YEAR ROSIE RIOT, THE LEAD SINGER OF MY FAVORITE BAND STEGOSOUR, WENT MISSING! WE EVENTUALLY FOUND HER...AND IN THE PROCESS WOUND UP UNCOVERING A CONSPIRACY IN THE MUSIC INDUSTRY RUN BY NONE OTHER THAN MEGA-PRODUCER RICK BLAZE!
BANDS WERE GOING MISSING AND HIS LABEL WAS BRAINWASHING THEM TO TAKE THE MESSAGE OUT OF THEIR MUSIC! IT WAS NUTS!
THAT ALL HAPPENED ABOUT NINE MONTHS AGO. SO NOW WE'RE ALL WORKING WITH ROSIE TO TAKE THIS OPERATION DOWN... FROM THE INSIDE!

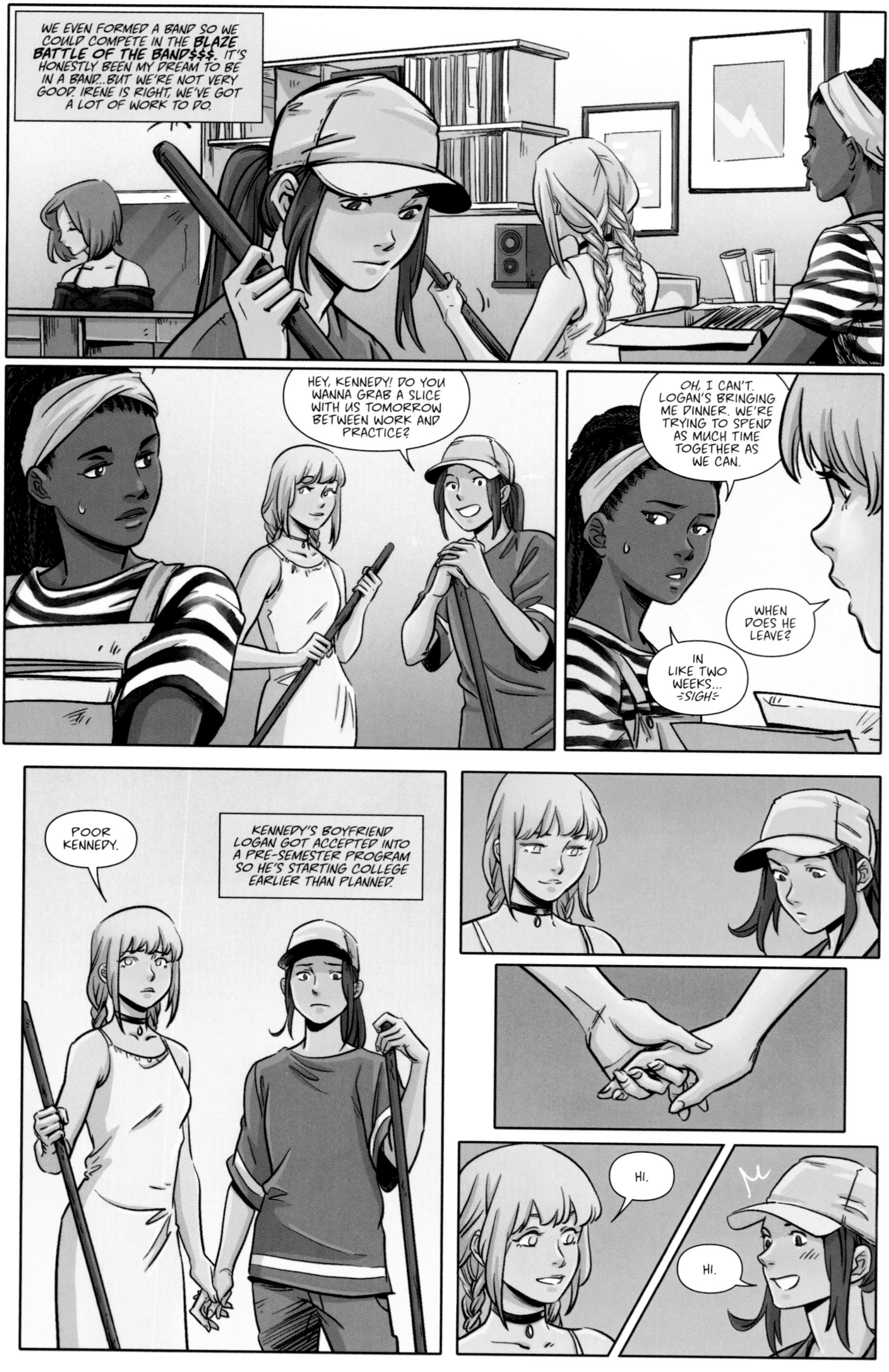
WE EVEN FORMED A BAND SO WE COULD COMPETE IN THE BLAZE BATTLE OF THE BAND$$$. IT'S HONESTLY BEEN MY DREAM TO BE IN A BAND...BUT WE'RE NOT VERY GOOD. IRENE IS RIGHT, WE'VE GOT A LOT OF WORK TO DO.
HEY, KENNEDY! DO YOU WANNA GRAB A SLICE WITH US TOMORROW BETWEEN WORK AND PRACTICE?
OH, I CAN'T. LOGAN'S BRINGING ME DINNER. WE'RE TRYING TO SPEND AS MUCH TIME TOGETHER AS WE CAN.
WHEN DOES HE LEAVE?
IN LIKE TWO WEEKS... =SIGH=
POOR KENNEDY.
KENNEDY'S BOYFRIEND LOGAN GOT ACCEPTED INTO A PRE-SEMESTER PROGRAM SO HE'S STARTING COLLEGE EARLIER THAN PLANNED.
HI.
HI.

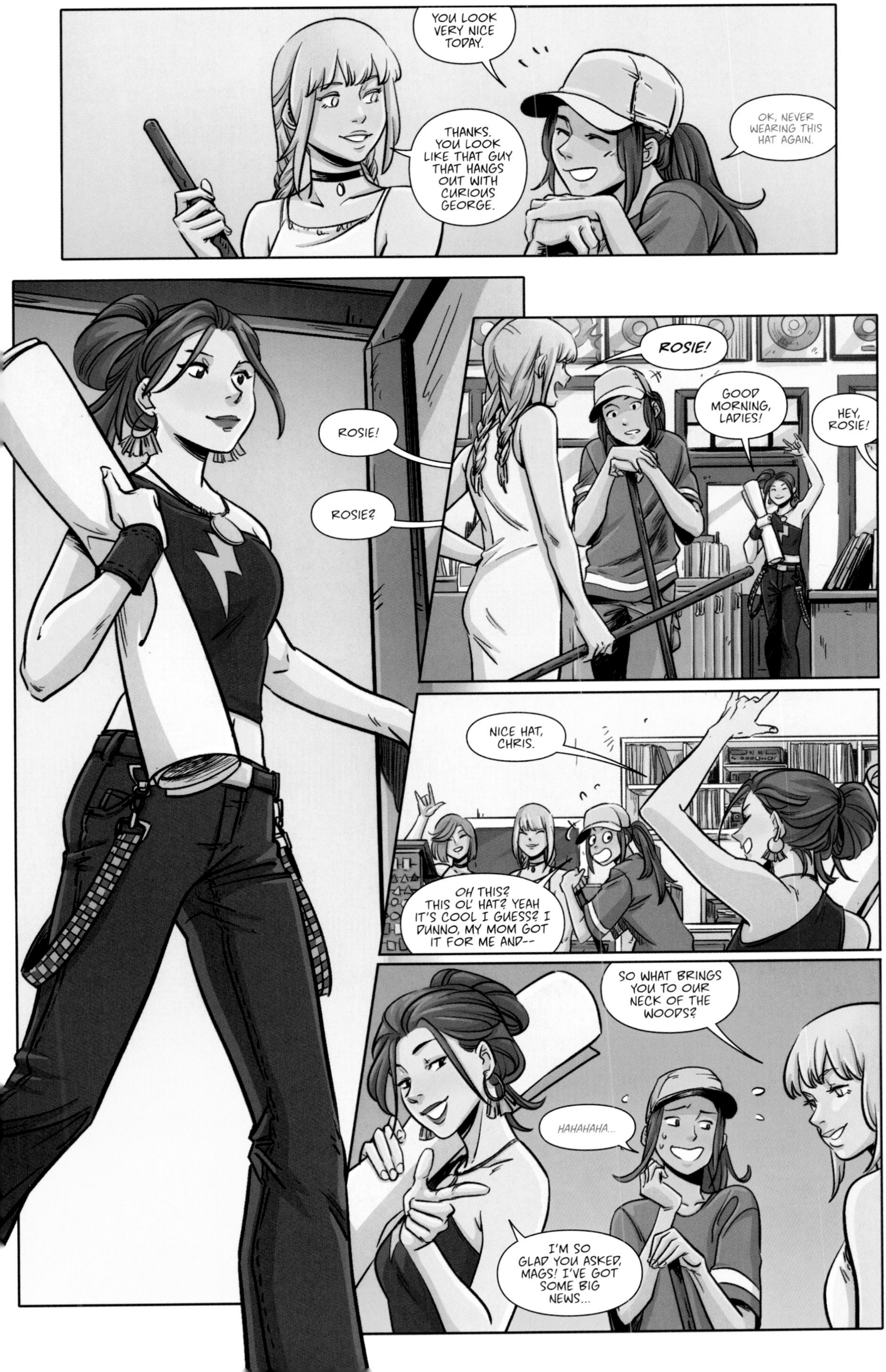
YOU LOOK VERY NICE TODAY.
THANKS. YOU LOOK LIKE THAT GUY THAT HANGS OUT WITH CURIOUS GEORGE.
OK, NEVER WEARING THIS HAT AGAIN.
ROSIE!
ROSIE!
ROSIE?
GOOD MORNING, LADIES!
HEY, ROSIE!
NICE HAT, CHRIS.
OH THIS? THIS OL' HAT? YEAH IT'S COOL I GUESS? I DUNNO, MY MOM GOT IT FOR ME AND--
SO WHAT BRINGS YOU TO OUR NECK OF THE WOODS?
HAHAHAHA...
I'M SO GLAD YOU ASKED, MAGS! I'VE GOT SOME BIG NEWS...

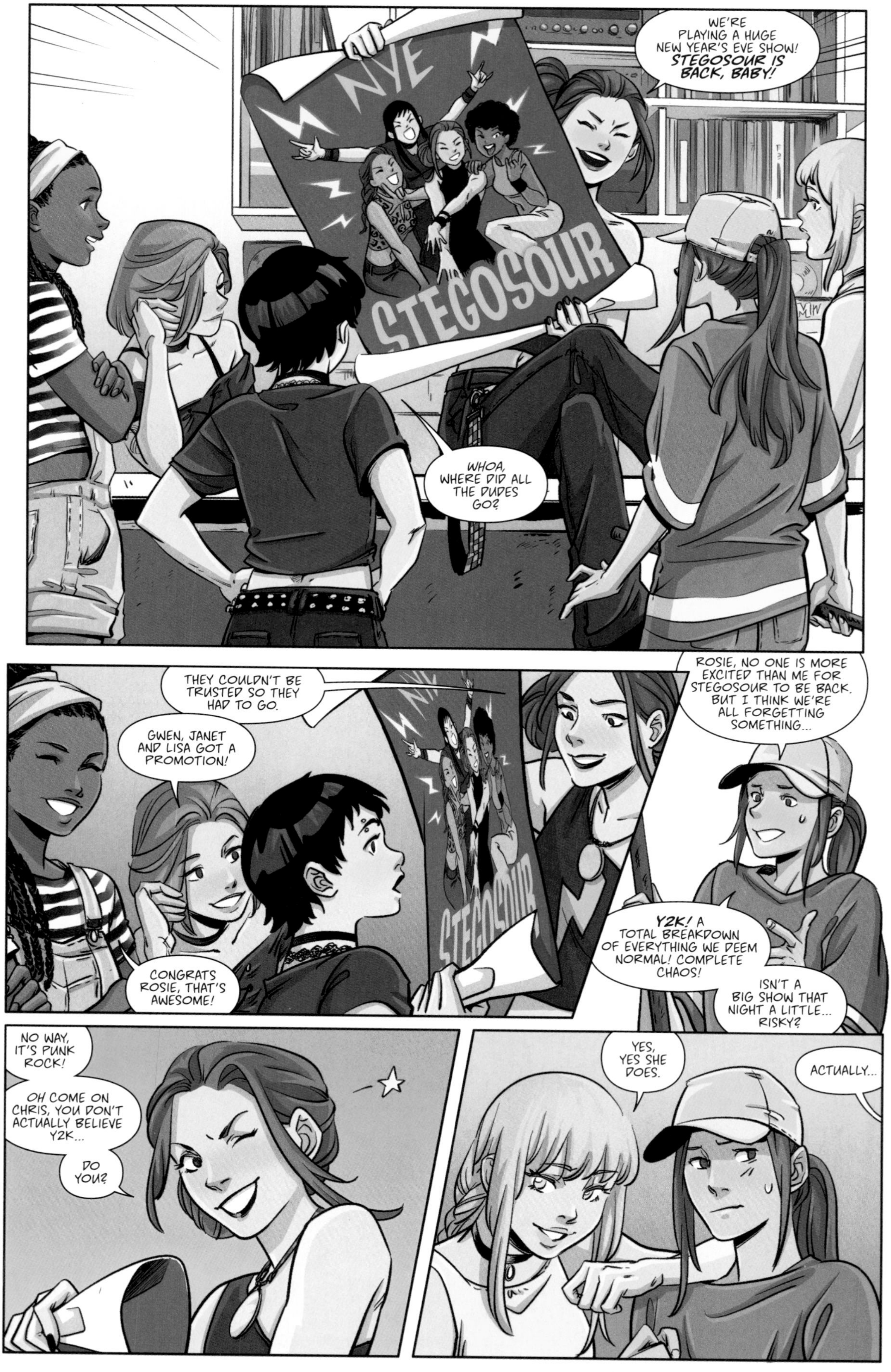

WE'RE PLAYING A HUGE NEW YEAR'S EVE SHOW! ***STEGOSOUR IS BACK, BABY!***
NYE
STEGOSOUR
WHOA, WHERE DID ALL THE DUDES GO?
THEY COULDN'T BE TRUSTED SO THEY HAD TO GO.
GWEN, JANET AND LISA GOT A PROMOTION!
CONGRATS ROSIE, THAT'S AWESOME!
ROSIE, NO ONE IS MORE EXCITED THAN ME FOR STEGOSOUR TO BE BACK. BUT I THINK WE'RE ALL FORGETTING SOMETHING...
Y2K! A TOTAL BREAKDOWN OF EVERYTHING WE DEEM NORMAL! COMPLETE CHAOS!
ISN'T A BIG SHOW THAT NIGHT A LITTLE... RISKY?
NO WAY, IT'S PUNK ROCK!
OH COME ON CHRIS, YOU DON'T ACTUALLY BELIEVE Y2K...
DO YOU?
YES, YES SHE DOES.
ACTUALLY...

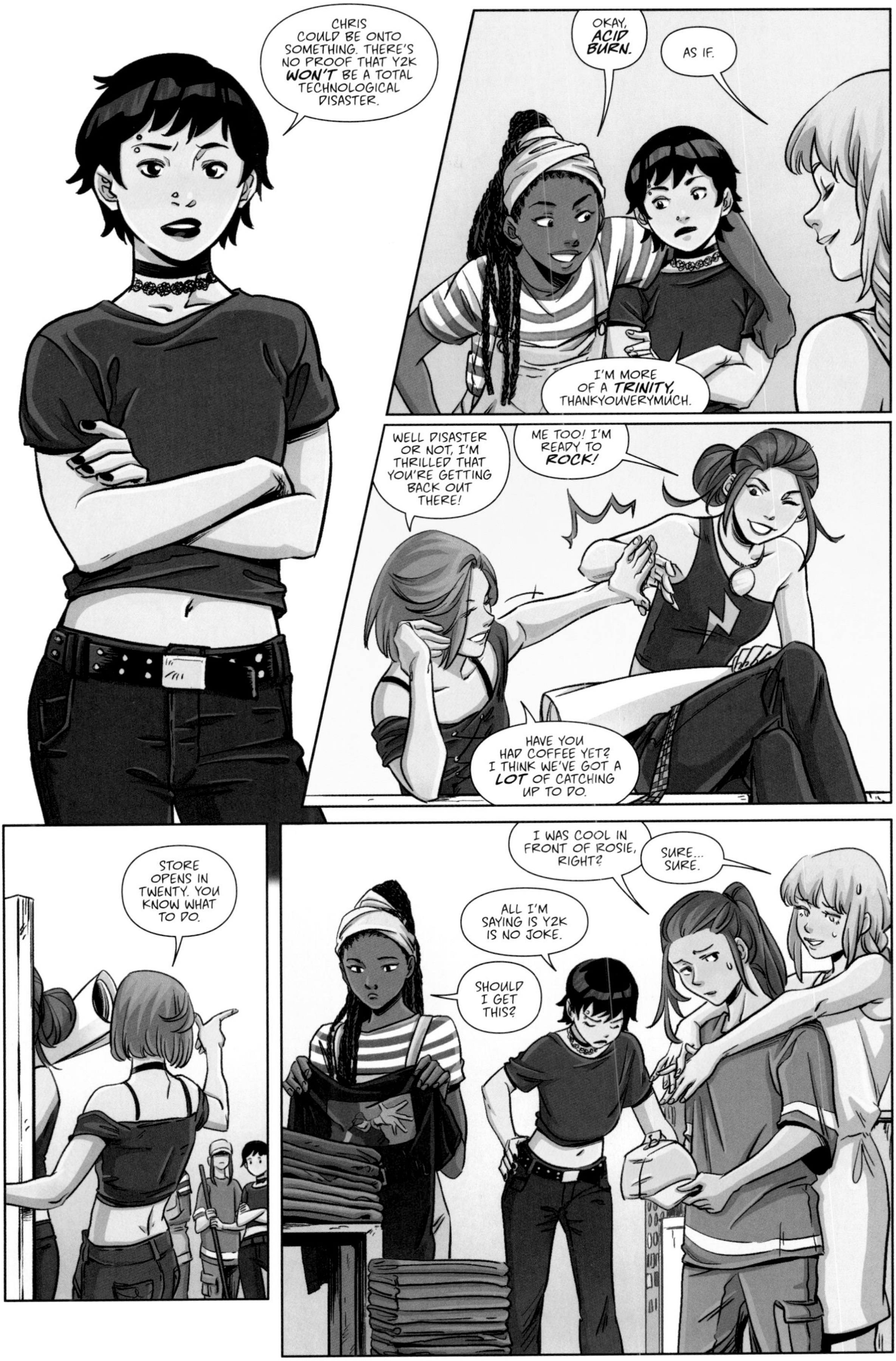
CHRIS COULD BE ONTO SOMETHING. THERE'S NO PROOF THAT Y2K *WON'T* BE A TOTAL TECHNOLOGICAL DISASTER.
OKAY, *ACID BURN.*
AS IF.
I'M MORE OF A *TRINITY,* THANKYOUVERYMUCH.
WELL DISASTER OR NOT, I'M THRILLED THAT YOU'RE GETTING BACK OUT THERE!
ME TOO! I'M READY TO *ROCK!*
HAVE YOU HAD COFFEE YET? I THINK WE'VE GOT A *LOT* OF CATCHING UP TO DO.
STORE OPENS IN TWENTY. YOU KNOW WHAT TO DO.
I WAS COOL IN FRONT OF ROSIE, RIGHT?
SURE... SURE.
ALL I'M SAYING IS Y2K IS NO JOKE.
SHOULD I GET THIS?

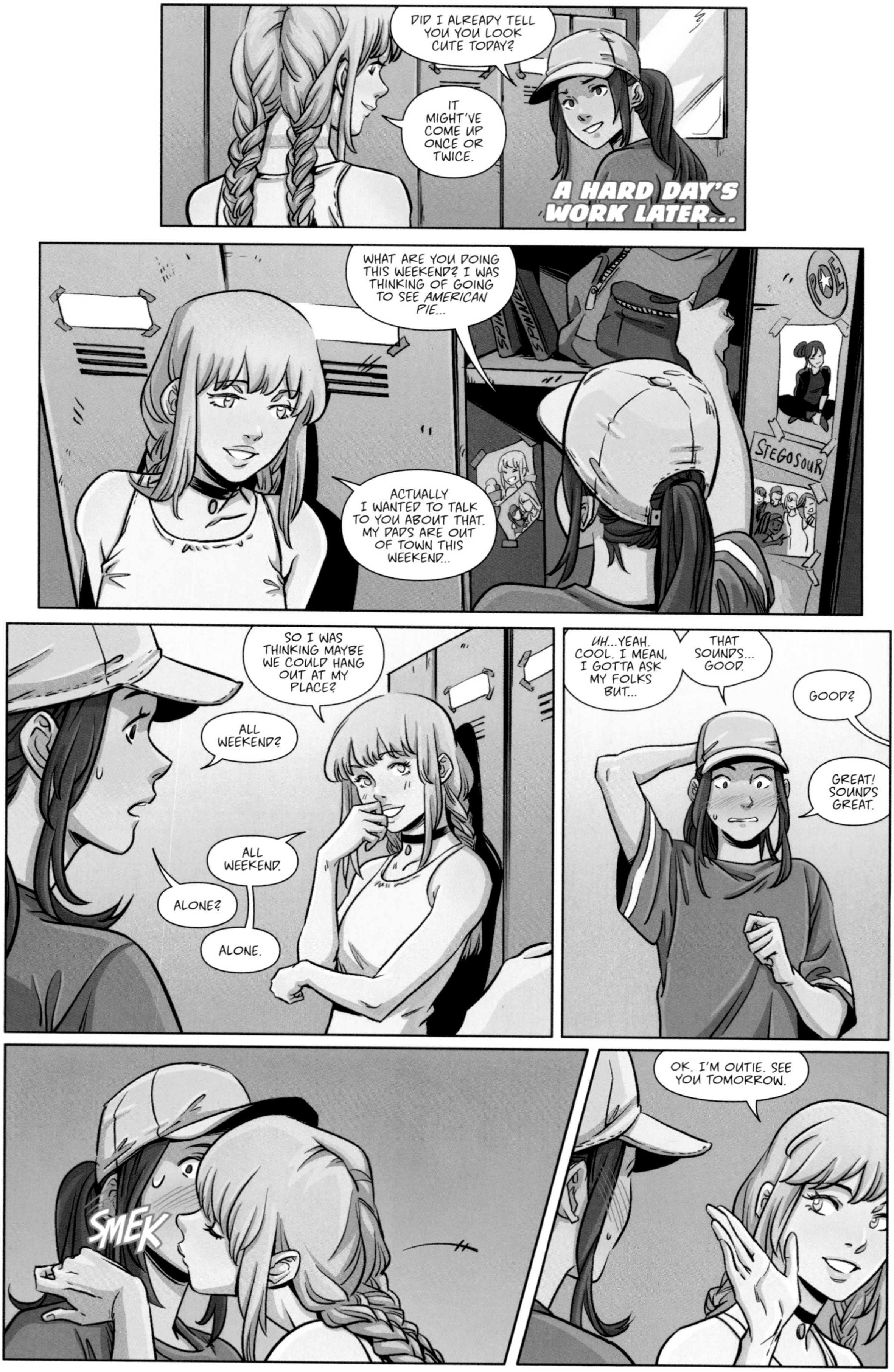
DID I ALREADY TELL YOU YOU LOOK CUTE TODAY?
IT MIGHT'VE COME UP ONCE OR TWICE.
A HARD DAY'S WORK LATER...
WHAT ARE YOU DOING THIS WEEKEND? I WAS THINKING OF GOING TO SEE AMERICAN PIE...
ACTUALLY I WANTED TO TALK TO YOU ABOUT THAT. MY DADS ARE OUT OF TOWN THIS WEEKEND...
POE
STEGOSOUR
SPINNOUT
SO I WAS THINKING MAYBE WE COULD HANG OUT AT MY PLACE?
ALL WEEKEND?
ALL WEEKEND.
ALONE?
ALONE.
UH...YEAH. COOL. I MEAN, I GOTTA ASK MY FOLKS BUT...
THAT SOUNDS... GOOD.
GOOD?
GREAT! SOUNDS GREAT.
SMEK
OK. I'M OUTIE. SEE YOU TOMORROW.

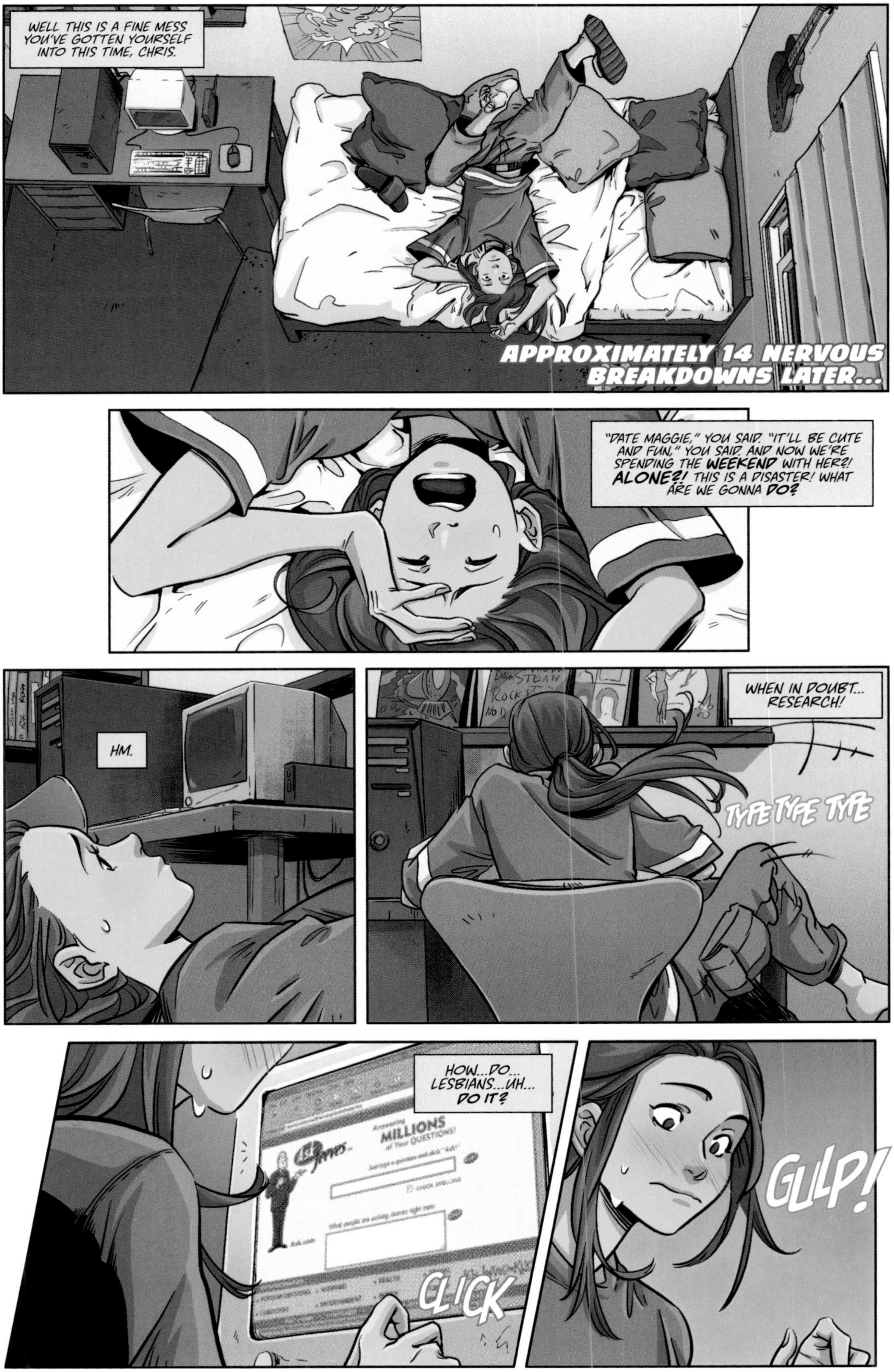
WELL THIS IS A FINE MESS YOU'VE GOTTEN YOURSELF INTO THIS TIME, CHRIS.
APPROXIMATELY 14 NERVOUS BREAKDOWNS LATER...
"DATE MAGGIE," YOU SAID. "IT'LL BE CUTE AND FUN," YOU SAID. AND NOW WE'RE SPENDING THE WEEKEND WITH HER?! ALONE?! THIS IS A DISASTER! WHAT ARE WE GONNA DO?
HM.
WHEN IN DOUBT... RESEARCH!
TYPE TYPE TYPE
HOW...DO... LESBIANS...UH... DO IT?
Answering MILLIONS of Your QUESTIONS!
CLICK
GULP!

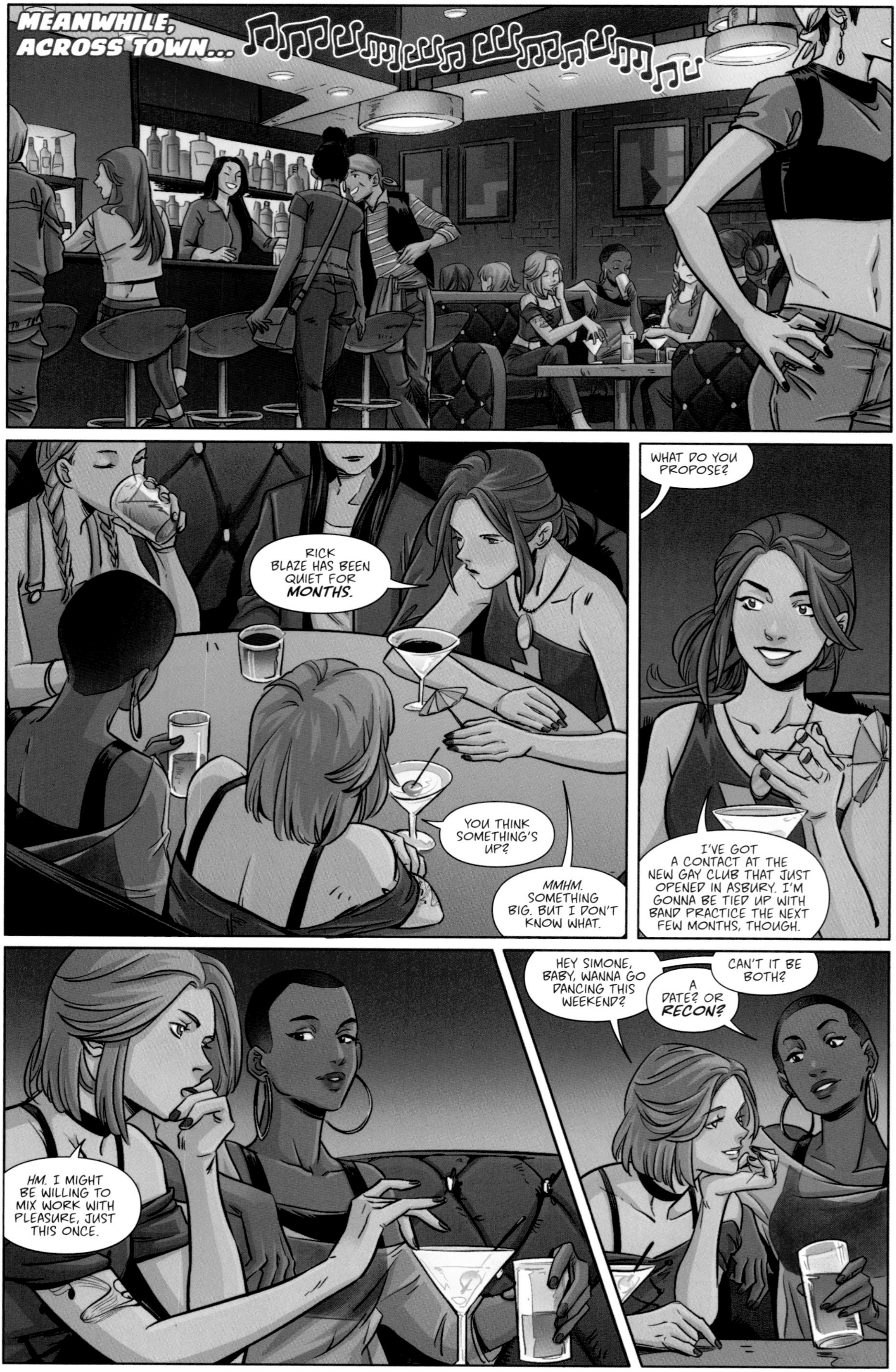
MEANWHILE, ACROSS TOWN...
RICK BLAZE HAS BEEN QUIET FOR MONTHS.
YOU THINK SOMETHING'S UP?
MMHM. SOMETHING BIG. BUT I DON'T KNOW WHAT.
WHAT DO YOU PROPOSE?
I'VE GOT A CONTACT AT THE NEW GAY CLUB THAT JUST OPENED IN ASBURY. I'M GONNA BE TIED UP WITH BAND PRACTICE THE NEXT FEW MONTHS, THOUGH.
HM. I MIGHT BE WILLING TO MIX WORK WITH PLEASURE, JUST THIS ONCE.
HEY SIMONE, BABY, WANNA GO DANCING THIS WEEKEND?
A DATE? OR RECON?
CAN'T IT BE BOTH?

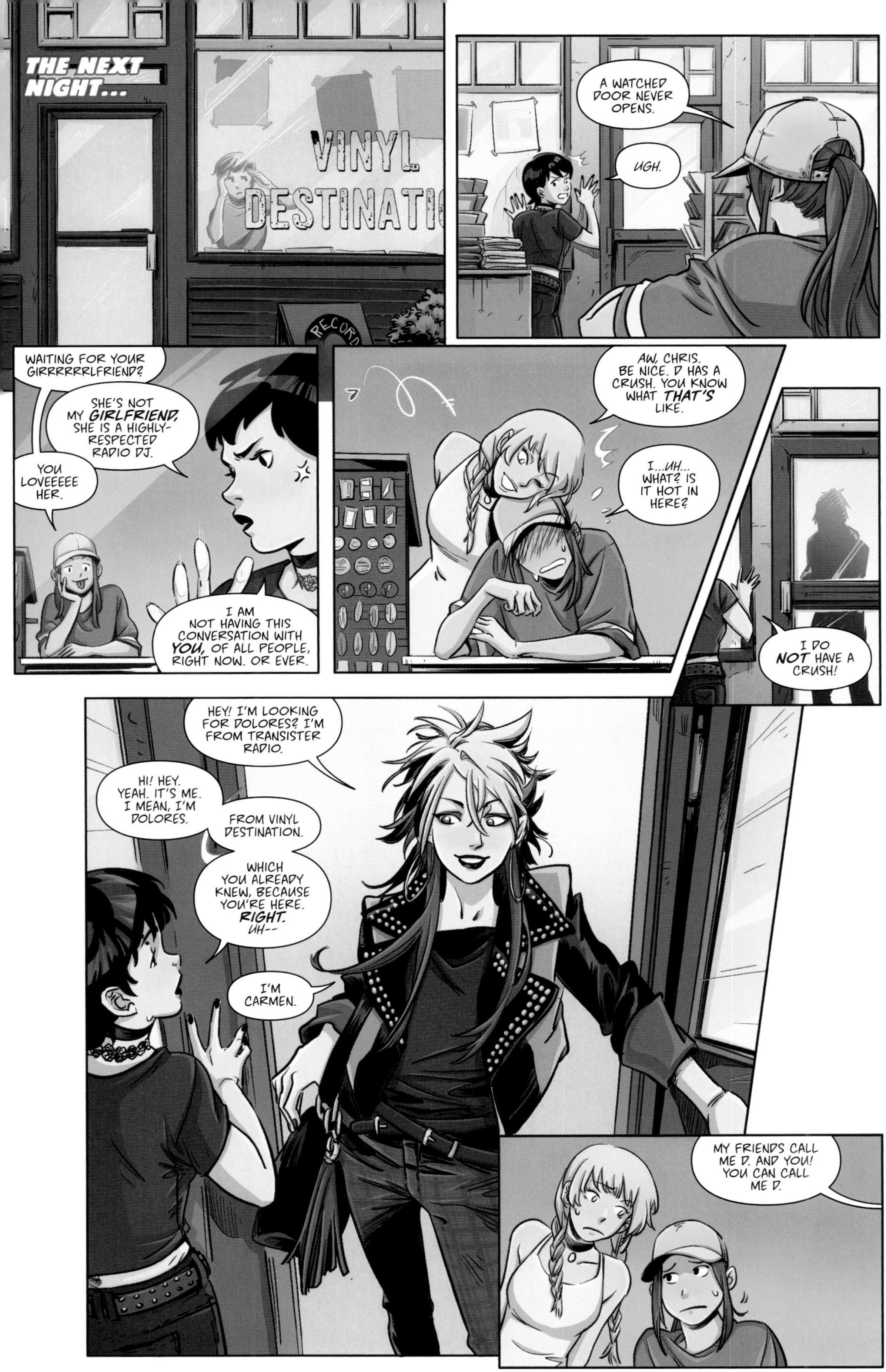
THE NEXT NIGHT...
VINYL DESTINATIO
A WATCHED DOOR NEVER OPENS.
UGH.
WAITING FOR YOUR GIRRRRRRLFRIEND?
SHE'S NOT MY GIRLFRIEND, SHE IS A HIGHLY-RESPECTED RADIO DJ.
YOU LOVEEEEE HER.
I AM NOT HAVING THIS CONVERSATION WITH YOU, OF ALL PEOPLE, RIGHT NOW. OR EVER.
AW, CHRIS. BE NICE. D HAS A CRUSH. YOU KNOW WHAT THAT'S LIKE.
I...UH... WHAT? IS IT HOT IN HERE?
I DO NOT HAVE A CRUSH!
HEY! I'M LOOKING FOR DOLORES? I'M FROM TRANSISTER RADIO.
HI! HEY. YEAH. IT'S ME. I MEAN, I'M DOLORES.
FROM VINYL DESTINATION.
WHICH YOU ALREADY KNEW, BECAUSE YOU'RE HERE. RIGHT. UH--
I'M CARMEN.
MY FRIENDS CALL ME D. AND YOU! YOU CAN CALL ME D.

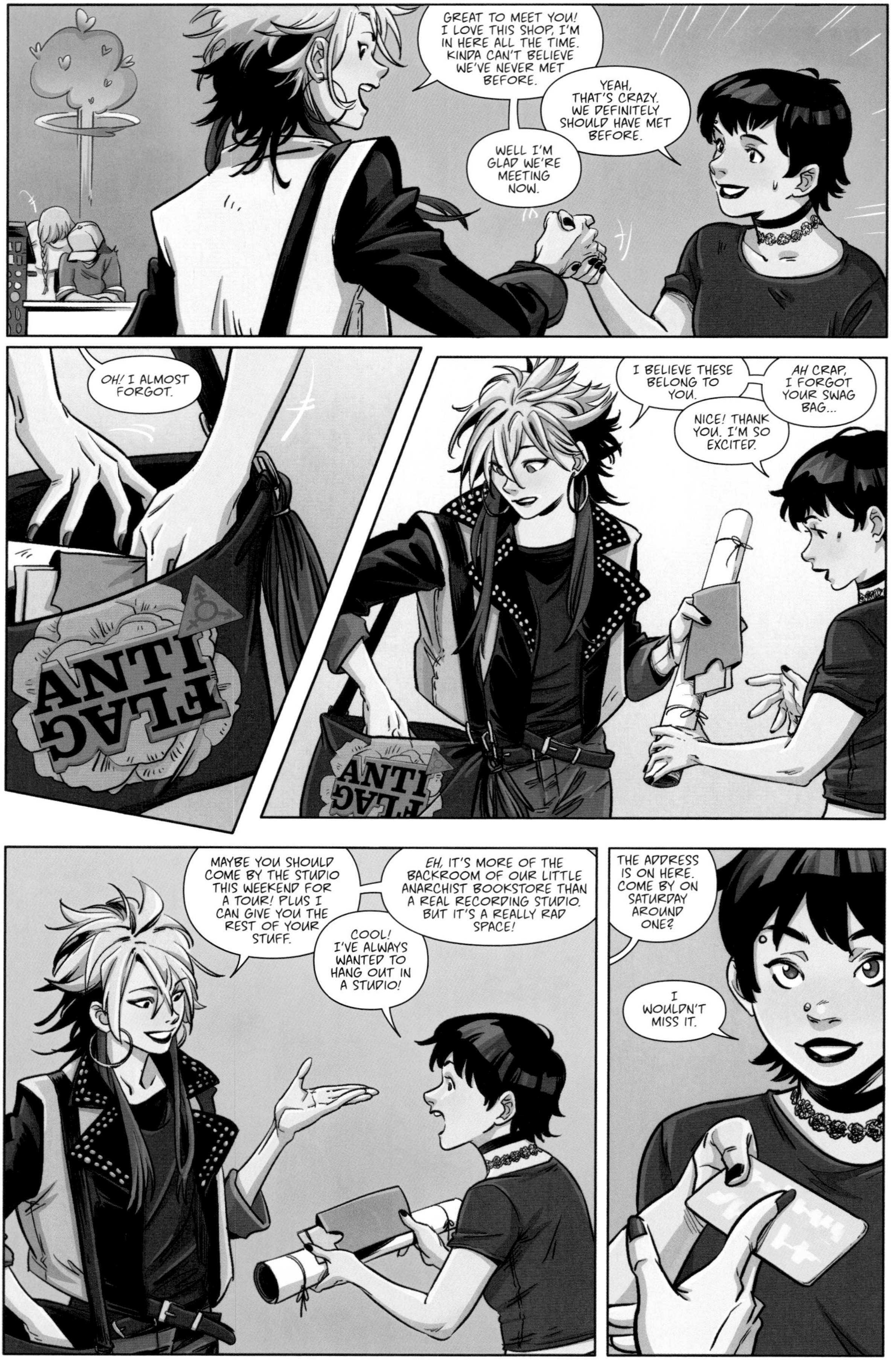
GREAT TO MEET YOU! I LOVE THIS SHOP, I'M IN HERE ALL THE TIME. KINDA CAN'T BELIEVE WE'VE NEVER MET BEFORE.
YEAH, THAT'S CRAZY. WE DEFINITELY SHOULD HAVE MET BEFORE.
WELL I'M GLAD WE'RE MEETING NOW.
OH! I ALMOST FORGOT.
ANTI FLAG
I BELIEVE THESE BELONG TO YOU.
AH CRAP, I FORGOT YOUR SWAG BAG...
NICE! THANK YOU. I'M SO EXCITED.
MAYBE YOU SHOULD COME BY THE STUDIO THIS WEEKEND FOR A TOUR! PLUS I CAN GIVE YOU THE REST OF YOUR STUFF.
EH, IT'S MORE OF THE BACKROOM OF OUR LITTLE ANARCHIST BOOKSTORE THAN A REAL RECORDING STUDIO. BUT IT'S A REALLY RAD SPACE!
COOL! I'VE ALWAYS WANTED TO HANG OUT IN A STUDIO!
THE ADDRESS IS ON HERE. COME BY ON SATURDAY AROUND ONE?
I WOULDN'T MISS IT.

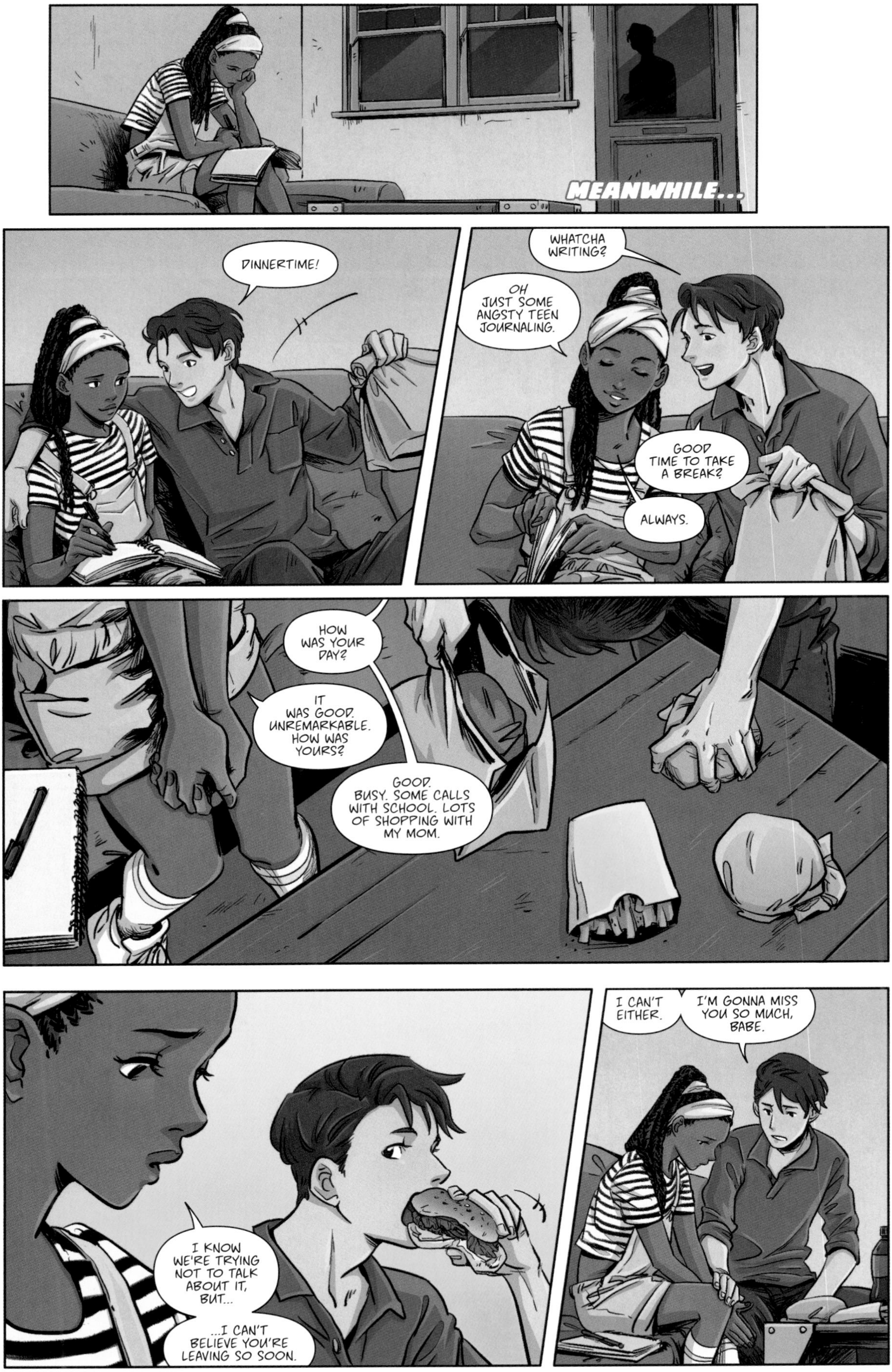
MEANWHILE...
DINNERTIME!
WHATCHA WRITING?
OH JUST SOME ANGSTY TEEN JOURNALING.
GOOD TIME TO TAKE A BREAK?
ALWAYS.
HOW WAS YOUR DAY?
IT WAS GOOD. UNREMARKABLE. HOW WAS YOURS?
GOOD. BUSY. SOME CALLS WITH SCHOOL. LOTS OF SHOPPING WITH MY MOM.
I KNOW WE'RE TRYING NOT TO TALK ABOUT IT, BUT...
...I CAN'T BELIEVE YOU'RE LEAVING SO SOON.
I'M GONNA MISS YOU SO MUCH, BABE.
I CAN'T EITHER.

HEY. LOOK AT ME.

I LOVE YOU. NOTHING'S GONNA CHANGE.

I KNOW. I LOVE YOU TOO.

AND I KNEW I HAD TO PREPARE FOR THIS, YOU LEAVING.

I JUST DIDN'T THINK IT WOULD BE SO SOON.

I KNOW. EVERYTHING IS HAPPENING SO QUICKLY.

I FEEL REALLY OUT OF MY LEAGUE.

DON'T BE SILLY. YOU'RE SO SMART AND SO TALENTED.

YOU'RE READY FOR THIS.

I'M SO PROUD OF YOU, LOGAN.

I'M REALLY EXCITED TO GO, BUT I'M GOING TO MISS YOU SO MUCH.

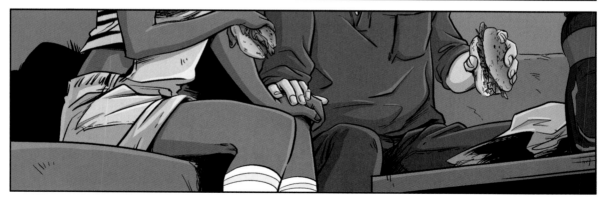

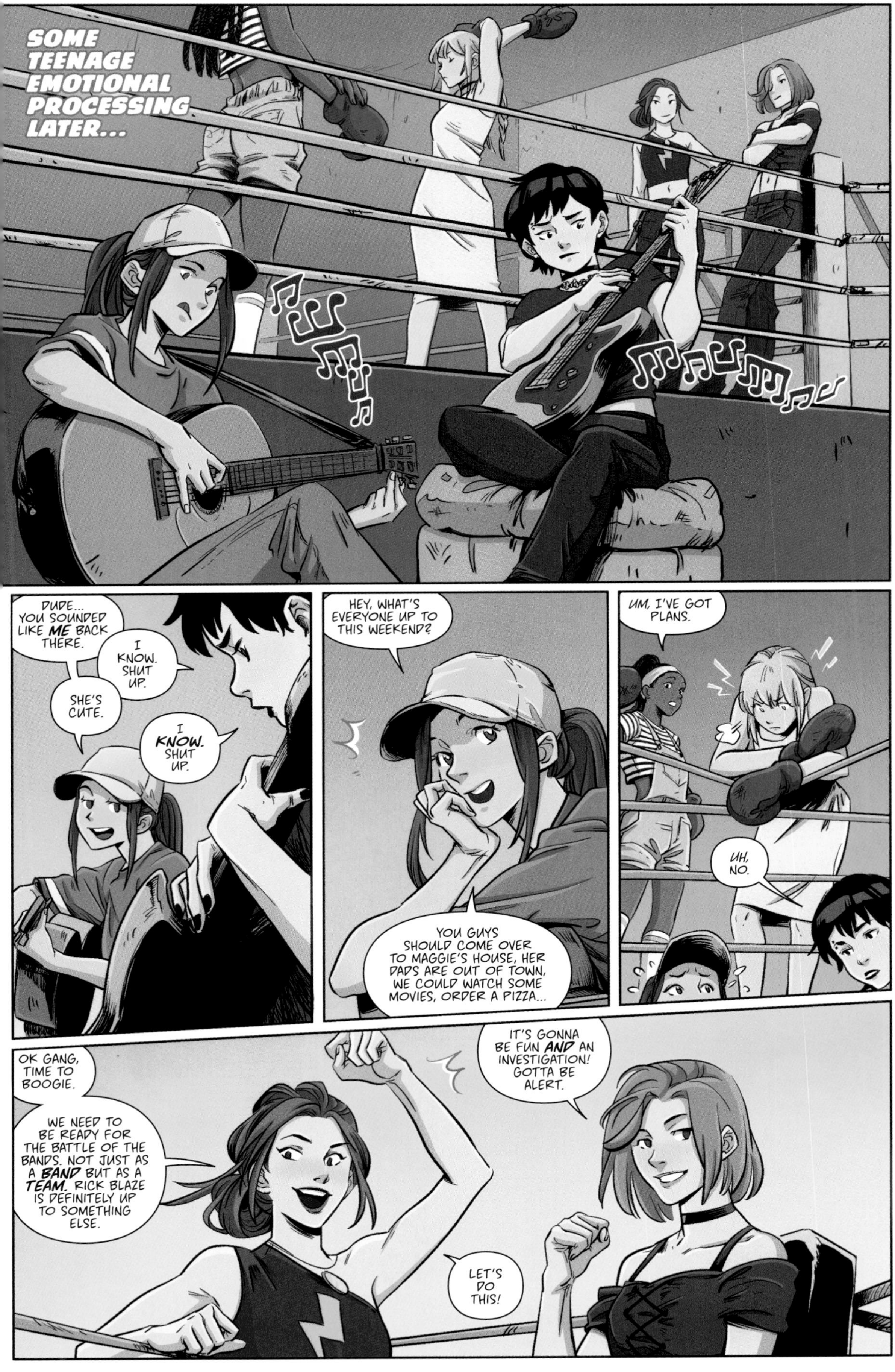
SOME TEENAGE EMOTIONAL PROCESSING LATER...
DUDE... YOU SOUNDED LIKE ME BACK THERE.
I KNOW. SHUT UP.
SHE'S CUTE.
I KNOW. SHUT UP.
HEY, WHAT'S EVERYONE UP TO THIS WEEKEND?
YOU GUYS SHOULD COME OVER TO MAGGIE'S HOUSE, HER DADS ARE OUT OF TOWN, WE COULD WATCH SOME MOVIES, ORDER A PIZZA...
UM, I'VE GOT PLANS.
UH, NO.
OK GANG, TIME TO BOOGIE.
WE NEED TO BE READY FOR THE BATTLE OF THE BANDS. NOT JUST AS A BAND BUT AS A TEAM. RICK BLAZE IS DEFINITELY UP TO SOMETHING ELSE.
IT'S GONNA BE FUN AND AN INVESTIGATION! GOTTA BE ALERT.
LET'S DO THIS!

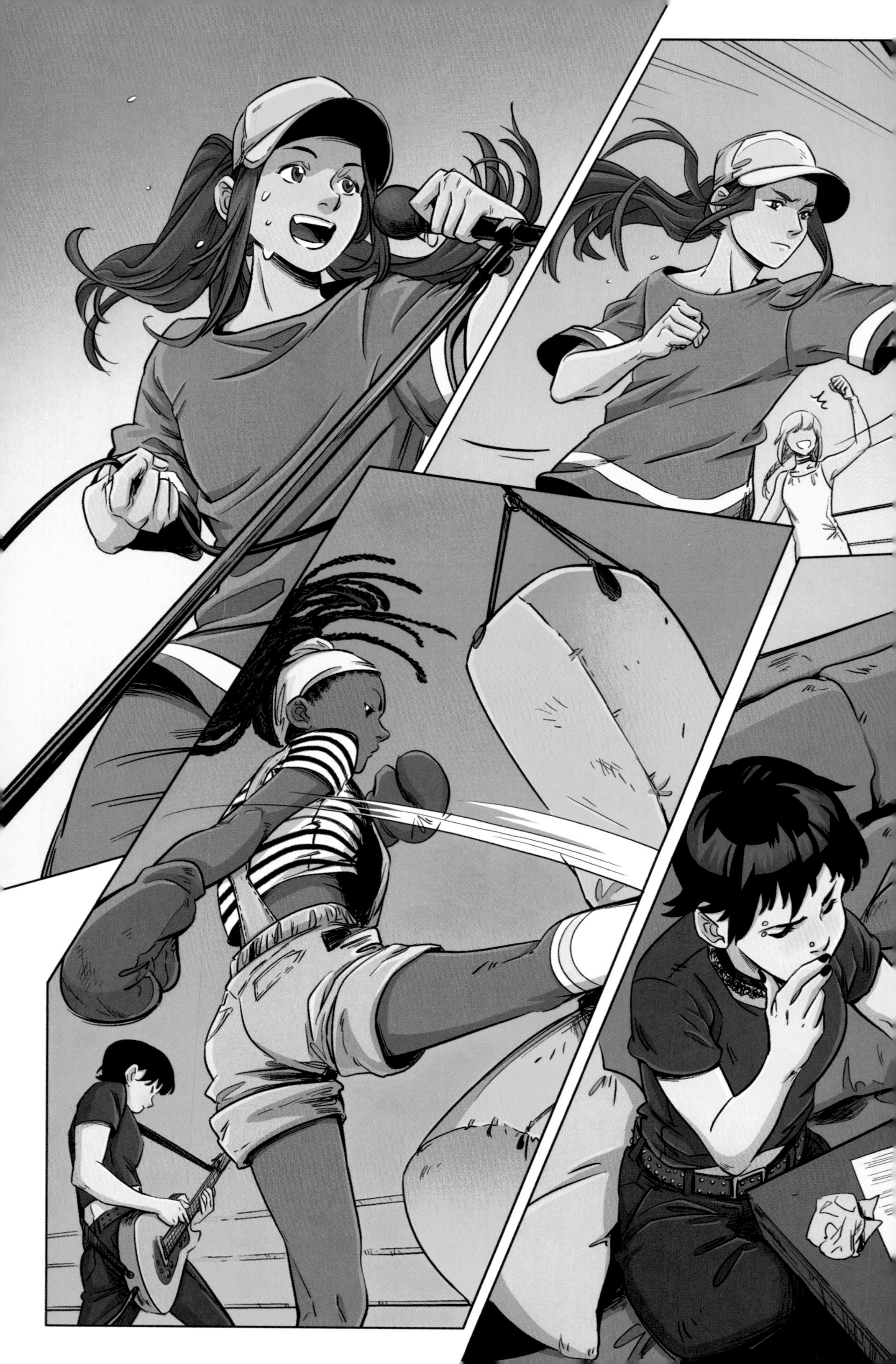

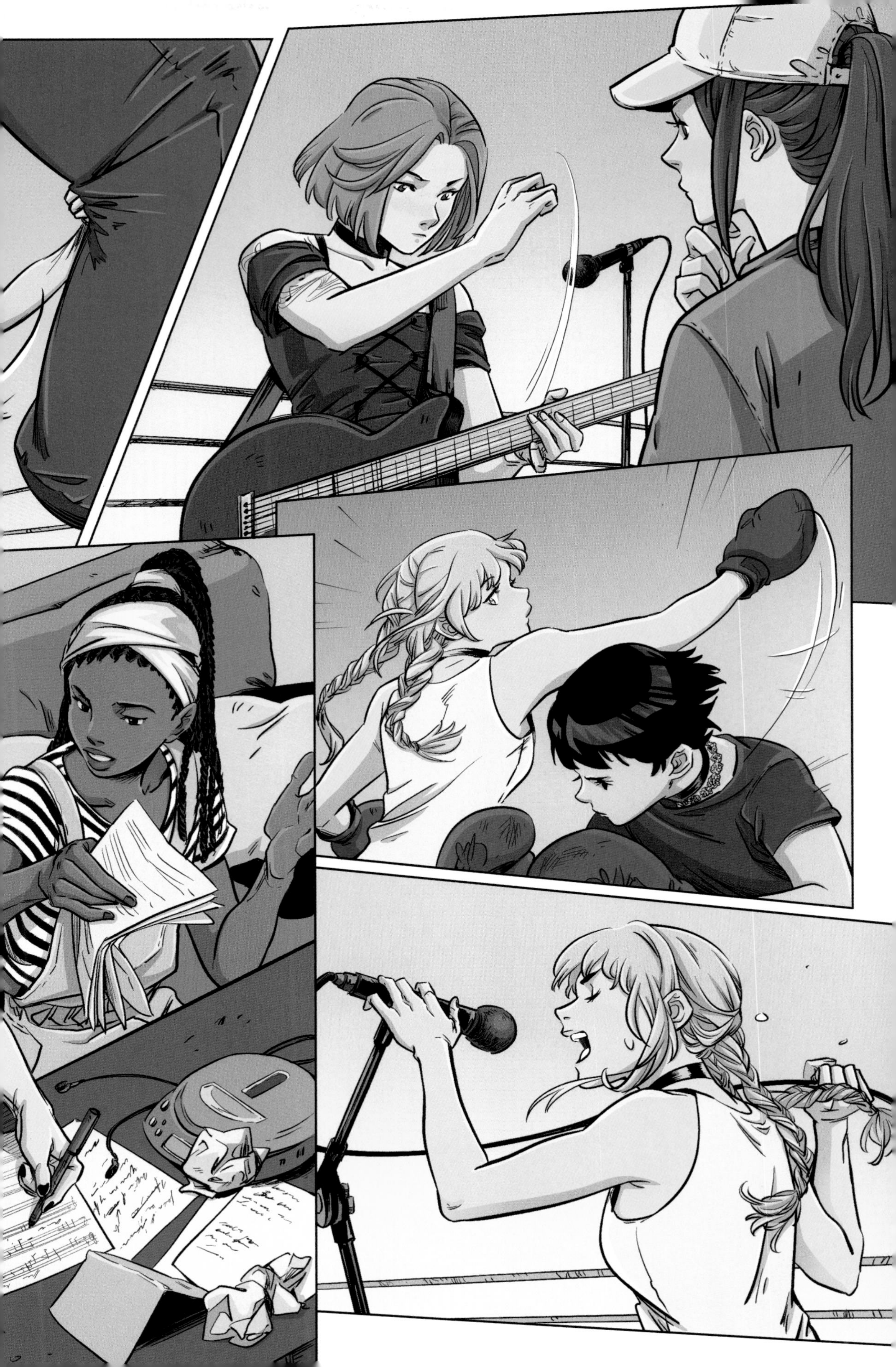

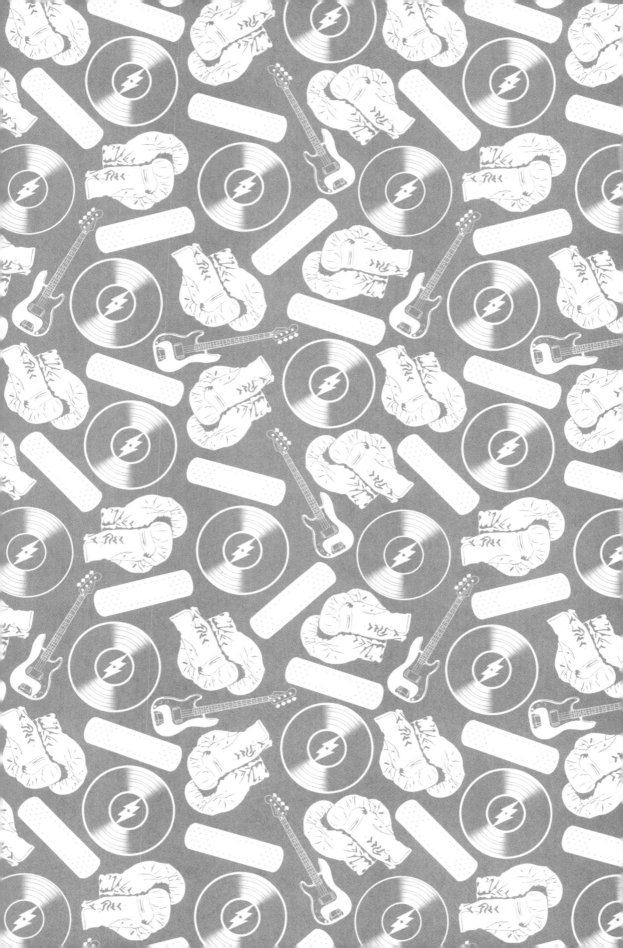

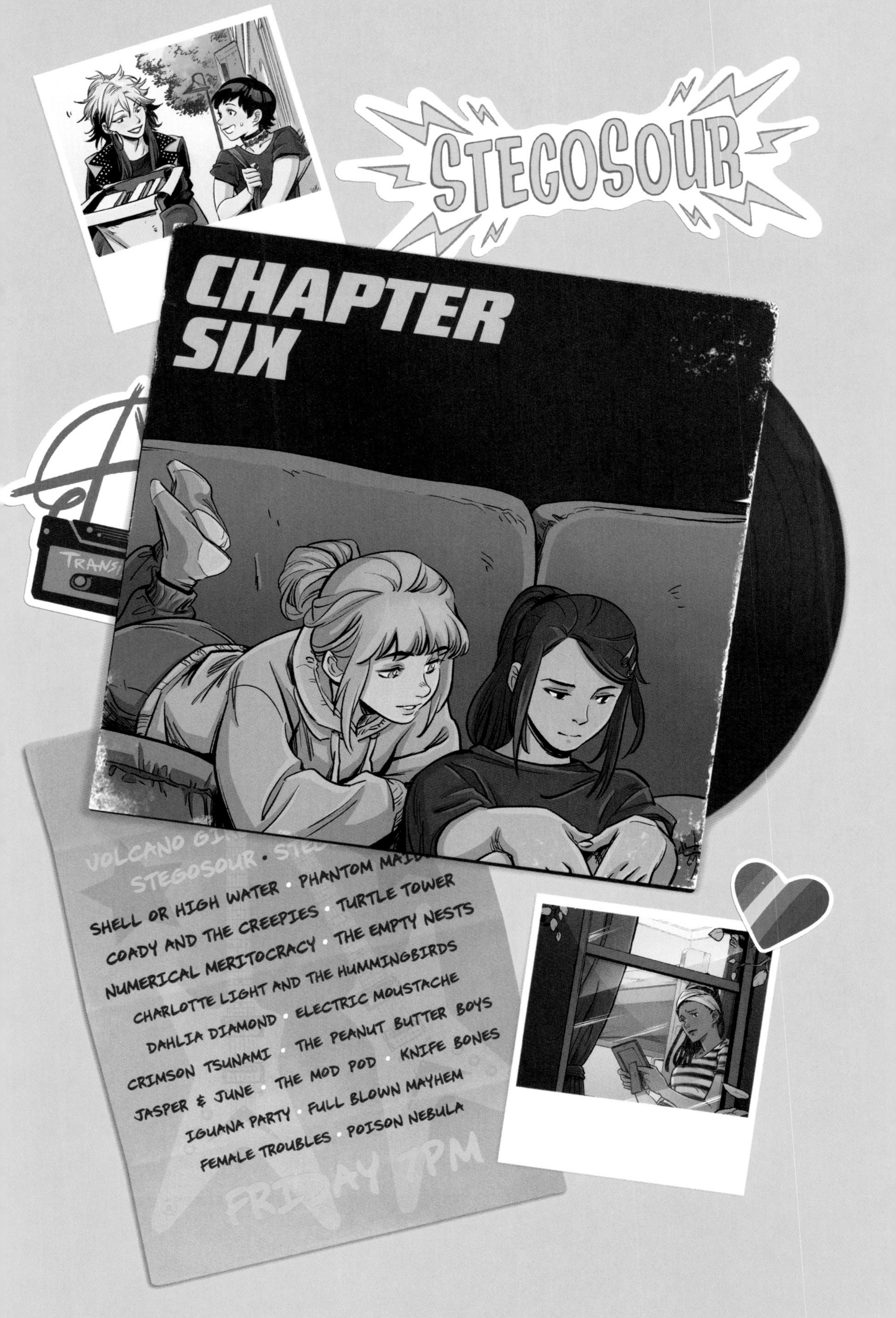

STEGOSOUR
CHAPTER SIX
STEGOSOUR
SHELL OR HIGH WATER • PHANTOM
CODY AND THE CREEPIES • TURTLE TOWER
NUMERICAL MERITOCRACY • THE EMPTY NESTS
CHARLOTTE LIGHT AND THE HUMMINGBIRDS
DAHLIA DIAMOND • ELECTRIC MOUSTACHE
CRIMSON TSUNAMI • THE PEANUT BUTTER BOYS
JASPER & JUNE • THE MOD POD • KNIFE BONES
IGUANA PARTY • FULL BLOWN MAYHEM
FEMALE TROUBLES • POISON NEBULA
FRIDAY 7PM

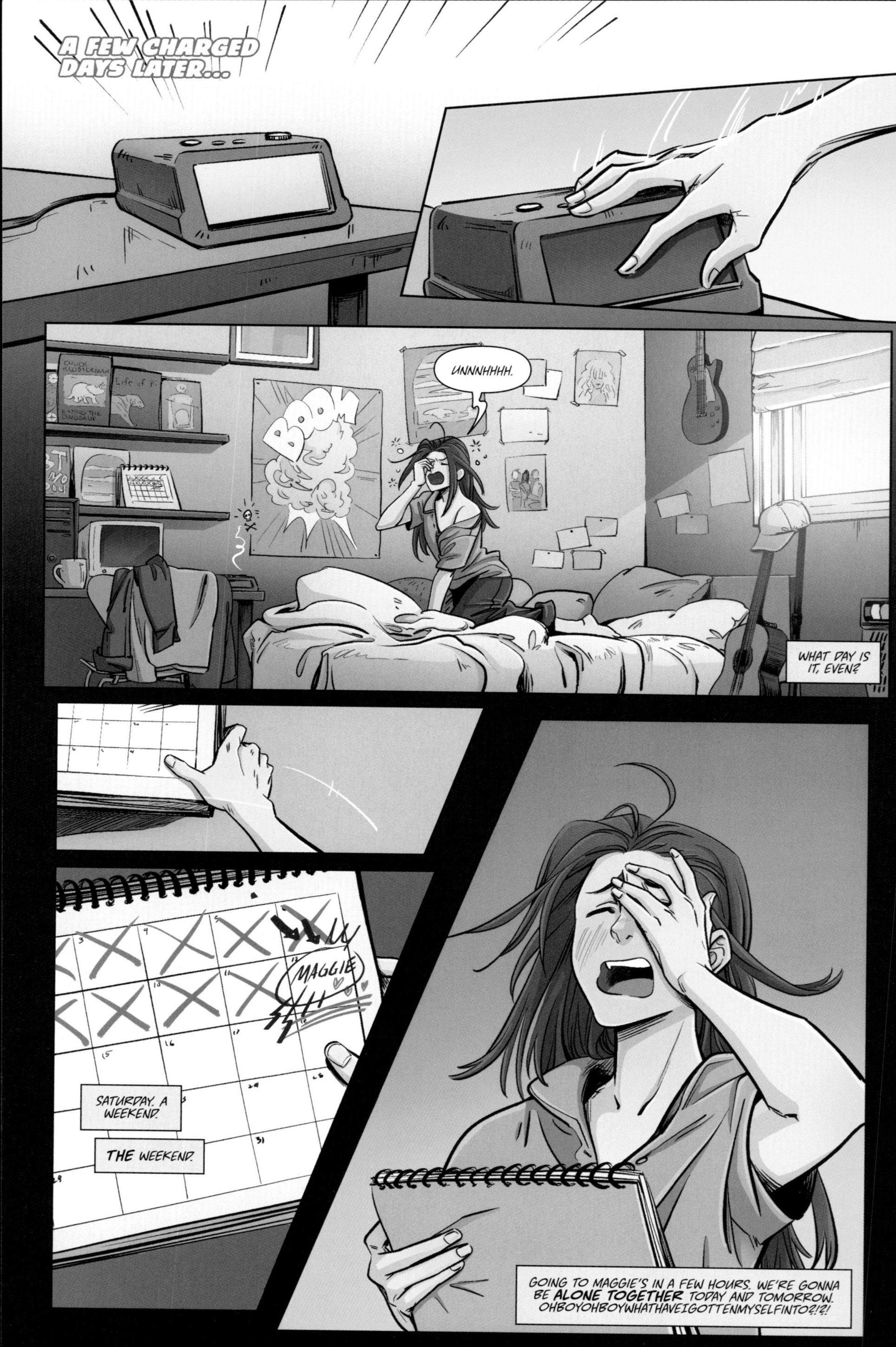
A FEW CHARGED DAYS LATER...
UNNNHHHH.
WHAT DAY IS IT, EVEN?
MAGGIE
SATURDAY. A WEEKEND.
THE WEEKEND.
GOING TO MAGGIE'S IN A FEW HOURS. WE'RE GONNA BE ALONE TOGETHER TODAY AND TOMORROW. OHBOYOHBOYWHATHAVEIGOTTENMYSELFINTO?!?!

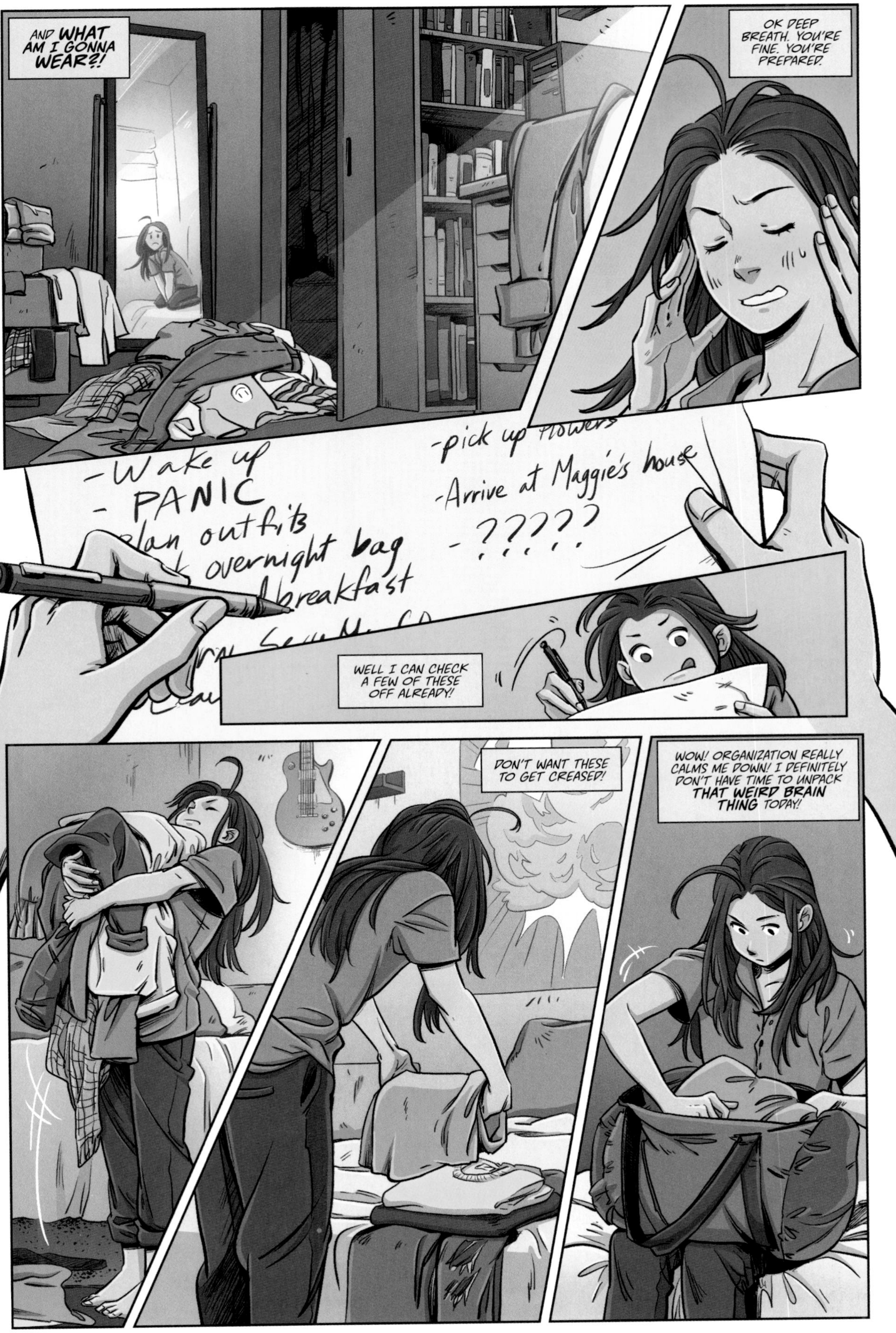
AND WHAT AM I GONNA WEAR?!
OK DEEP BREATH. YOU'RE FINE. YOU'RE PREPARED.
-Wake up
- PANIC
-pick up flowers
-Arrive at Maggie's house
- ?????
WELL I CAN CHECK A FEW OF THESE OFF ALREADY!
DON'T WANT THESE TO GET CREASED!
WOW! ORGANIZATION REALLY CALMS ME DOWN! I DEFINITELY DON'T HAVE TIME TO UNPACK THAT WEIRD BRAIN THING TODAY!

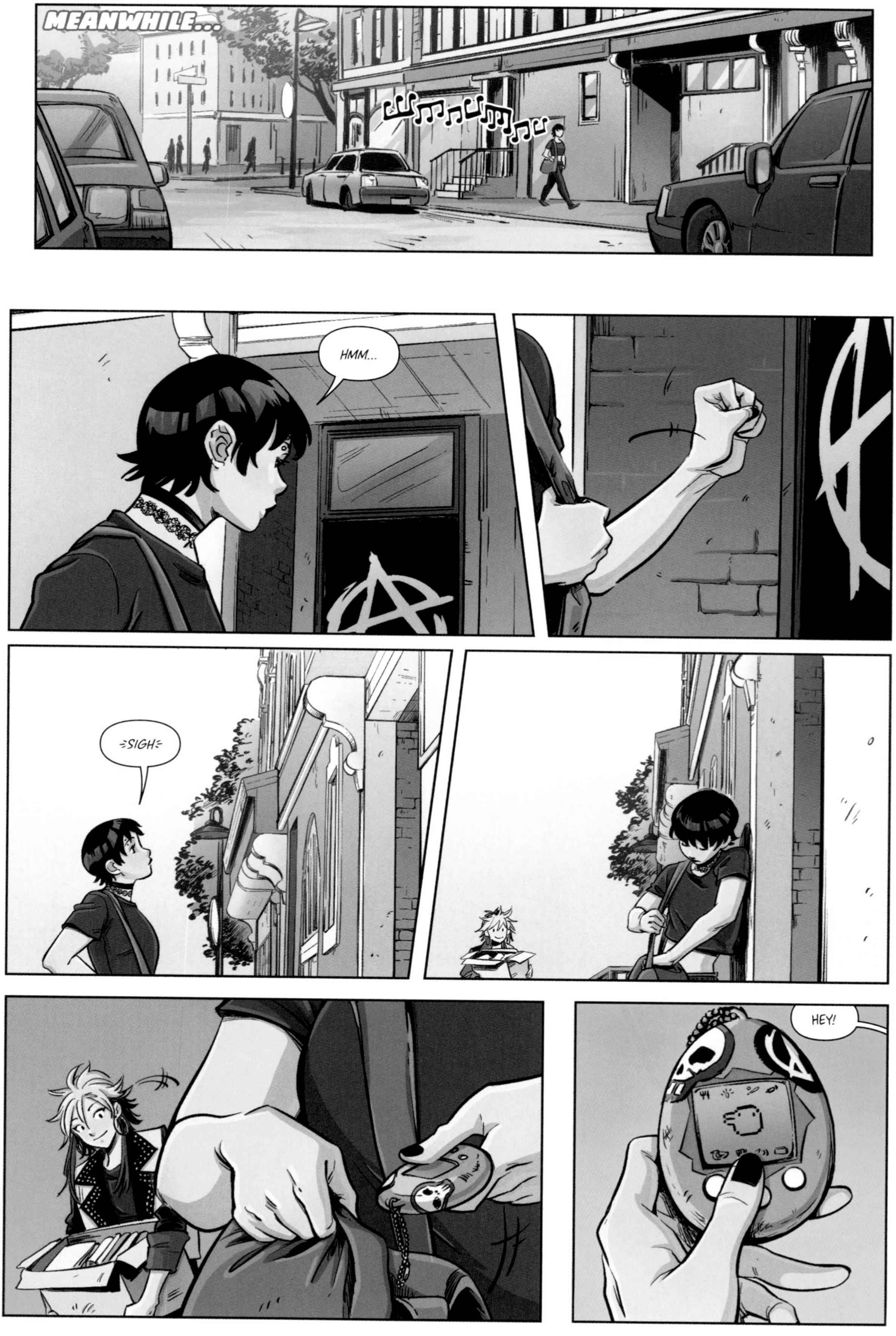
MEANWHILE...
HMM...
SIGH
HEY!

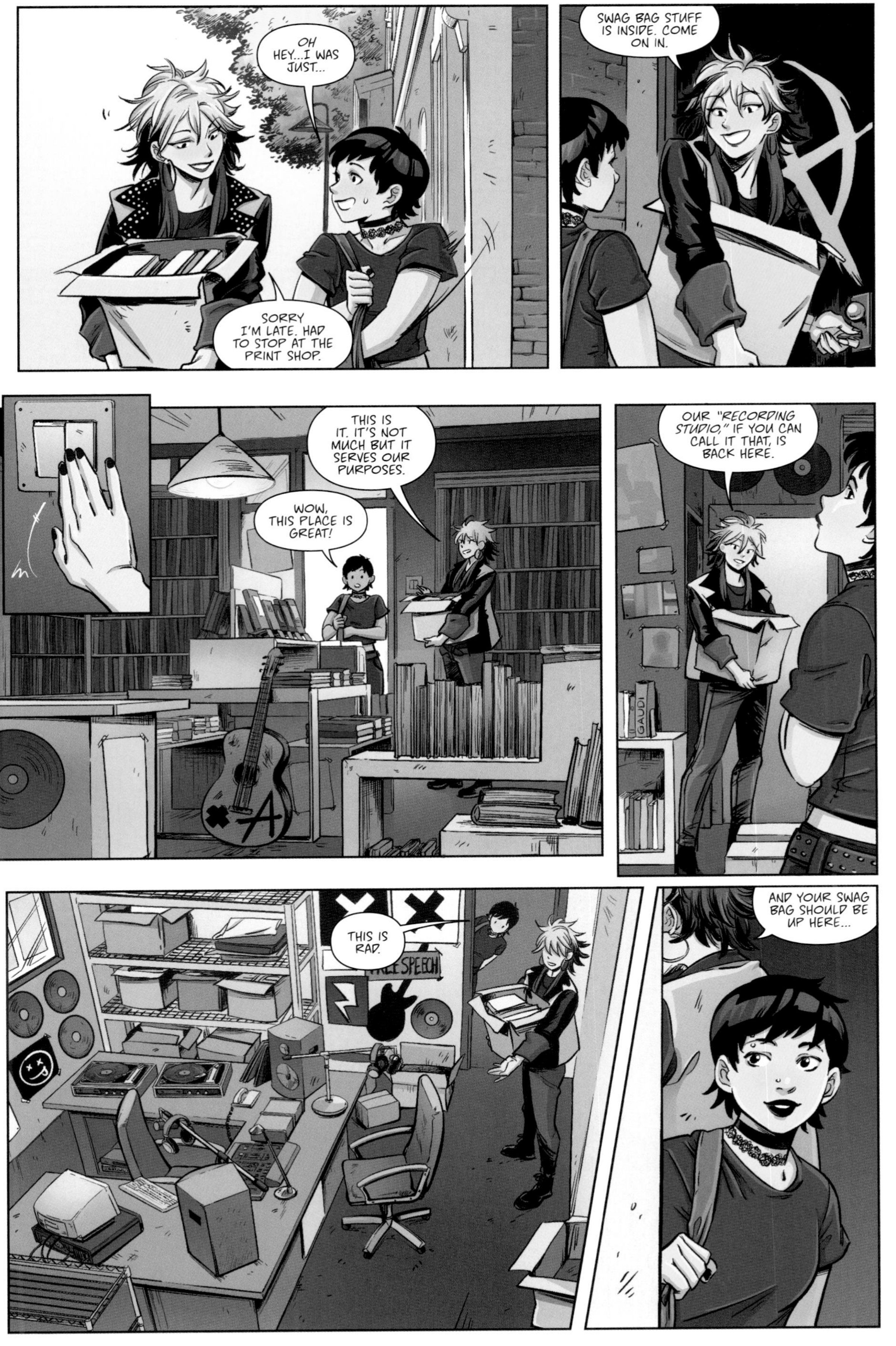

OH HEY...I WAS JUST...
SORRY I'M LATE. HAD TO STOP AT THE PRINT SHOP.
SWAG BAG STUFF IS INSIDE. COME ON IN.
THIS IS IT. IT'S NOT MUCH BUT IT SERVES OUR PURPOSES.
WOW, THIS PLACE IS GREAT!
OUR "RECORDING STUDIO," IF YOU CAN CALL IT THAT, IS BACK HERE.
GAUDI
THIS IS RAD.
FREE SPEECH
AND YOUR SWAG BAG SHOULD BE UP HERE...

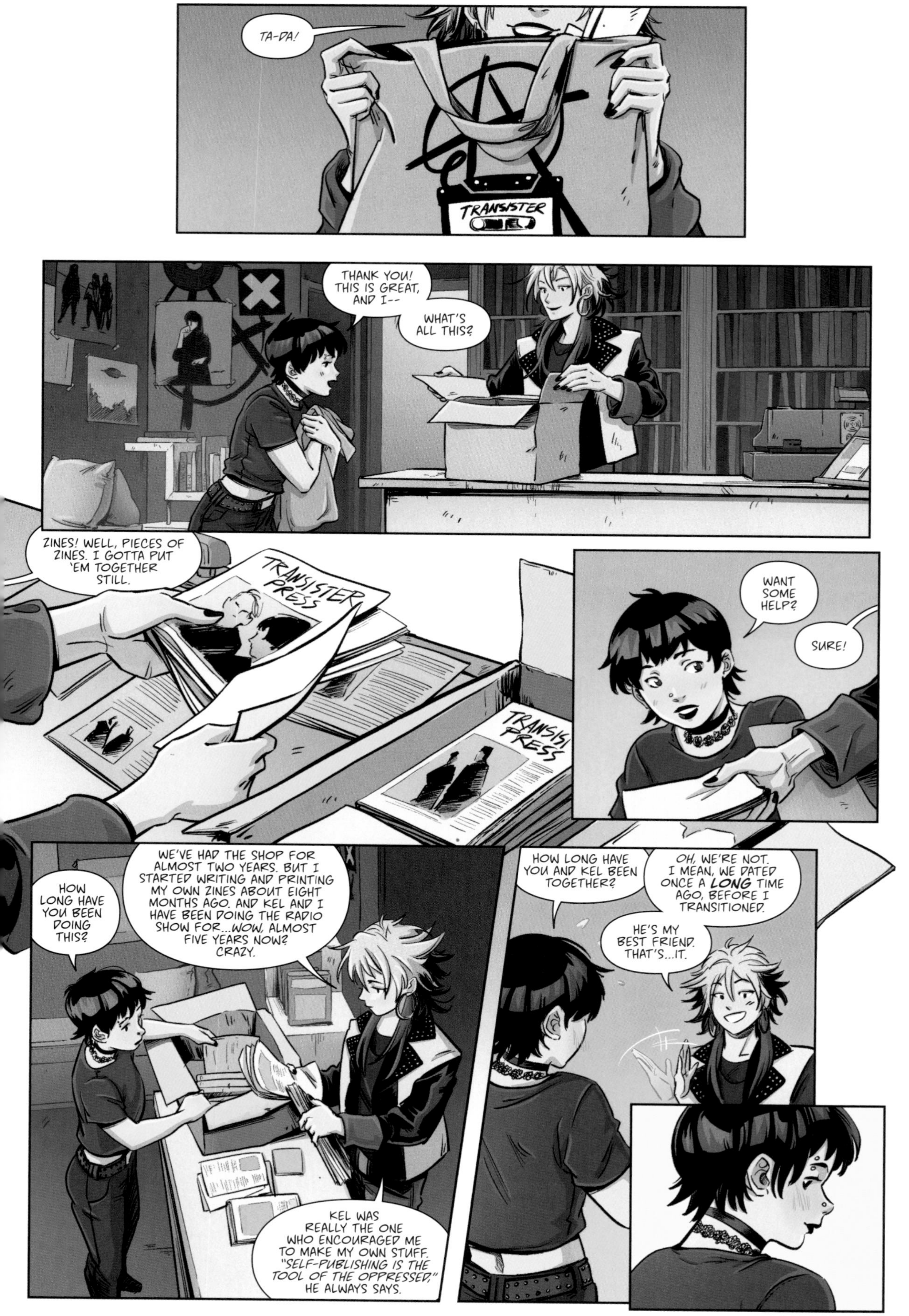
TA-DA!
TRANSISTER
THANK YOU! THIS IS GREAT, AND I--
WHAT'S ALL THIS?
ZINES! WELL, PIECES OF ZINES. I GOTTA PUT 'EM TOGETHER STILL.
TRANSISTER PRESS
WANT SOME HELP?
SURE!
HOW LONG HAVE YOU BEEN DOING THIS?
WE'VE HAD THE SHOP FOR ALMOST TWO YEARS. BUT I STARTED WRITING AND PRINTING MY OWN ZINES ABOUT EIGHT MONTHS AGO. AND KEL AND I HAVE BEEN DOING THE RADIO SHOW FOR...WOW, ALMOST FIVE YEARS NOW? CRAZY.
KEL WAS REALLY THE ONE WHO ENCOURAGED ME TO MAKE MY OWN STUFF. *"SELF-PUBLISHING IS THE TOOL OF THE OPPRESSED,"* HE ALWAYS SAYS.
HOW LONG HAVE YOU AND KEL BEEN TOGETHER?
OH, WE'RE NOT. I MEAN, WE DATED ONCE A **LONG** TIME AGO, BEFORE I TRANSITIONED.
HE'S MY BEST FRIEND. THAT'S...IT.

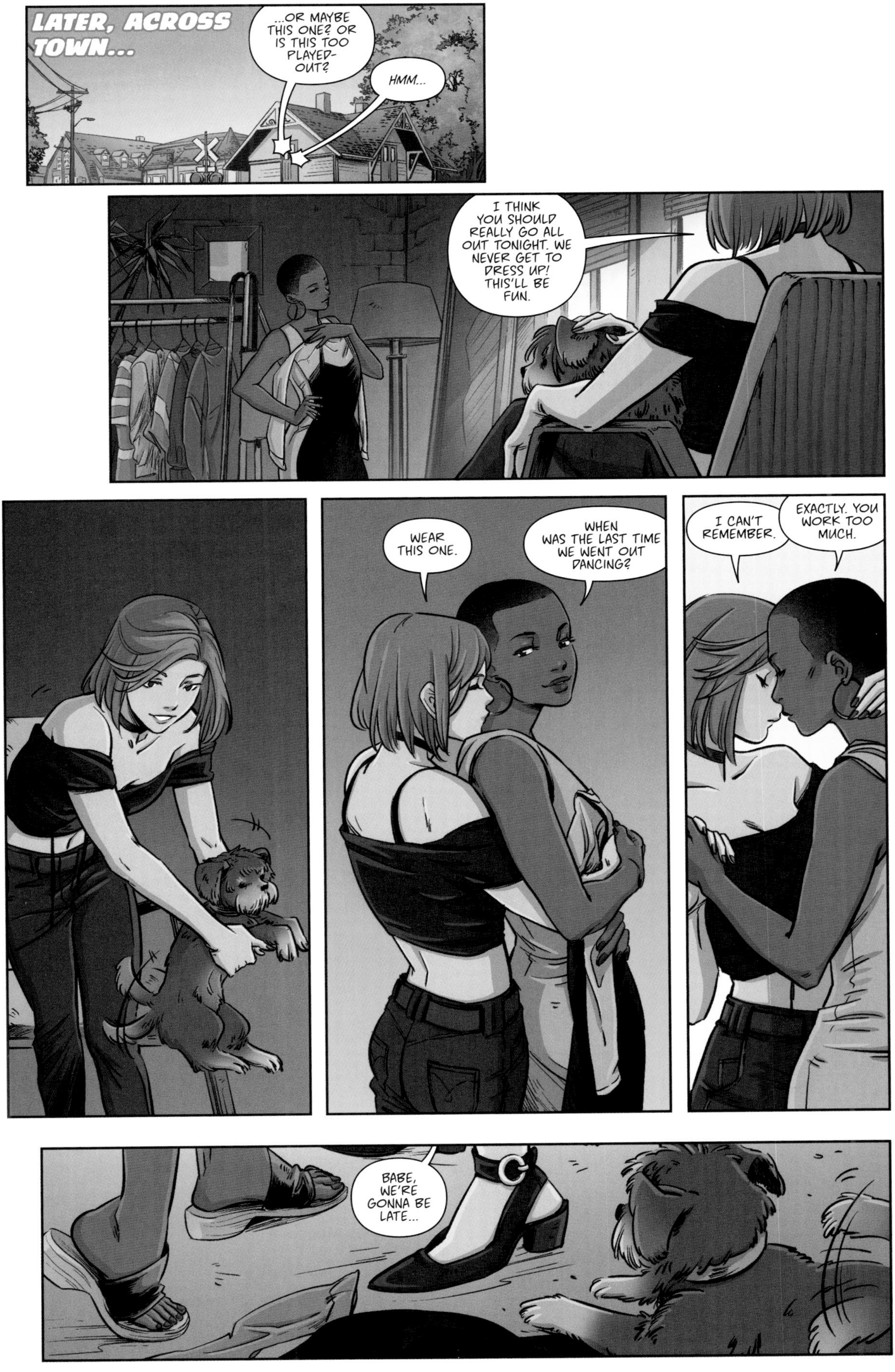

LATER, ACROSS TOWN...
...OR MAYBE THIS ONE? OR IS THIS TOO PLAYED-OUT?
HMM...
I THINK YOU SHOULD REALLY GO ALL OUT TONIGHT. WE NEVER GET TO DRESS UP! THIS'LL BE FUN.
WEAR THIS ONE.
WHEN WAS THE LAST TIME WE WENT OUT DANCING?
I CAN'T REMEMBER.
EXACTLY. YOU WORK TOO MUCH.
BABE, WE'RE GONNA BE LATE...

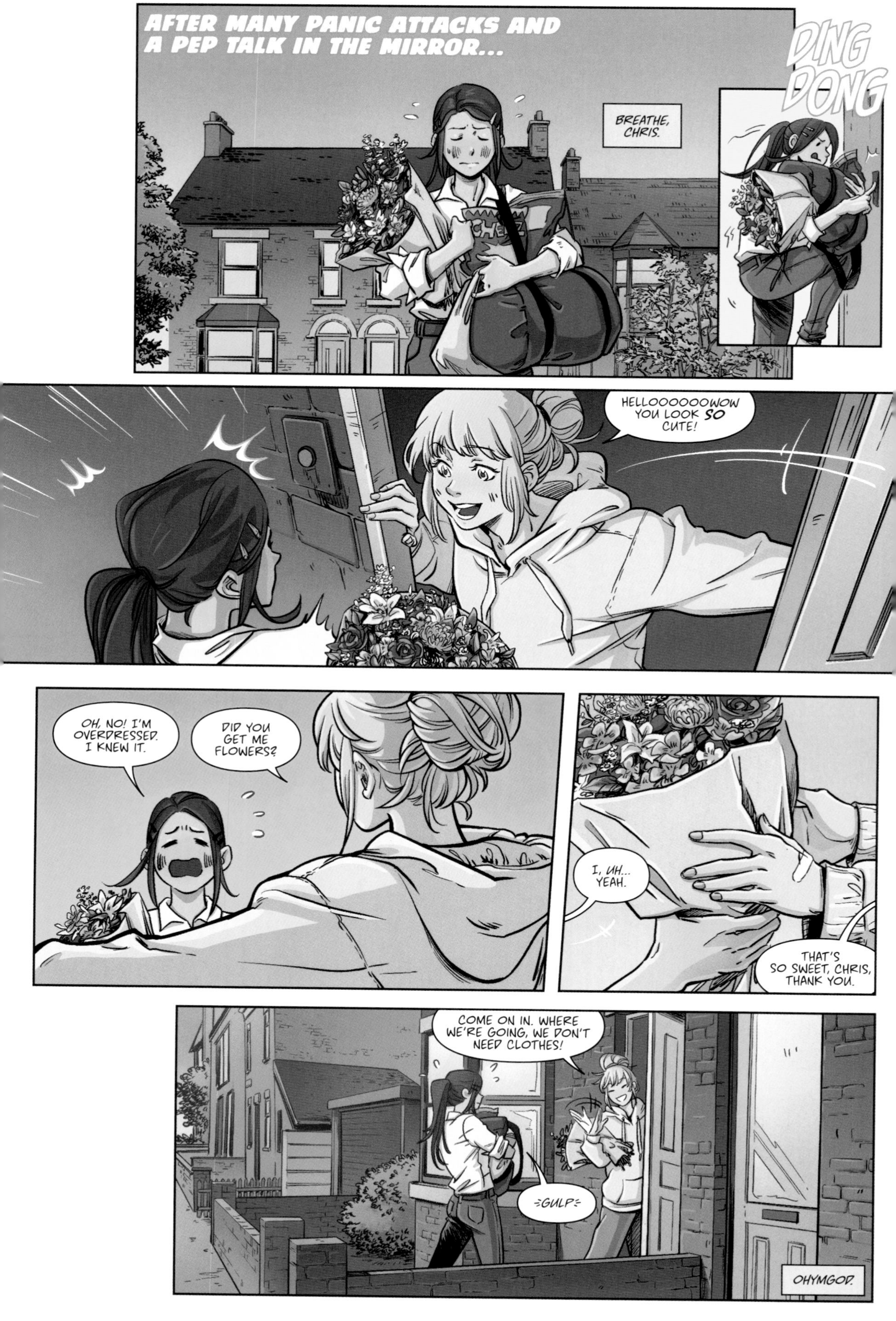
AFTER MANY PANIC ATTACKS AND A PEP TALK IN THE MIRROR...
BREATHE, CHRIS.
DING DONG
HELLOOOOOOWOW YOU LOOK SO CUTE!
OH, NO! I'M OVERDRESSED. I KNEW IT.
DID YOU GET ME FLOWERS?
I, UH... YEAH.
THAT'S SO SWEET, CHRIS, THANK YOU.
COME ON IN. WHERE WE'RE GOING, WE DON'T NEED CLOTHES!
GULP
OHYMGOD.

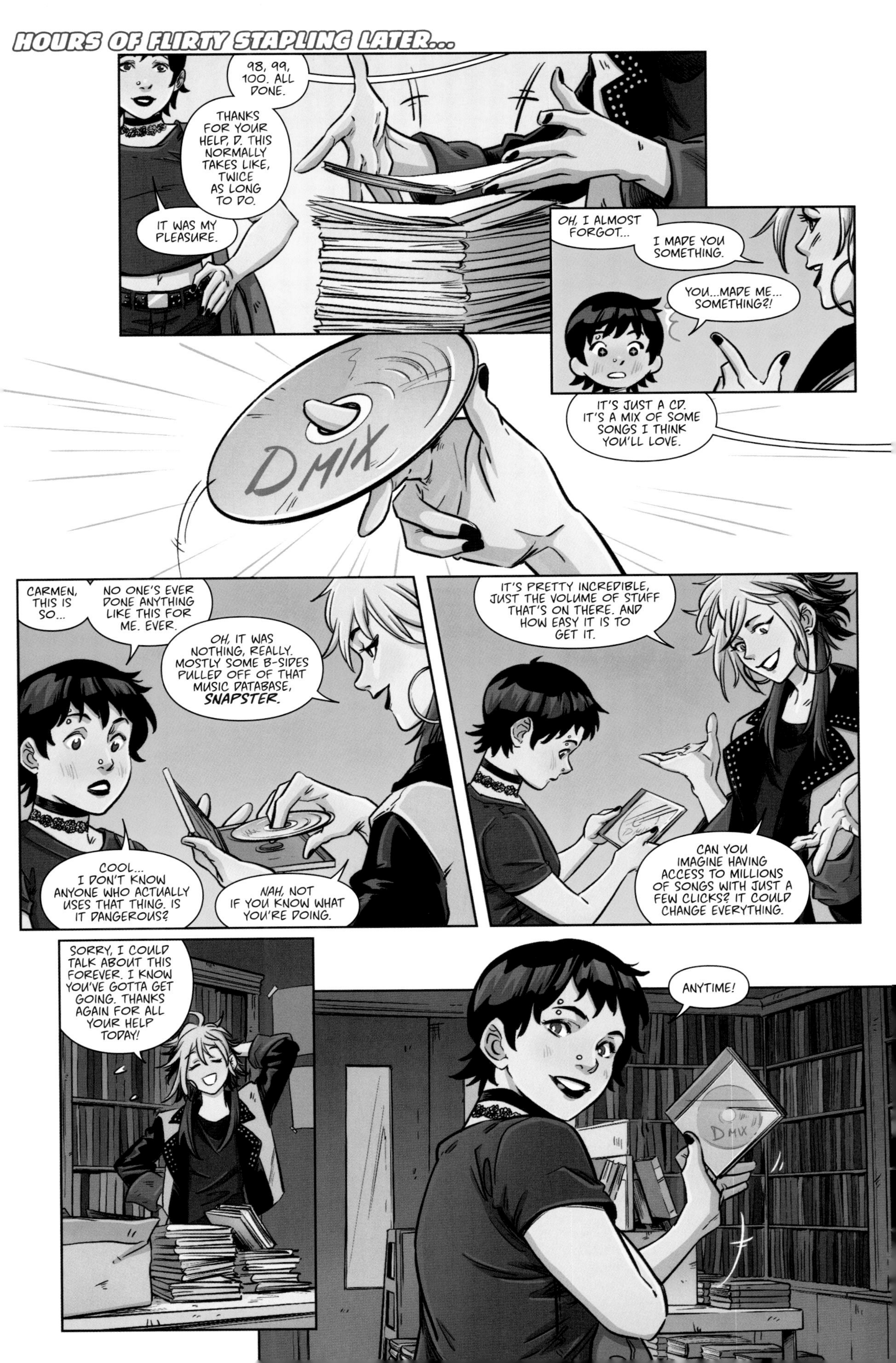
HOURS OF FLIRTY STAPLING LATER...
98, 99, 100. ALL DONE.
THANKS FOR YOUR HELP, D. THIS NORMALLY TAKES LIKE, TWICE AS LONG TO DO.
IT WAS MY PLEASURE.
OH, I ALMOST FORGOT...
I MADE YOU SOMETHING.
YOU...MADE ME... SOMETHING?!
D MIX
IT'S JUST A CD. IT'S A MIX OF SOME SONGS I THINK YOU'LL LOVE.
CARMEN, THIS IS SO...
NO ONE'S EVER DONE ANYTHING LIKE THIS FOR ME. EVER.
OH, IT WAS NOTHING, REALLY. MOSTLY SOME B-SIDES PULLED OFF OF THAT MUSIC DATABASE, SNAPSTER.
COOL... I DON'T KNOW ANYONE WHO ACTUALLY USES THAT THING. IS IT DANGEROUS?
NAH, NOT IF YOU KNOW WHAT YOU'RE DOING.
IT'S PRETTY INCREDIBLE, JUST THE VOLUME OF STUFF THAT'S ON THERE. AND HOW EASY IT IS TO GET IT.
CAN YOU IMAGINE HAVING ACCESS TO MILLIONS OF SONGS WITH JUST A FEW CLICKS? IT COULD CHANGE EVERYTHING.
SORRY, I COULD TALK ABOUT THIS FOREVER. I KNOW YOU'VE GOTTA GET GOING. THANKS AGAIN FOR ALL YOUR HELP TODAY!
ANYTIME!
D MIX

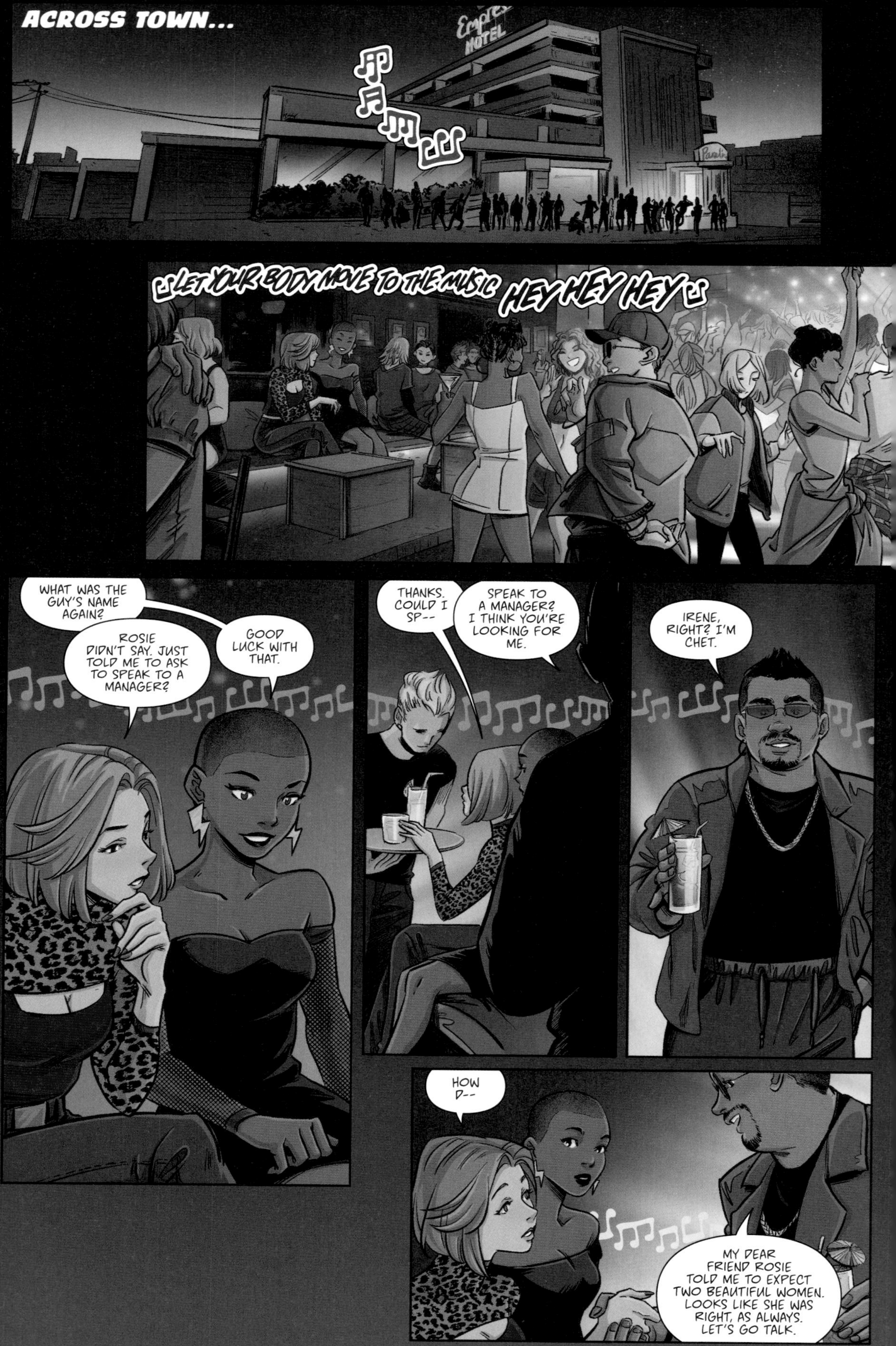
ACROSS TOWN...
EMPRESS HOTEL
LET YOUR BODY MOVE TO THE MUSIC HEY HEY HEY
WHAT WAS THE GUY'S NAME AGAIN?
ROSIE DIDN'T SAY. JUST TOLD ME TO ASK TO SPEAK TO A MANAGER?
GOOD LUCK WITH THAT.
THANKS. COULD I SP--
SPEAK TO A MANAGER? I THINK YOU'RE LOOKING FOR ME.
IRENE, RIGHT? I'M CHET.
HOW D--
MY DEAR FRIEND ROSIE TOLD ME TO EXPECT TWO BEAUTIFUL WOMEN. LOOKS LIKE SHE WAS RIGHT, AS ALWAYS. LET'S GO TALK.

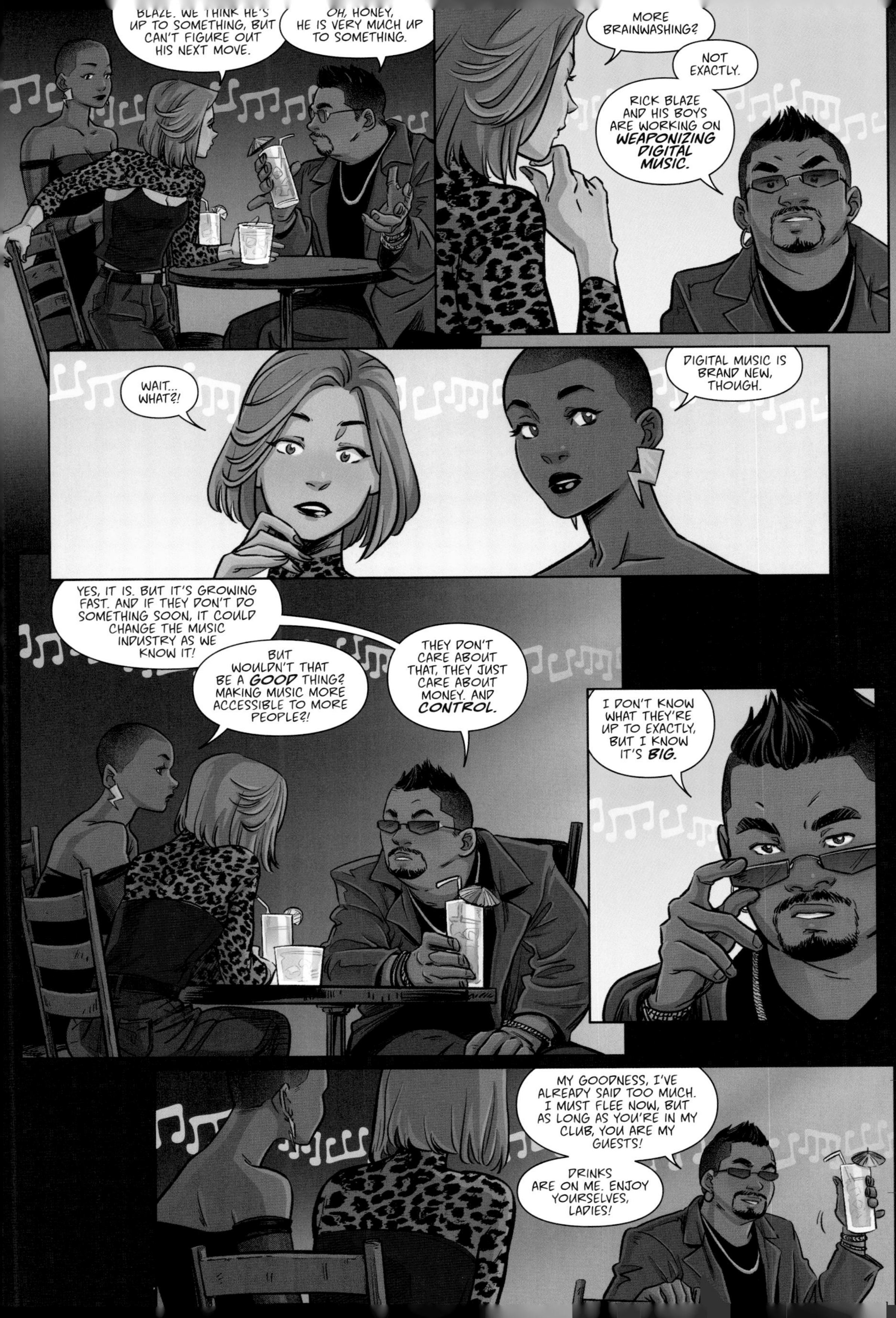
BLAZE. WE THINK HE'S UP TO SOMETHING, BUT CAN'T FIGURE OUT HIS NEXT MOVE.
OH, HONEY, HE IS VERY MUCH UP TO SOMETHING.
MORE BRAINWASHING?
NOT EXACTLY.
RICK BLAZE AND HIS BOYS ARE WORKING ON **WEAPONIZING DIGITAL MUSIC.**
WAIT... WHAT?!
DIGITAL MUSIC IS BRAND NEW, THOUGH.
YES, IT IS. BUT IT'S GROWING FAST. AND IF THEY DON'T DO SOMETHING SOON, IT COULD CHANGE THE MUSIC INDUSTRY AS WE KNOW IT!
BUT WOULDN'T THAT BE A **GOOD** THING? MAKING MUSIC MORE ACCESSIBLE TO MORE PEOPLE?!
THEY DON'T CARE ABOUT THAT, THEY JUST CARE ABOUT MONEY. AND **CONTROL.**
I DON'T KNOW WHAT THEY'RE UP TO EXACTLY, BUT I KNOW IT'S **BIG.**
MY GOODNESS, I'VE ALREADY SAID TOO MUCH. I MUST FLEE NOW, BUT AS LONG AS YOU'RE IN MY CLUB, YOU ARE MY GUESTS!
DRINKS ARE ON ME. ENJOY YOURSELVES, LADIES!

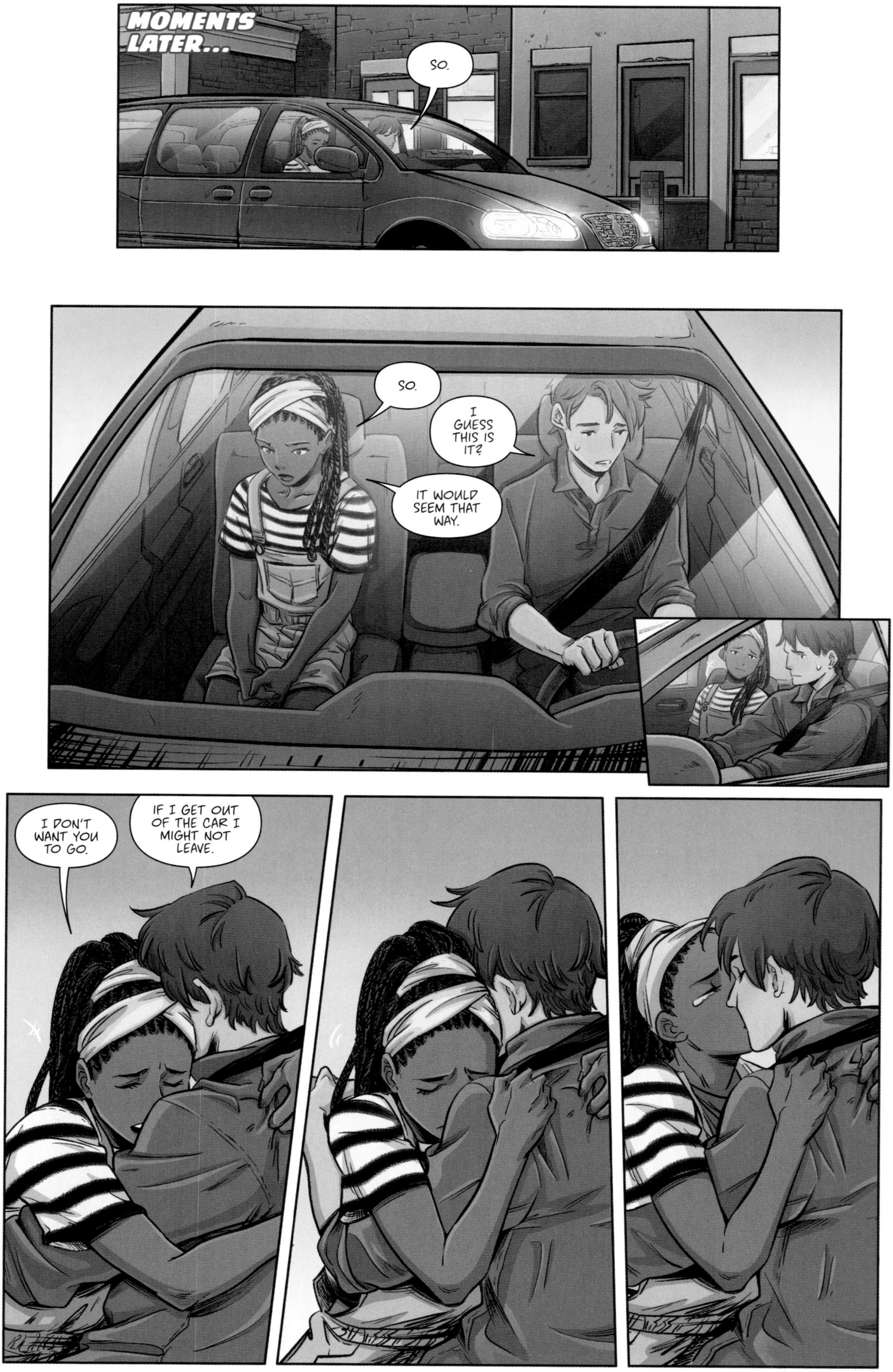
MOMENTS LATER...
SO.
SO.
I GUESS THIS IS IT?
IT WOULD SEEM THAT WAY.
I DON'T WANT YOU TO GO.
IF I GET OUT OF THE CAR I MIGHT NOT LEAVE.

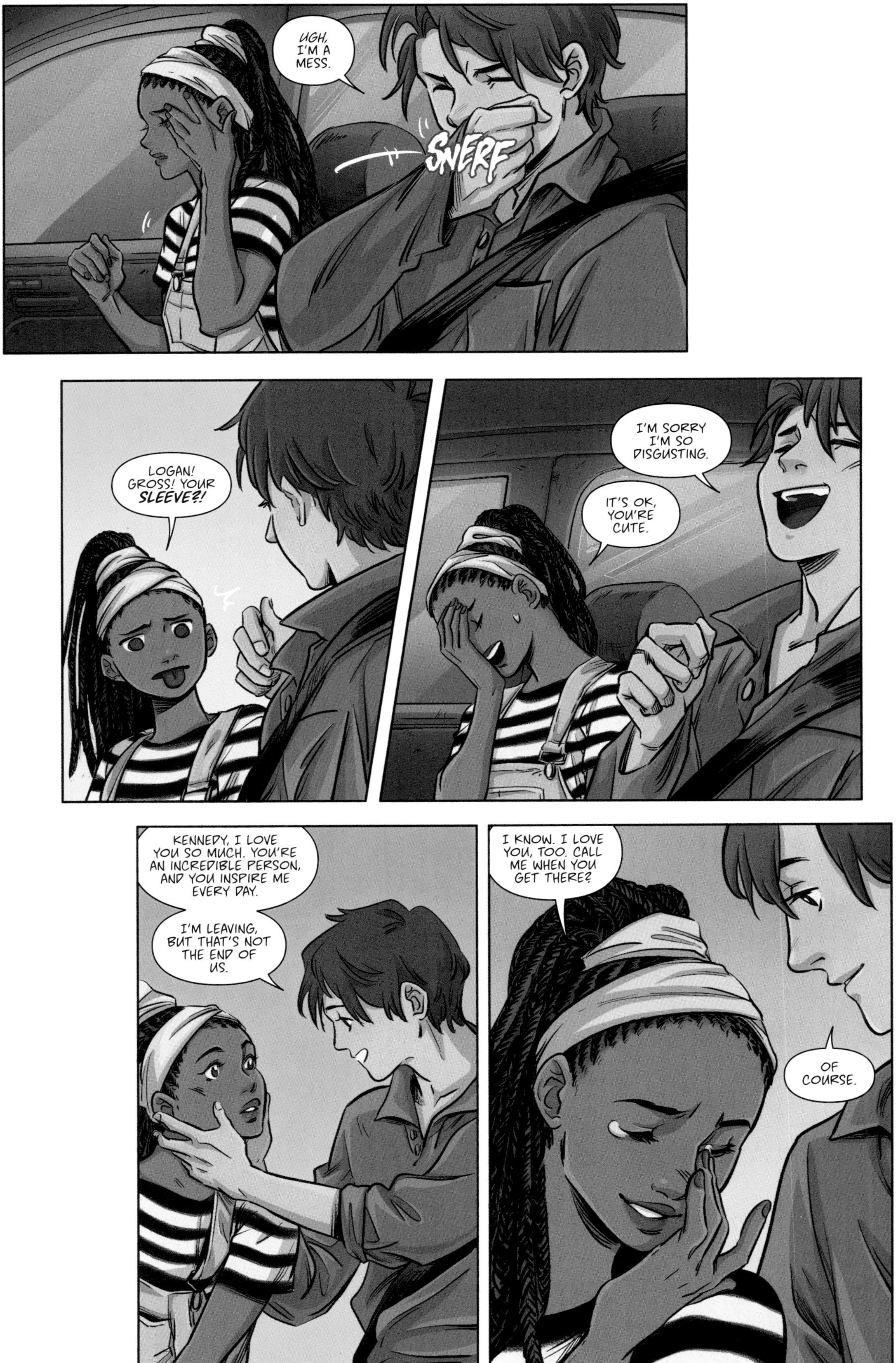
UGH, I'M A MESS.
SNERF
LOGAN! GROSS! YOUR SLEEVE?!
I'M SORRY I'M SO DISGUSTING.
IT'S OK, YOU'RE CUTE.
KENNEDY, I LOVE YOU SO MUCH. YOU'RE AN INCREDIBLE PERSON, AND YOU INSPIRE ME EVERY DAY.
I'M LEAVING, BUT THAT'S NOT THE END OF US.
I KNOW. I LOVE YOU, TOO. CALL ME WHEN YOU GET THERE?
OF COURSE.

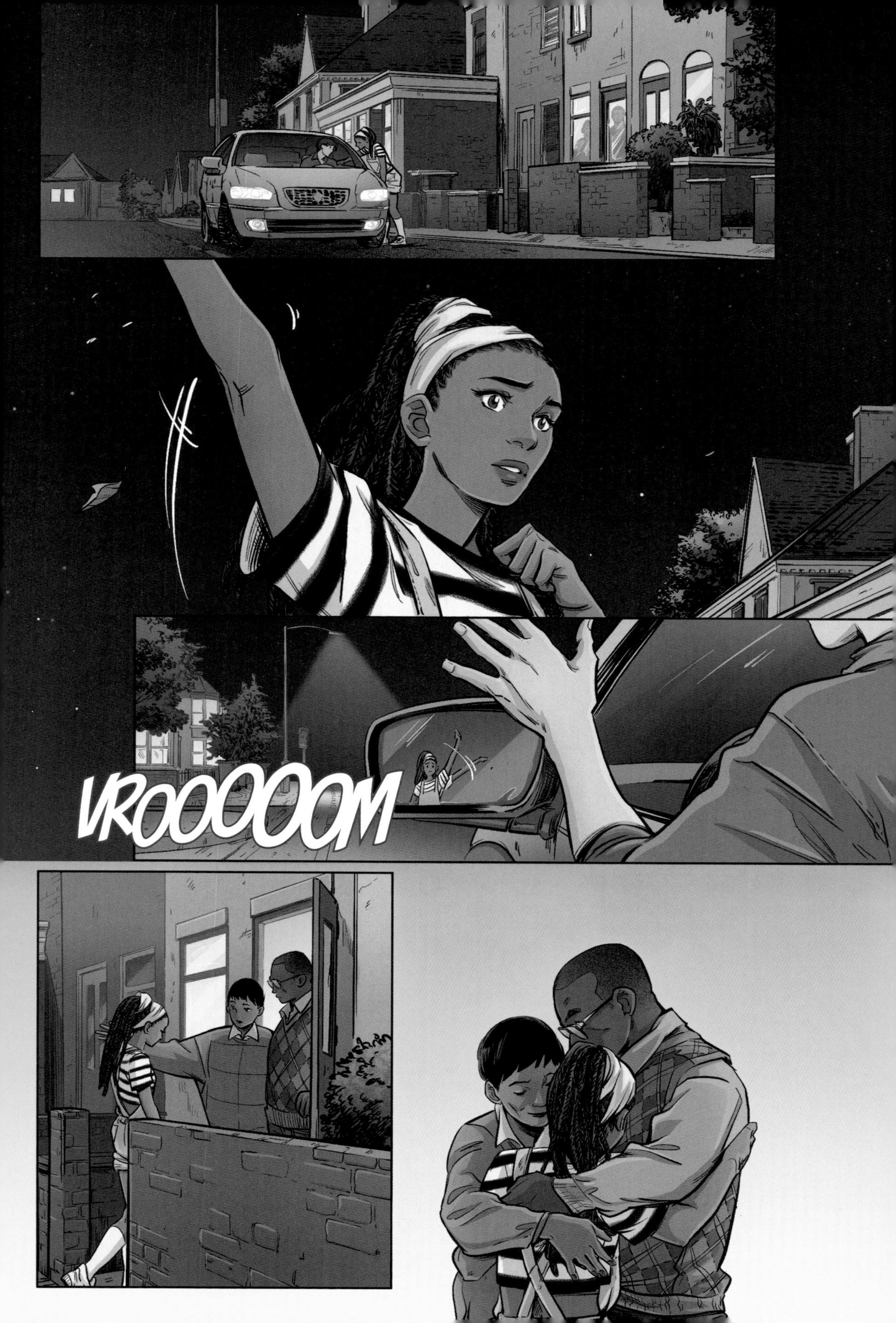
VROOOOOM

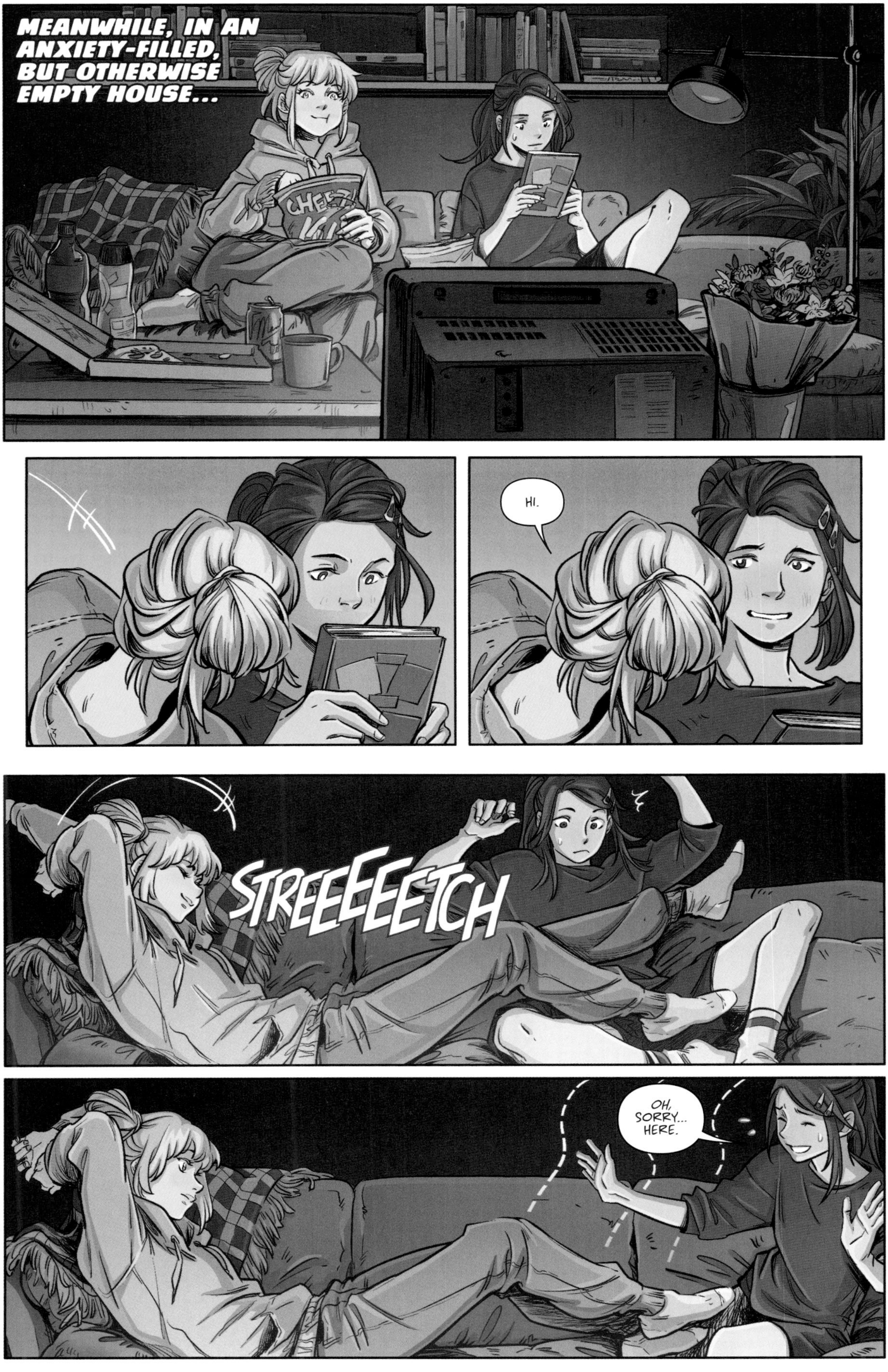
MEANWHILE, IN AN ANXIETY-FILLED, BUT OTHERWISE EMPTY HOUSE...
HI.
STREEEEEETCH
OH, SORRY... HERE.

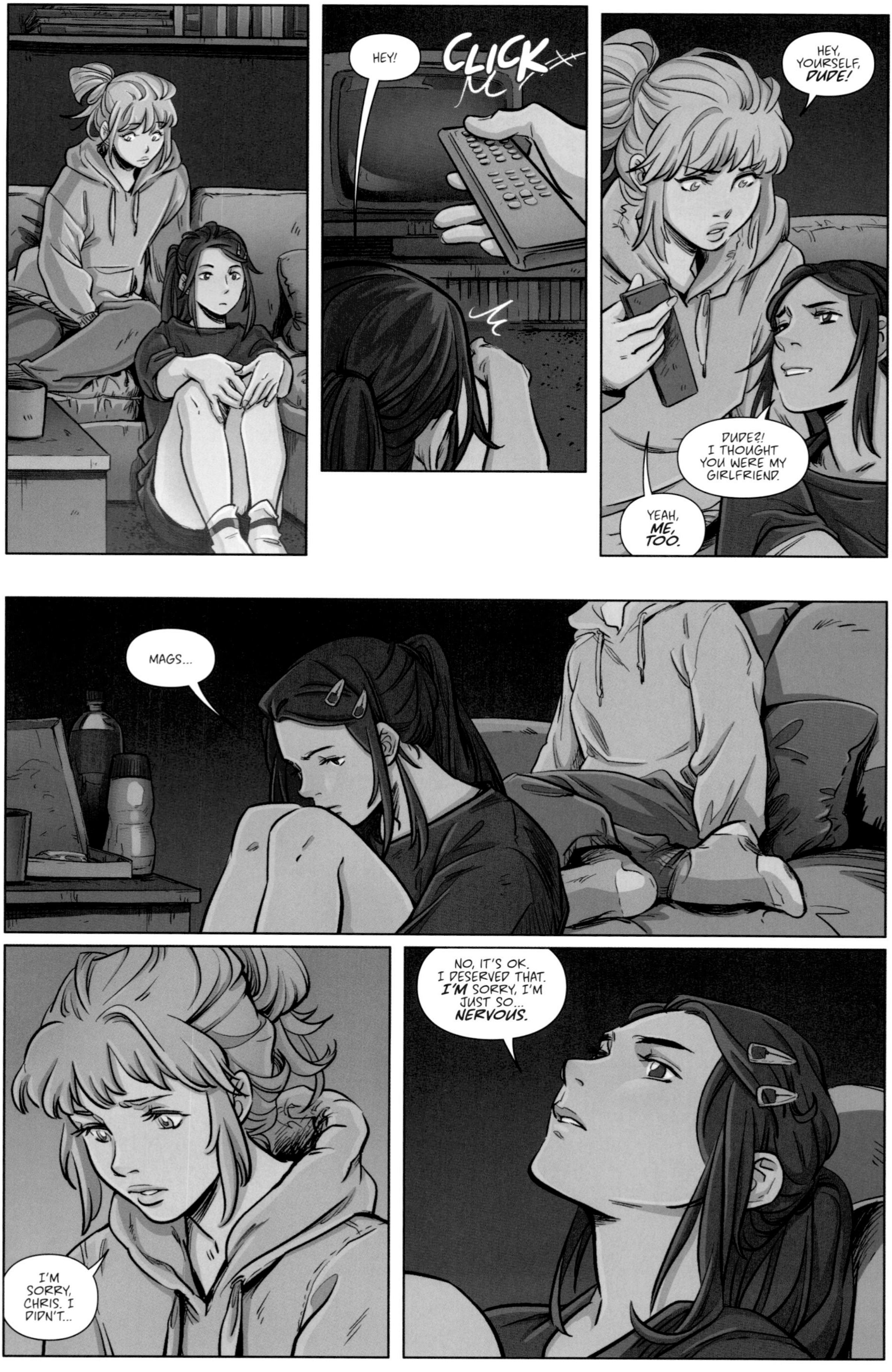
HEY!
CLICK
HEY, YOURSELF, DUDE!
DUDE?! I THOUGHT YOU WERE MY GIRLFRIEND.
YEAH, ME, TOO.
MAGS...
I'M SORRY, CHRIS. I DIDN'T...
NO, IT'S OK. I DESERVED THAT. I'M SORRY, I'M JUST SO... NERVOUS.

IT'S OK. THERE'S NOTHING TO BE NERVOUS ABOUT. IT'S JUST ME.

I'M NOT SCARY, AM I?

NO. YOU'RE NOT SCARY.

DO YOU WANT ME TO PUT THE MOVIE BACK ON?

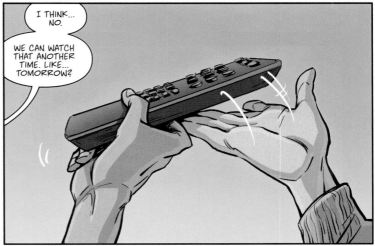

I THINK... NO.

WE CAN WATCH THAT ANOTHER TIME. LIKE... TOMORROW?

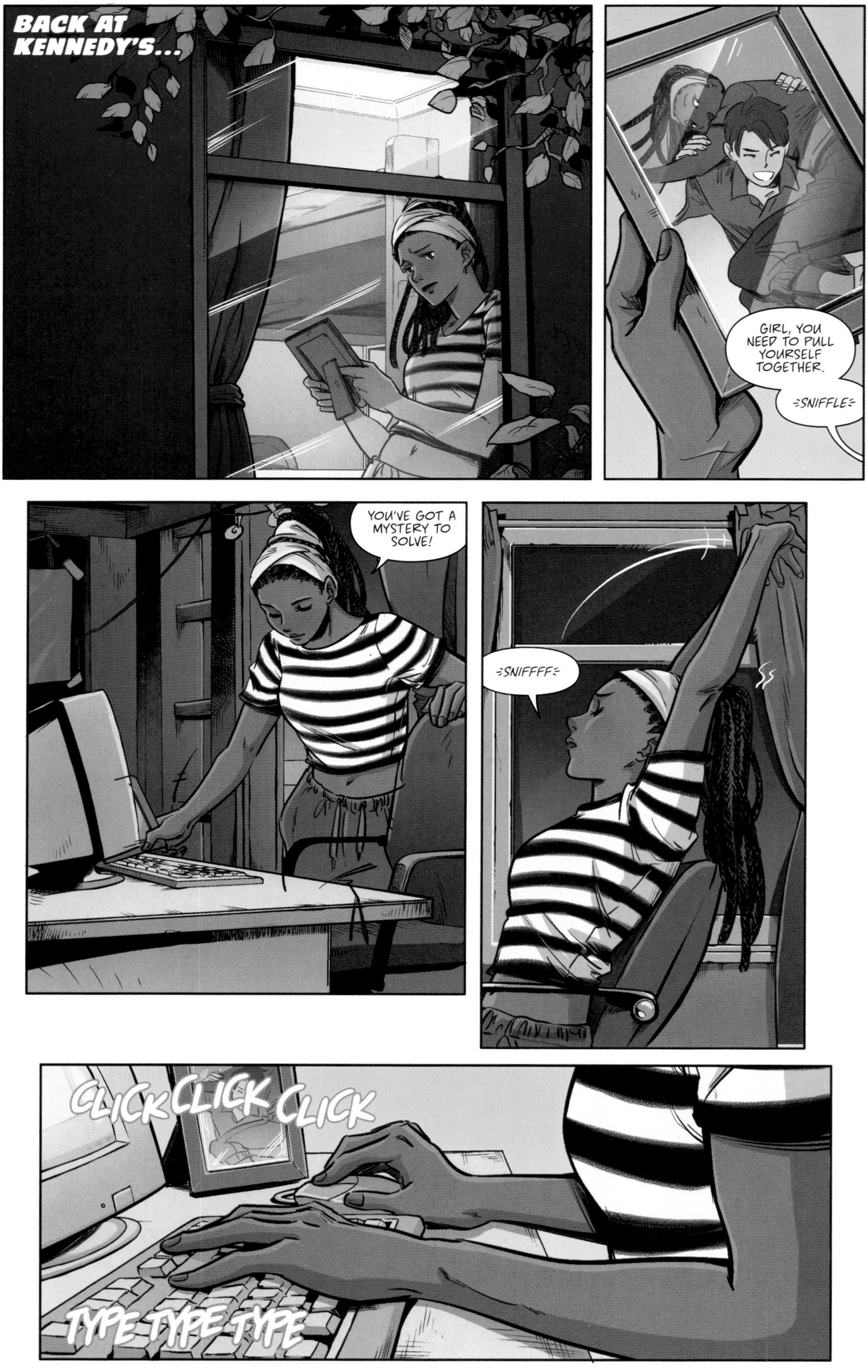
BACK AT KENNEDY'S...
GIRL, YOU NEED TO PULL YOURSELF TOGETHER.
=SNIFFLE=
YOU'VE GOT A MYSTERY TO SOLVE!
=SNIFFFF=
CLICK CLICK CLICK
TYPE TYPE TYPE

HOME   POST   SEARCH   EXPAND

NEWSIC: Music News You Can Use

"Genie in a Bottle" still #1!!
New Dixie Chicks on the way
Who will win a Moonman at the VMAs??
Snapster growing despite legal objections
INCREDIBLE FINDS AT THE ARTIST FORMERLY KNOWN AS PRINCE'S YARD SALE!!!
DESTINY'S CHILD!!!
weird Snapster thing, has ne1 else noticed?
just discovered TILT on SHORT MUSIC FOR SHORT PEOPLE, holy crap....
More lawsuits filed against Woodstock 99 promoters
NOW THAT'S WHAT I CALL MUSIC 2???? How many of these can they even make?!?!

HMM...

CLICK

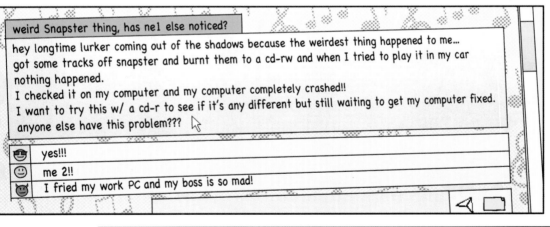

weird Snapster thing, has ne1 else noticed?

hey longtime lurker coming out of the shadows because the weirdest thing happened to me...
got some tracks off snapster and burnt them to a cd-rw and when I tried to play it in my car
nothing happened.
I checked it on my computer and my computer completely crashed!!
I want to try this w/ a cd-r to see if it's any different but still waiting to get my computer fixed.
anyone else have this problem???

	yes!!!
	me 2!!
	I fried my work PC and my boss is so mad!

WHOA!

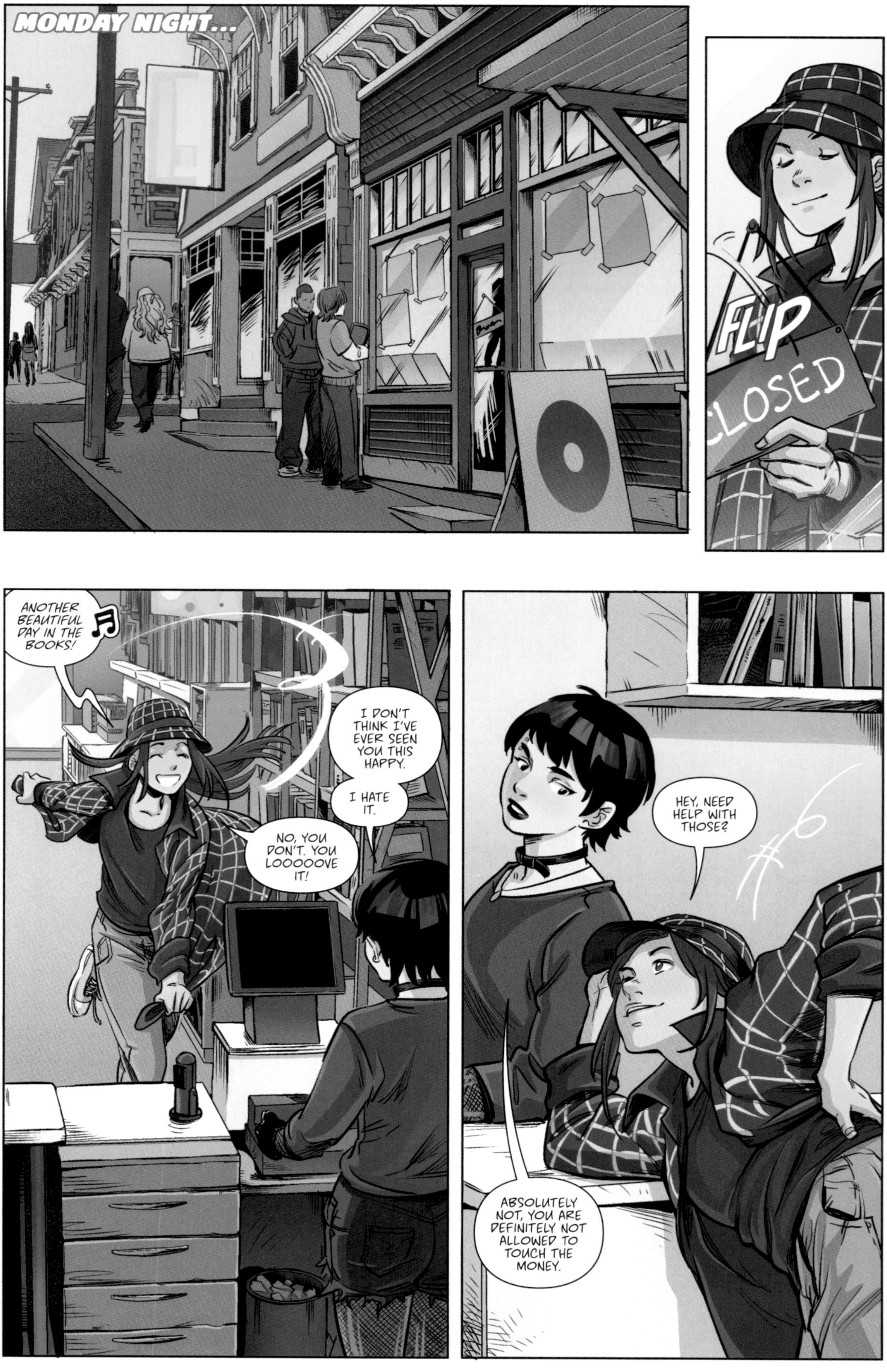
MONDAY NIGHT...
FLIP
CLOSED
ANOTHER BEAUTIFUL DAY IN THE BOOKS!
I DON'T THINK I'VE EVER SEEN YOU THIS HAPPY.
I HATE IT.
NO, YOU DON'T. YOU LOOOOOVE IT!
HEY, NEED HELP WITH THOSE?
ABSOLUTELY NOT, YOU ARE DEFINITELY NOT ALLOWED TO TOUCH THE MONEY.

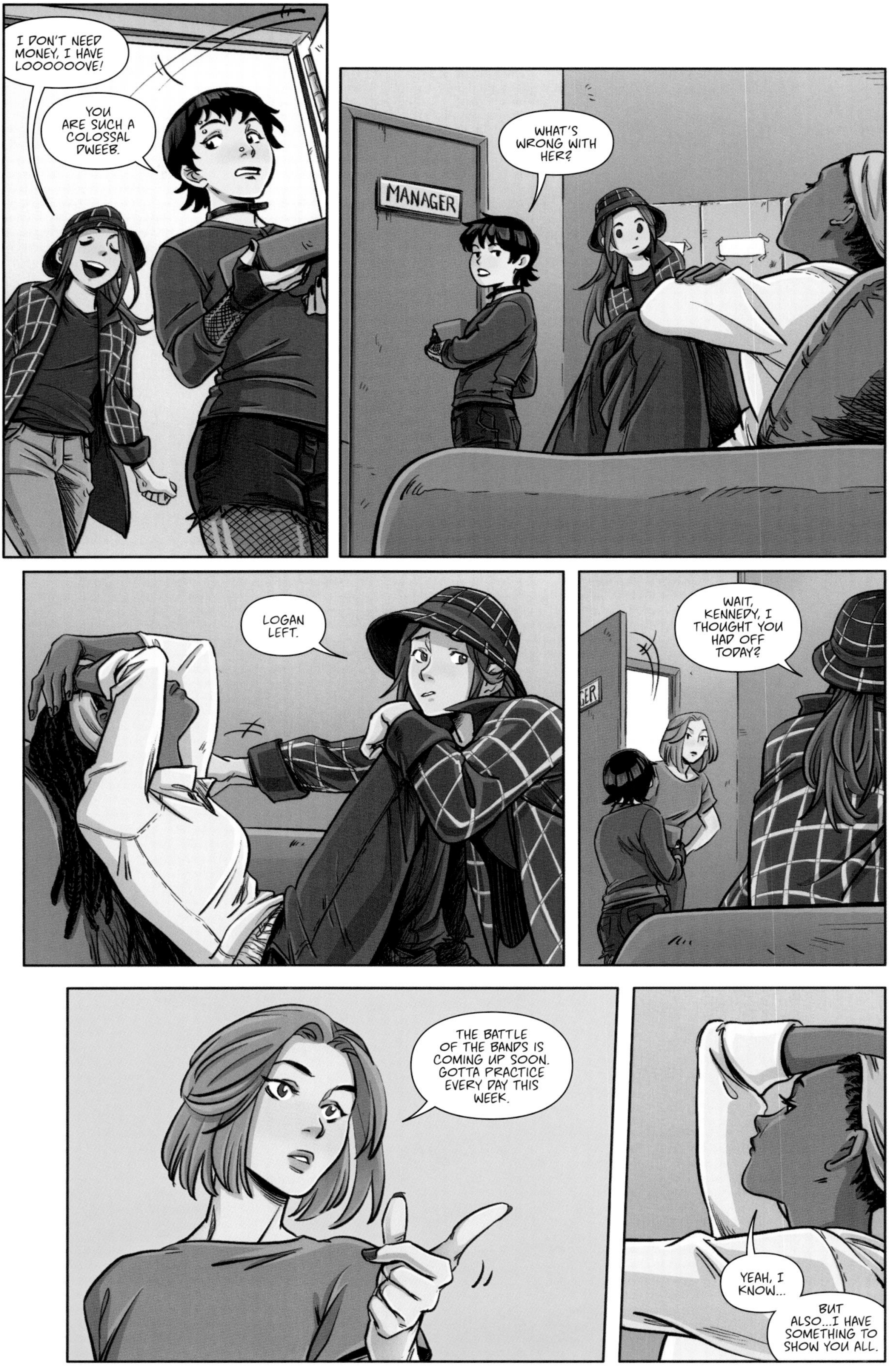

I DON'T NEED MONEY, I HAVE LOOOOOOVE!
YOU ARE SUCH A COLOSSAL DWEEB.
MANAGER
WHAT'S WRONG WITH HER?
LOGAN LEFT.
WAIT, KENNEDY, I THOUGHT YOU HAD OFF TODAY?
THE BATTLE OF THE BANDS IS COMING UP SOON. GOTTA PRACTICE EVERY DAY THIS WEEK.
YEAH, I KNOW...
BUT ALSO...I HAVE SOMETHING TO SHOW YOU ALL.

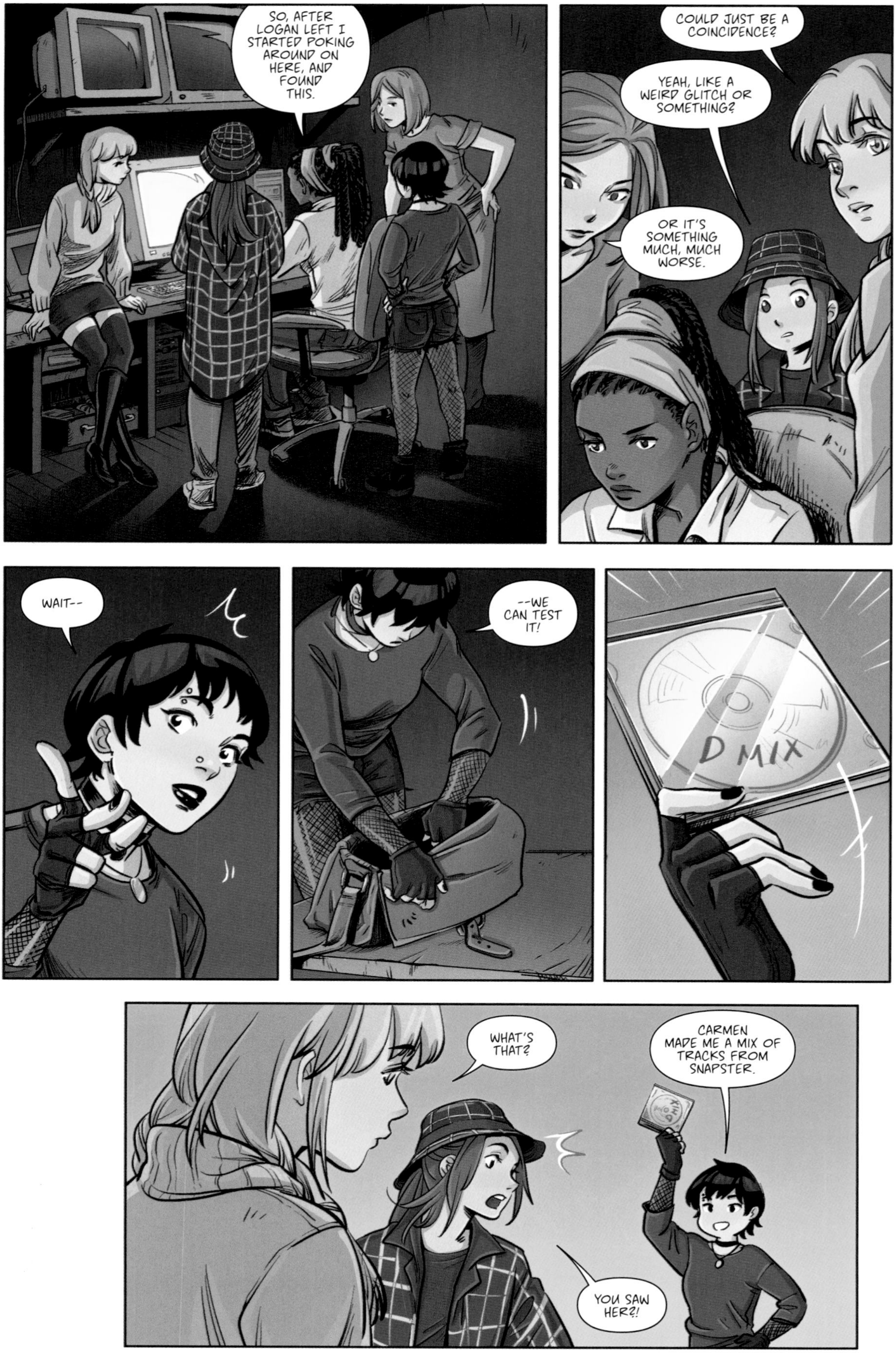
SO, AFTER LOGAN LEFT I STARTED POKING AROUND ON HERE, AND FOUND THIS.
COULD JUST BE A COINCIDENCE?
YEAH, LIKE A WEIRD GLITCH OR SOMETHING?
OR IT'S SOMETHING MUCH, MUCH WORSE.
WAIT--
--WE CAN TEST IT!
D MIX
WHAT'S THAT?
CARMEN MADE ME A MIX OF TRACKS FROM SNAPSTER.
YOU SAW HER?!

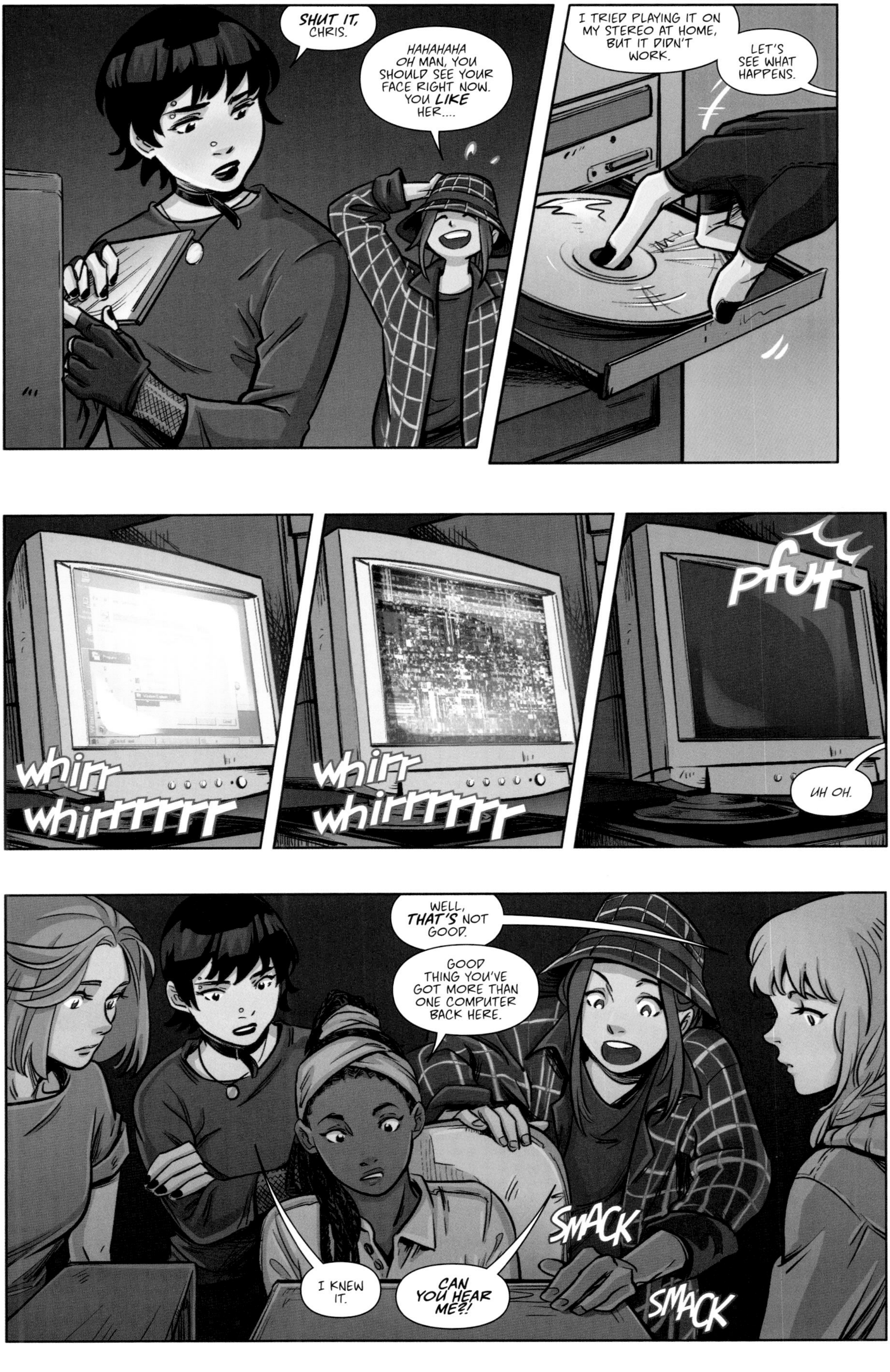
SHUT IT, CHRIS.
HAHAHAHA OH MAN, YOU SHOULD SEE YOUR FACE RIGHT NOW. YOU LIKE HER....
I TRIED PLAYING IT ON MY STEREO AT HOME, BUT IT DIDN'T WORK.
LET'S SEE WHAT HAPPENS.
whirr whirrrrrrr
whirr whirrrrrrr
pfut
UH OH.
WELL, THAT'S NOT GOOD.
GOOD THING YOU'VE GOT MORE THAN ONE COMPUTER BACK HERE.
I KNEW IT.
CAN YOU HEAR ME?!
SMACK
SMACK

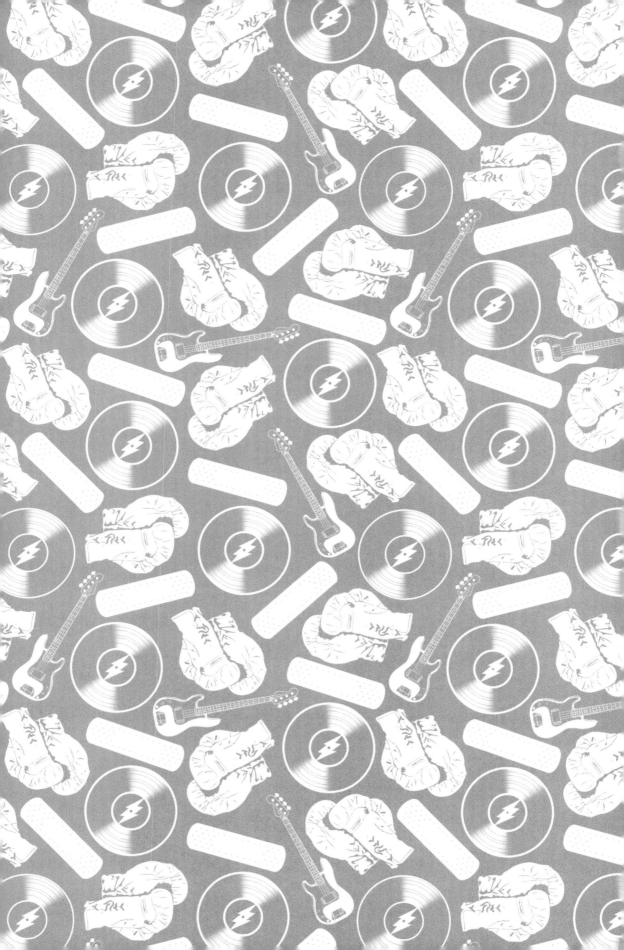

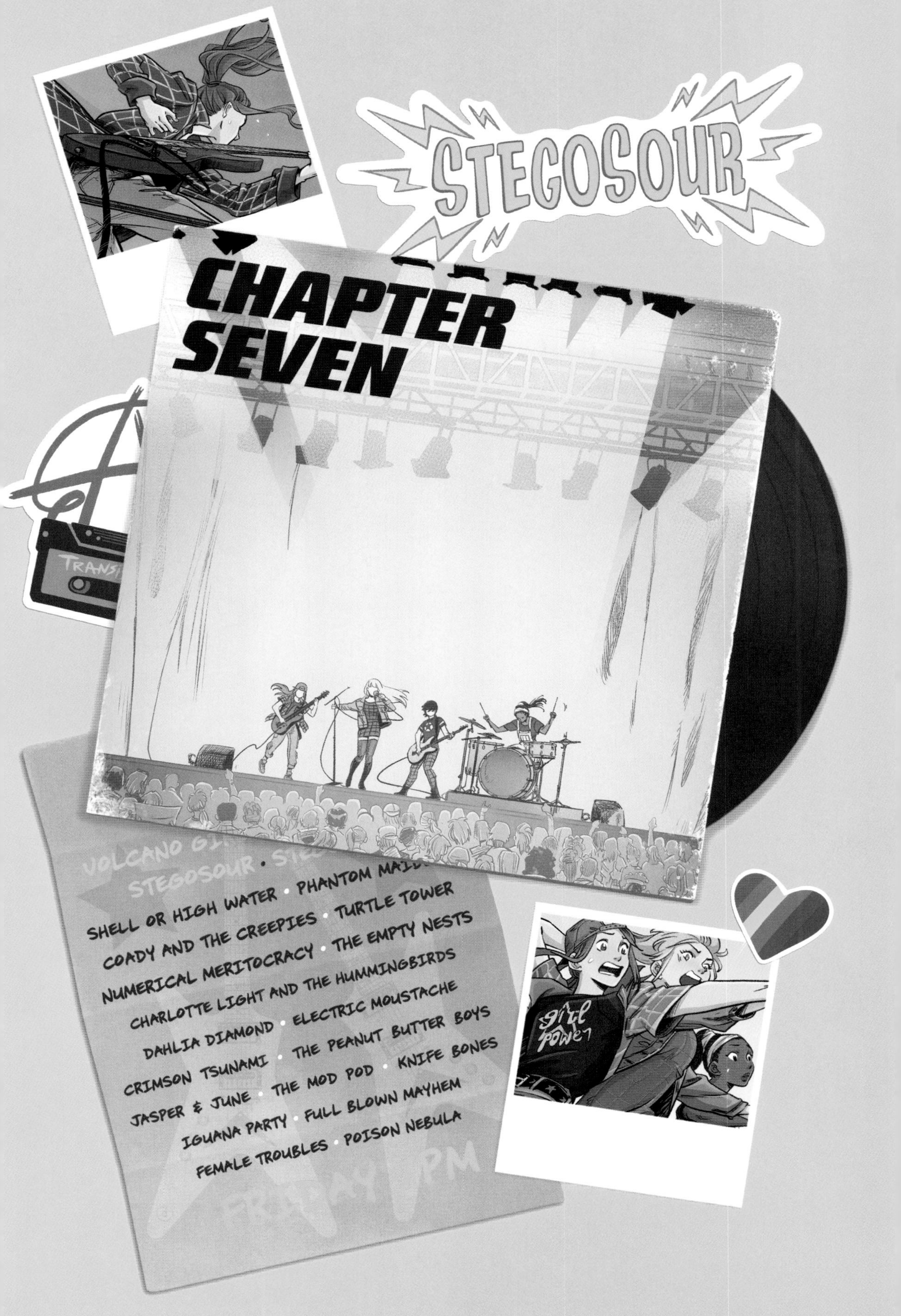
STEGOSOUR
CHAPTER SEVEN
STEGOSOUR
SHELL OR HIGH WATER • PHANTOM
COADY AND THE CREEPIES • TURTLE TOWER
NUMERICAL MERITOCRACY • THE EMPTY NESTS
CHARLOTTE LIGHT AND THE HUMMINGBIRDS
DAHLIA DIAMOND • ELECTRIC MOUSTACHE
CRIMSON TSUNAMI • THE PEANUT BUTTER BOYS
JASPER & JUNE • THE MOD POD • KNIFE BONES
IGUANA PARTY • FULL BLOWN MAYHEM
FEMALE TROUBLES • POISON NEBULA
girl power

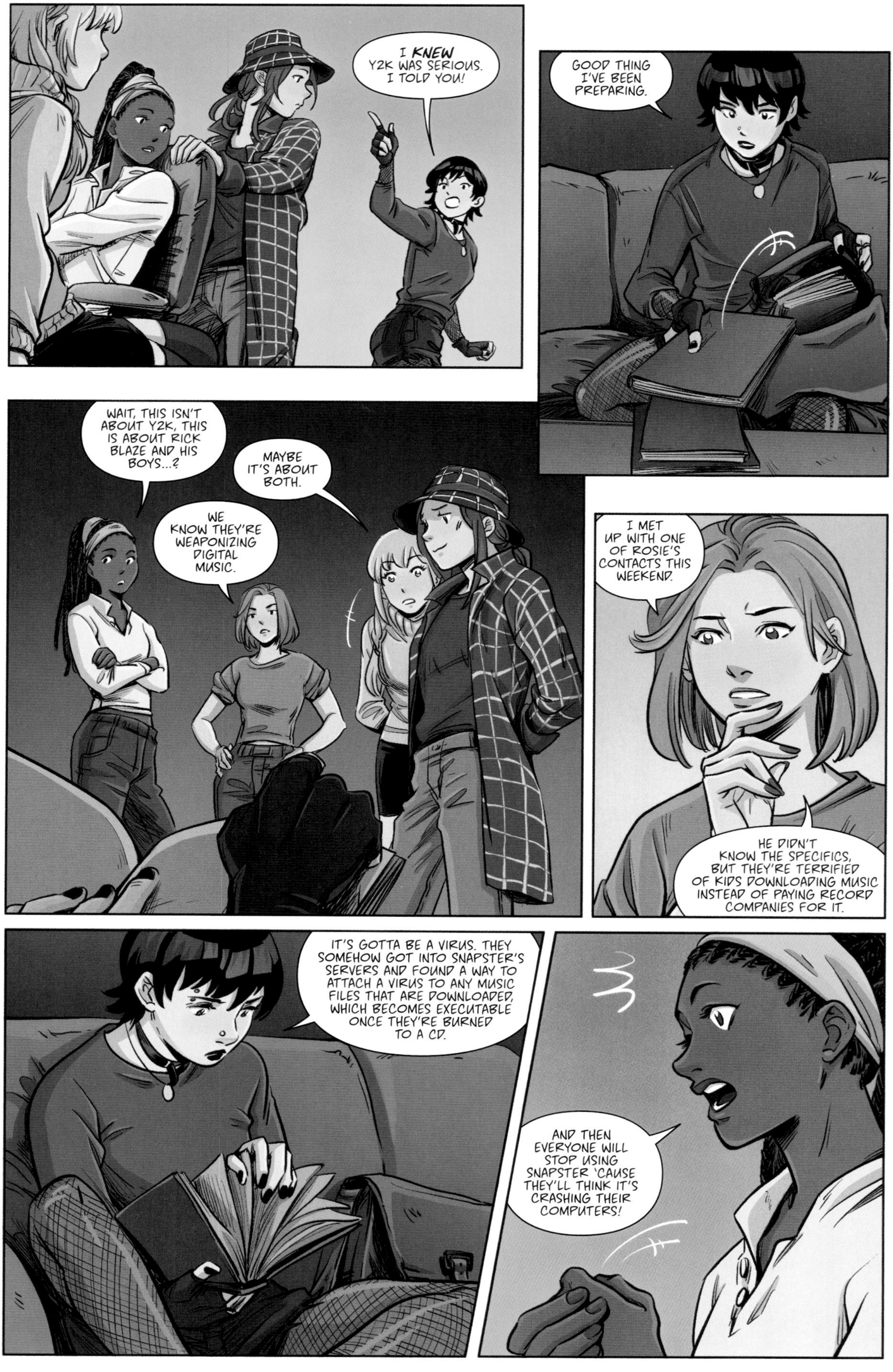
I KNEW Y2K WAS SERIOUS. I TOLD YOU!
GOOD THING I'VE BEEN PREPARING.
WAIT, THIS ISN'T ABOUT Y2K, THIS IS ABOUT RICK BLAZE AND HIS BOYS...?
MAYBE IT'S ABOUT BOTH.
WE KNOW THEY'RE WEAPONIZING DIGITAL MUSIC.
I MET UP WITH ONE OF ROSIE'S CONTACTS THIS WEEKEND.
HE DIDN'T KNOW THE SPECIFICS, BUT THEY'RE TERRIFIED OF KIDS DOWNLOADING MUSIC INSTEAD OF PAYING RECORD COMPANIES FOR IT.
IT'S GOTTA BE A VIRUS. THEY SOMEHOW GOT INTO SNAPSTER'S SERVERS AND FOUND A WAY TO ATTACH A VIRUS TO ANY MUSIC FILES THAT ARE DOWNLOADED, WHICH BECOMES EXECUTABLE ONCE THEY'RE BURNED TO A CD.
AND THEN EVERYONE WILL STOP USING SNAPSTER 'CAUSE THEY'LL THINK IT'S CRASHING THEIR COMPUTERS!

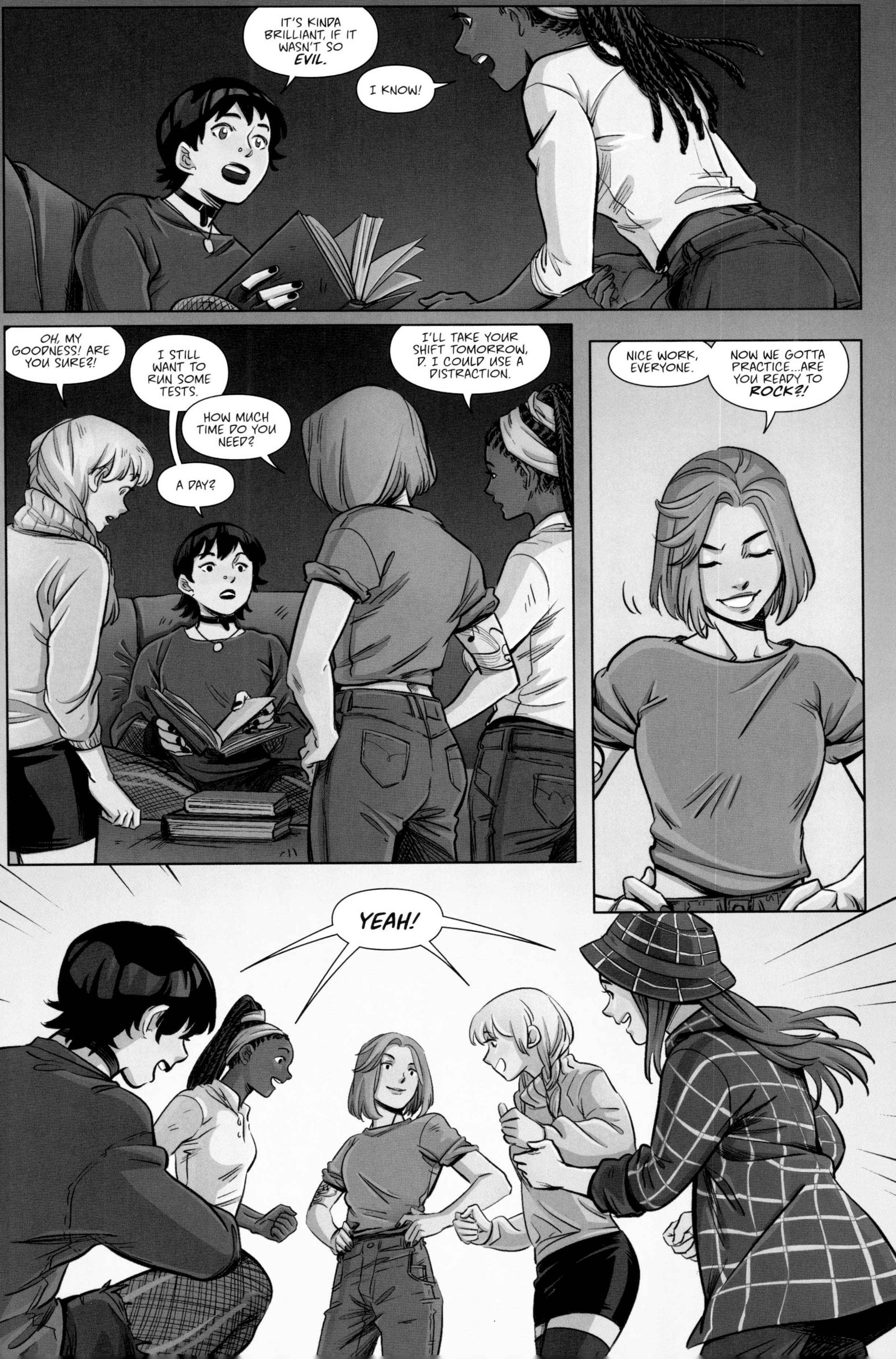
IT'S KINDA BRILLIANT, IF IT WASN'T SO EVIL.
I KNOW!
OH, MY GOODNESS! ARE YOU SURE?!
I STILL WANT TO RUN SOME TESTS.
HOW MUCH TIME DO YOU NEED?
A DAY?
I'LL TAKE YOUR SHIFT TOMORROW, D. I COULD USE A DISTRACTION.
NICE WORK, EVERYONE.
NOW WE GOTTA PRACTICE...ARE YOU READY TO ROCK?!
YEAH!

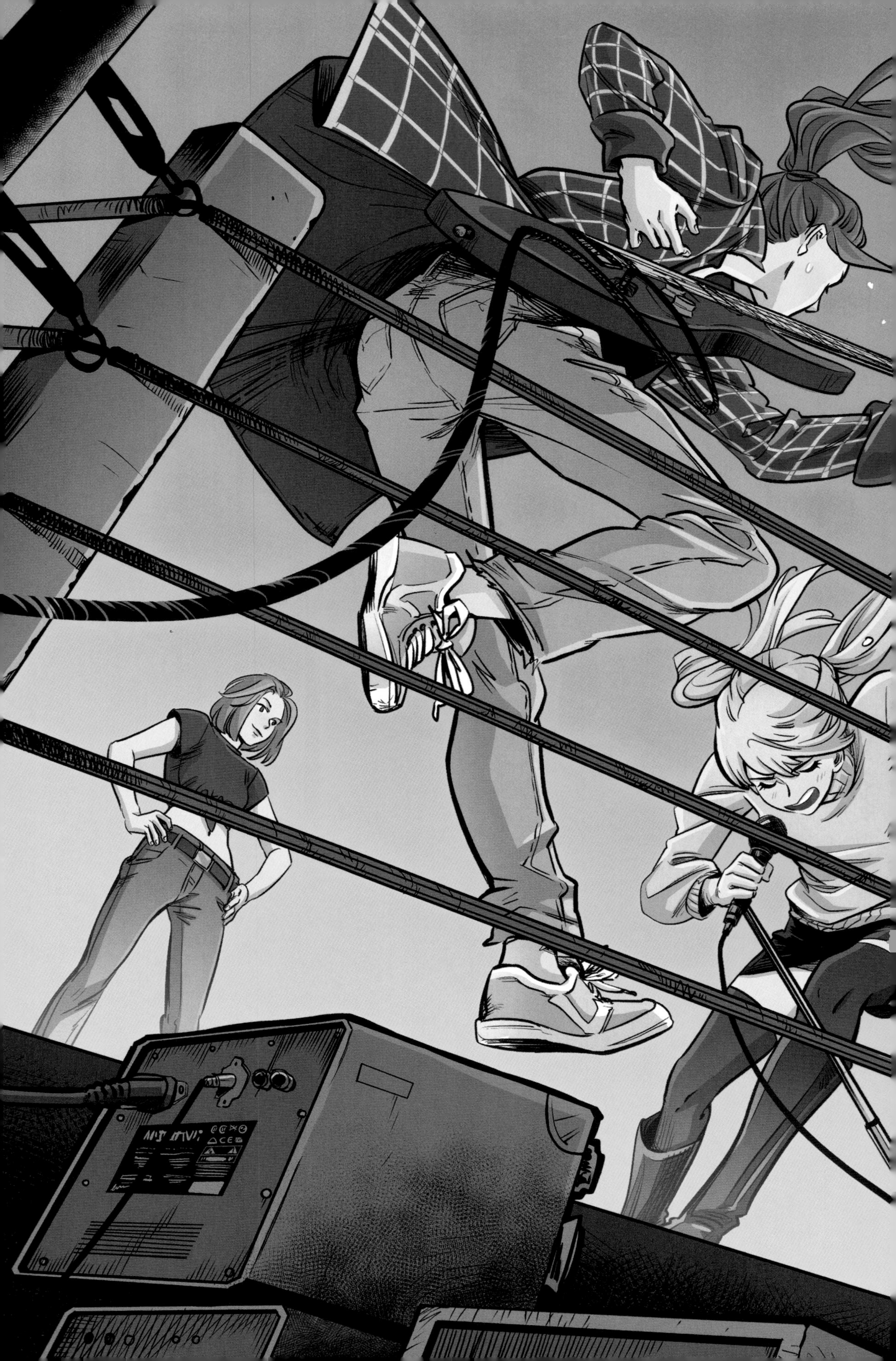

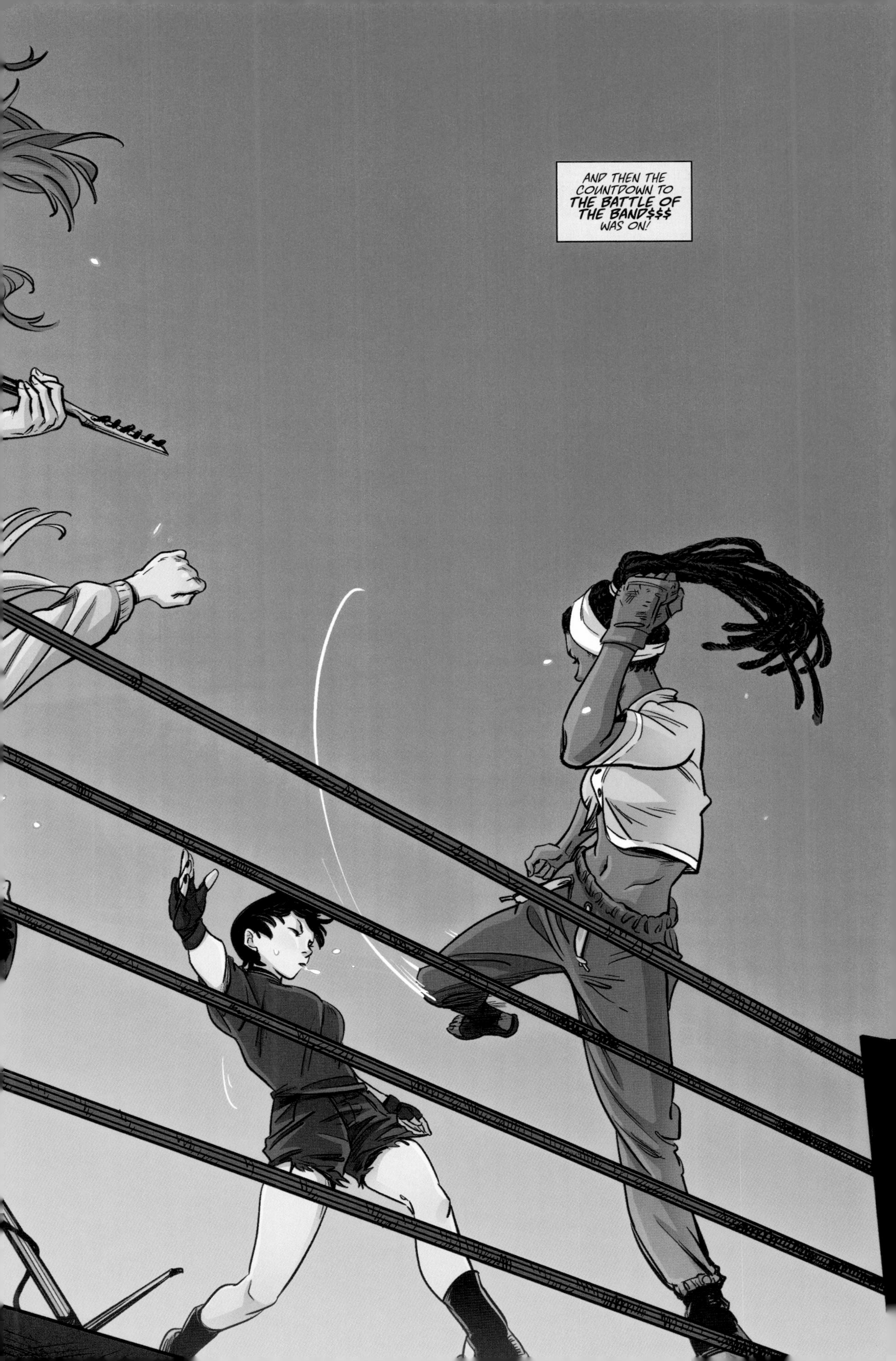
AND THEN THE COUNTDOWN TO **THE BATTLE OF THE BAND$$$** WAS ON!

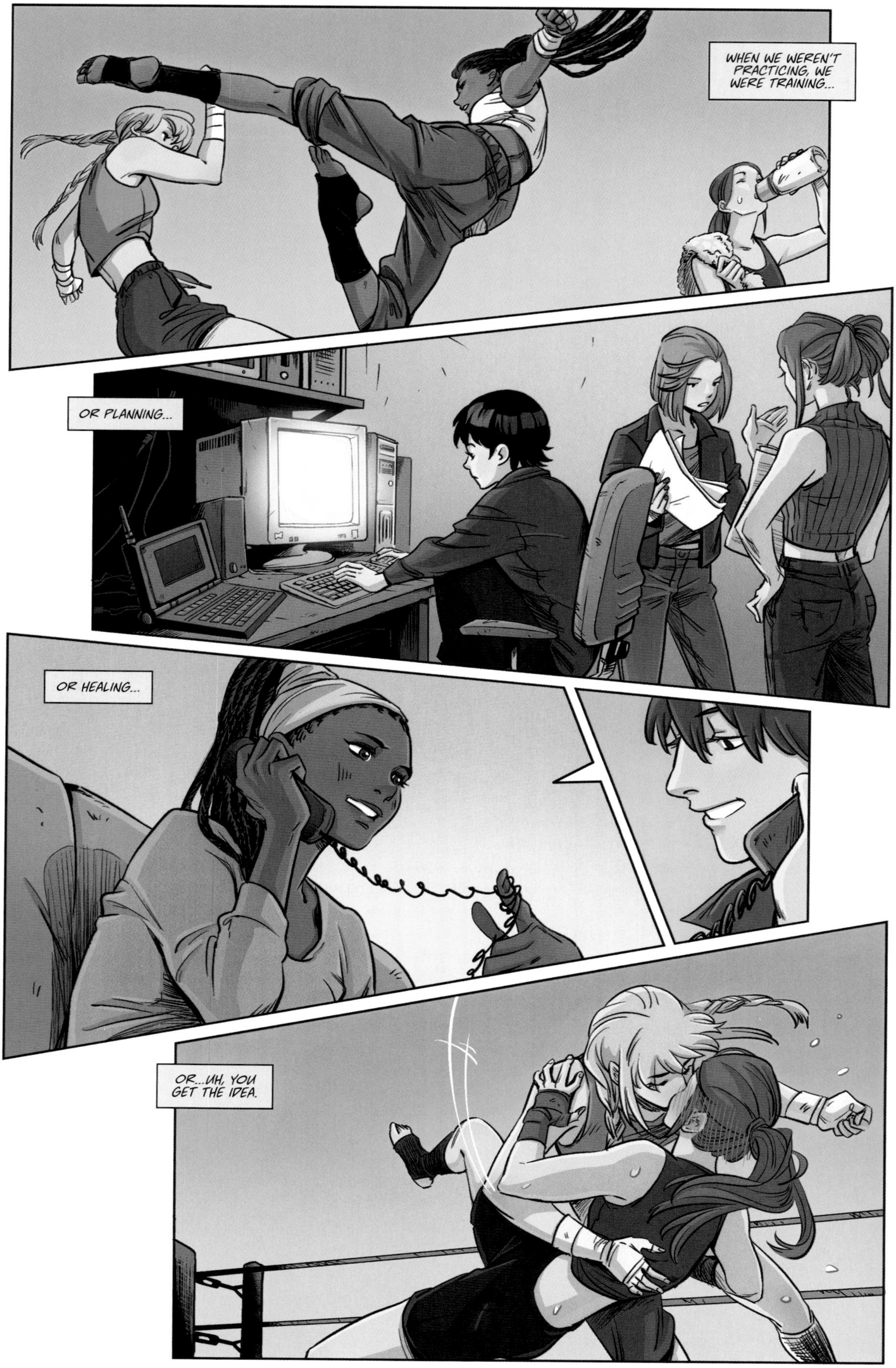
WHEN WE WEREN'T PRACTICING, WE WERE TRAINING...
OR PLANNING...
OR HEALING...
OR...UH, YOU GET THE IDEA.

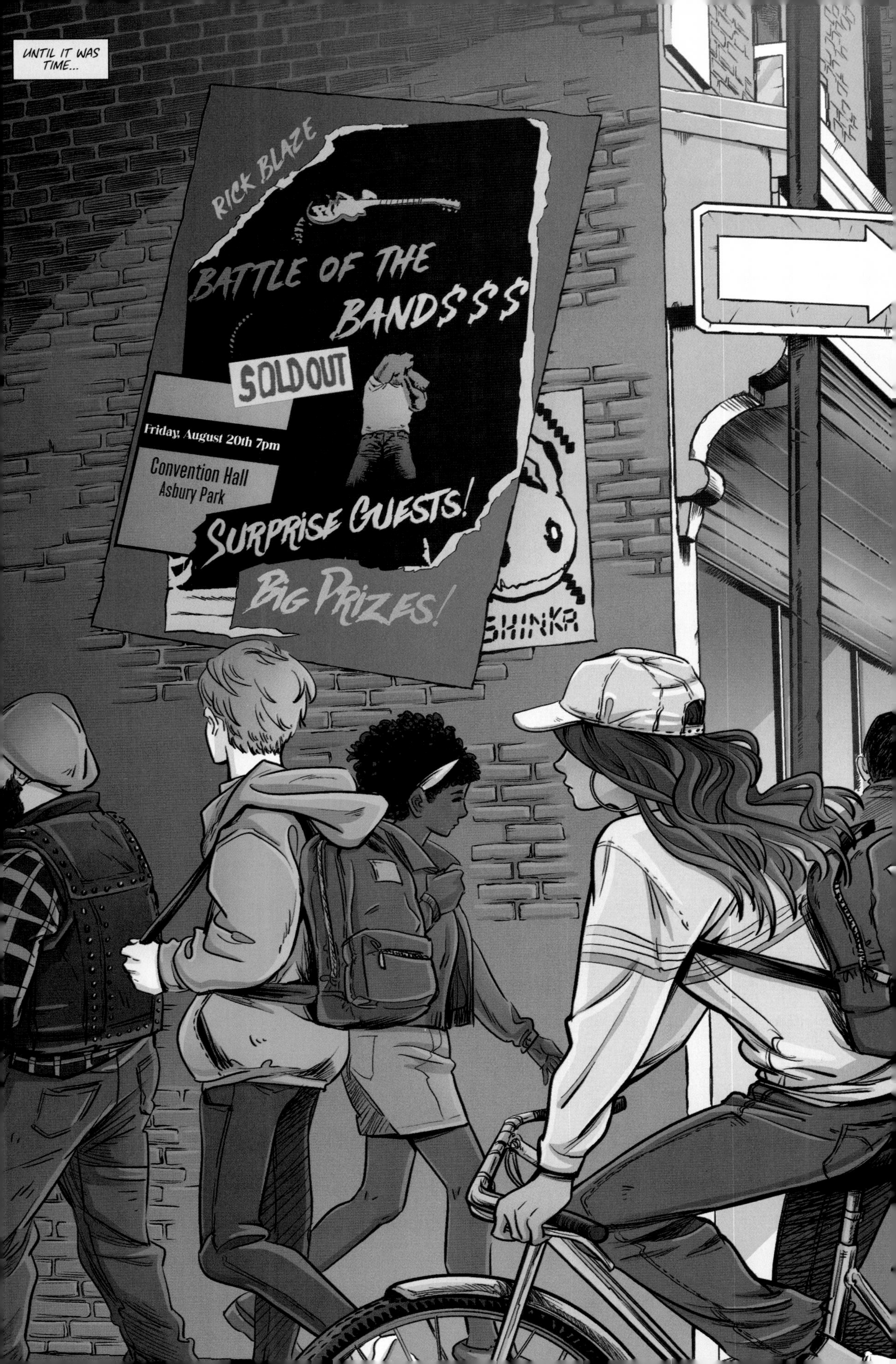
UNTIL IT WAS TIME...
RICK BLAZE
BATTLE OF THE BAND$$$
SOLD OUT
Friday, August 20th 7pm
Convention Hall
Asbury Park
SURPRISE GUESTS!
BIG PRIZES!
SHINKR

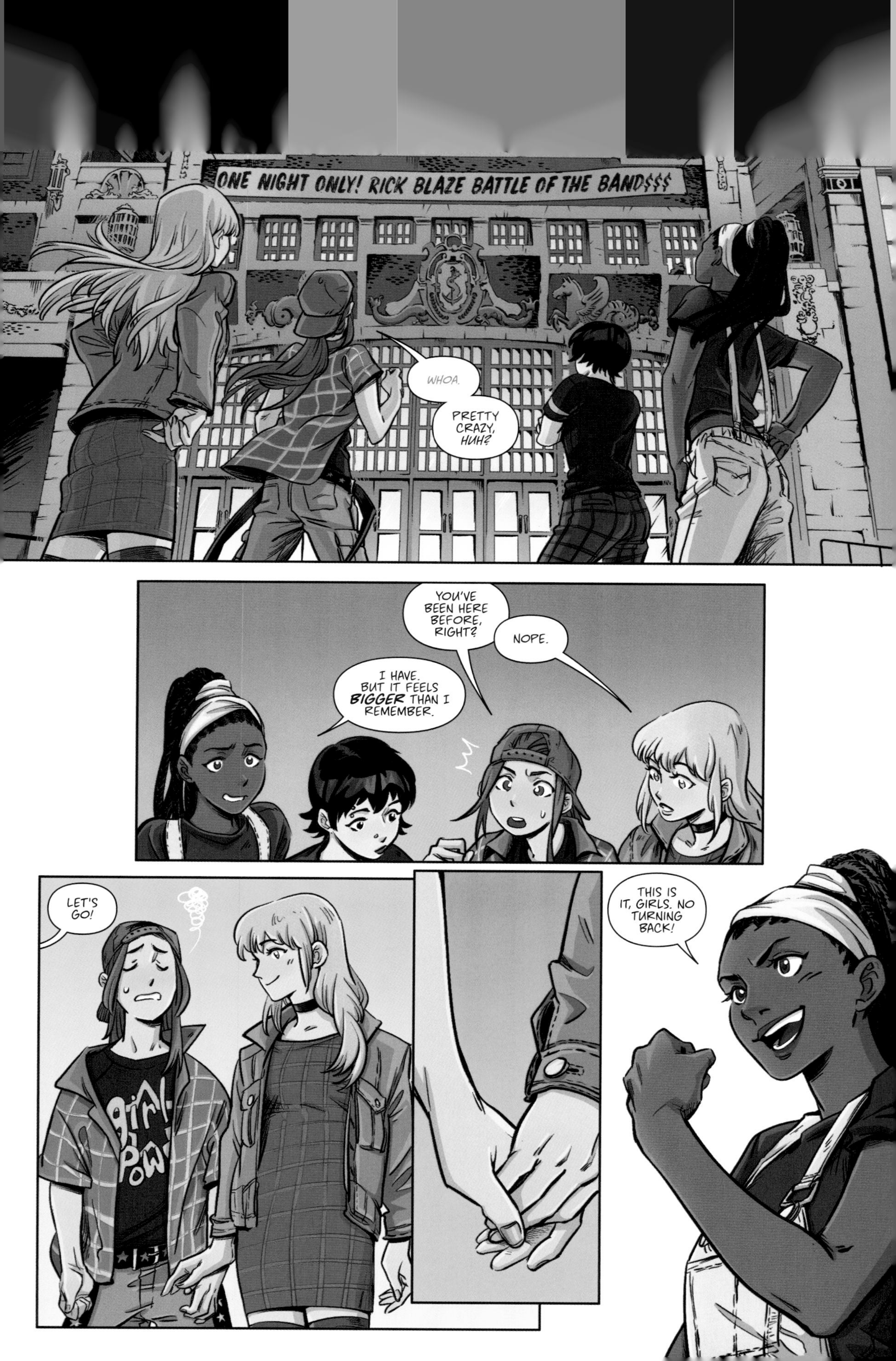
ONE NIGHT ONLY! RICK BLAZE BATTLE OF THE BAND$$$
WHOA.
PRETTY CRAZY, HUH?
YOU'VE BEEN HERE BEFORE, RIGHT?
NOPE.
I HAVE. BUT IT FEELS BIGGER THAN I REMEMBER.
LET'S GO!
THIS IS IT, GIRLS. NO TURNING BACK!
girl Power

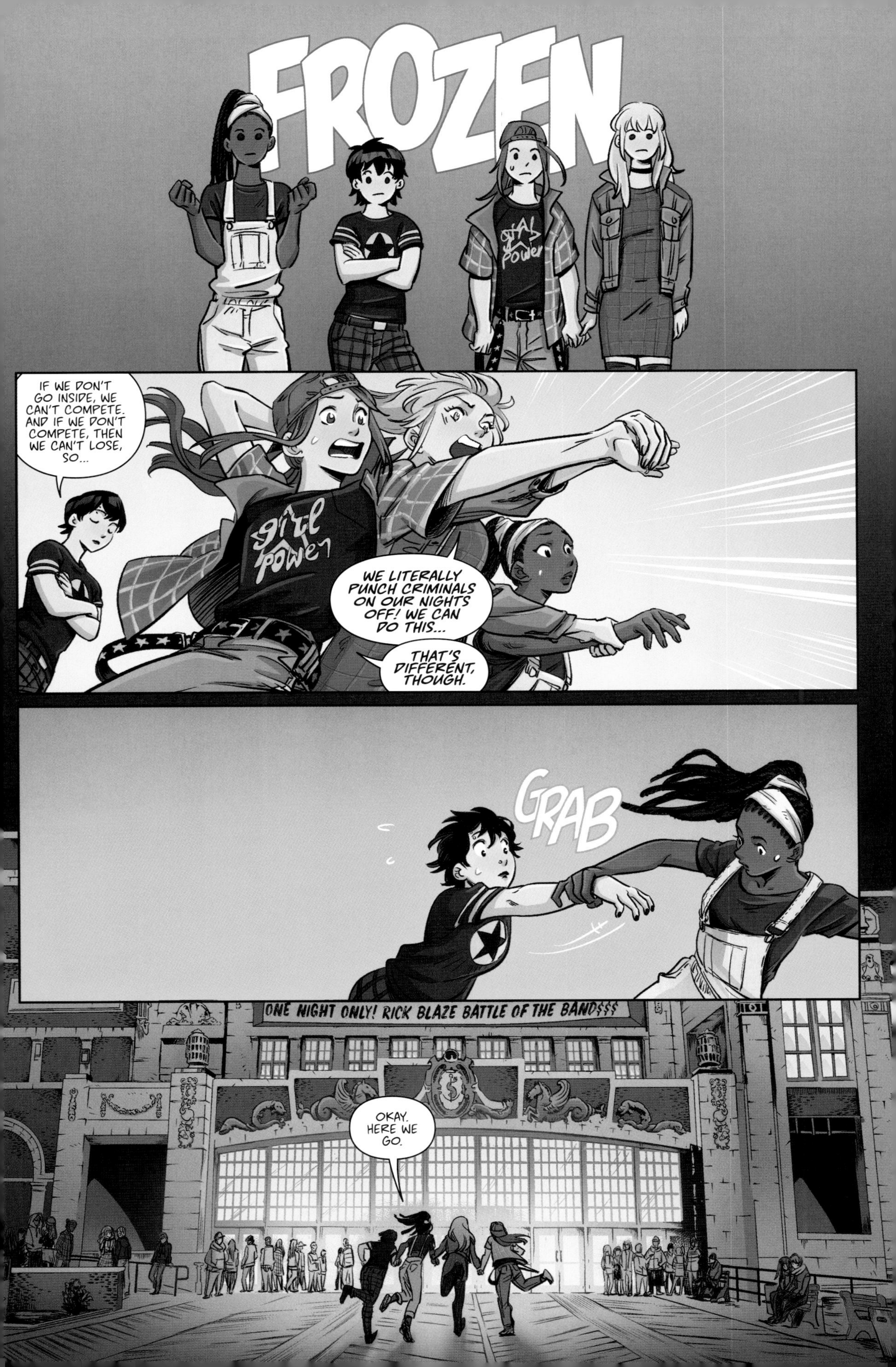
FROZEN
girl power
IF WE DON'T GO INSIDE, WE CAN'T COMPETE. AND IF WE DON'T COMPETE, THEN WE CAN'T LOSE, SO...
girl power
WE LITERALLY PUNCH CRIMINALS ON OUR NIGHTS OFF! WE CAN DO THIS...
THAT'S DIFFERENT, THOUGH.
GRAB
ONE NIGHT ONLY! RICK BLAZE BATTLE OF THE BAND$$$
OKAY. HERE WE GO.

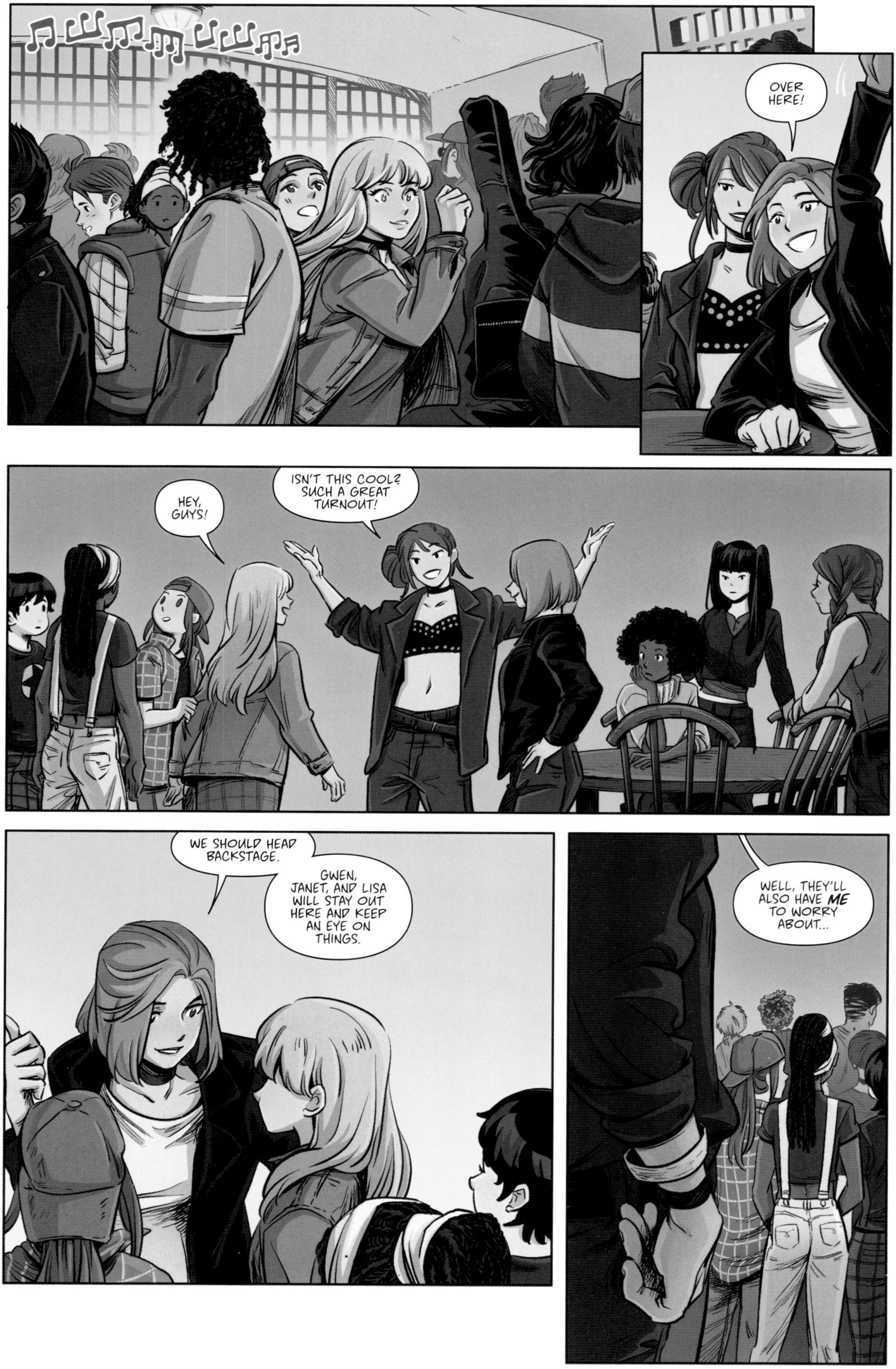
OVER HERE!
HEY, GUYS!
ISN'T THIS COOL? SUCH A GREAT TURNOUT!
WE SHOULD HEAD BACKSTAGE.
GWEN, JANET, AND LISA WILL STAY OUT HERE AND KEEP AN EYE ON THINGS.
WELL, THEY'LL ALSO HAVE ME TO WORRY ABOUT...

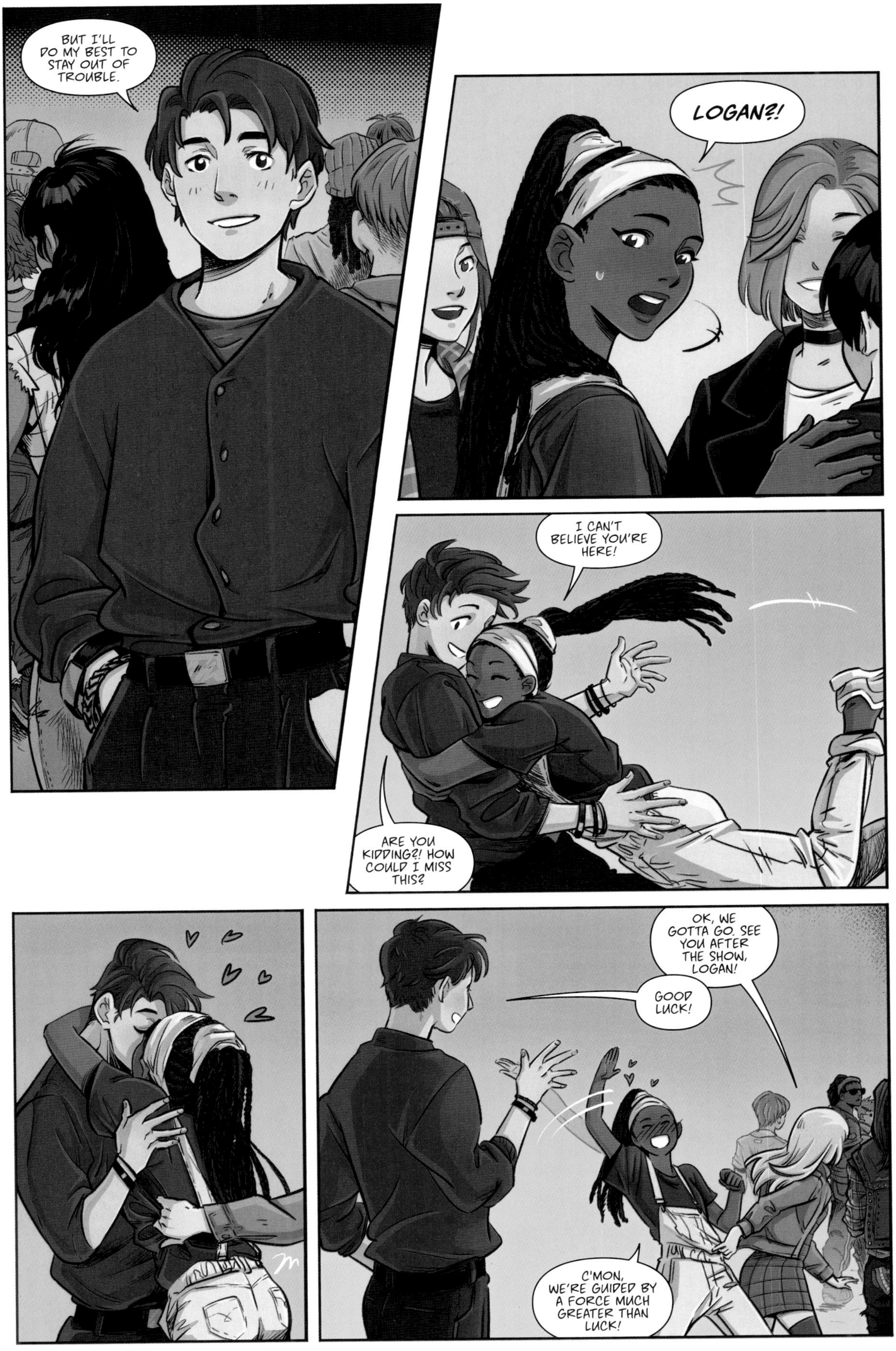
BUT I'LL DO MY BEST TO STAY OUT OF TROUBLE.
LOGAN?!
I CAN'T BELIEVE YOU'RE HERE!
ARE YOU KIDDING?! HOW COULD I MISS THIS?
OK, WE GOTTA GO. SEE YOU AFTER THE SHOW, LOGAN!
GOOD LUCK!
C'MON, WE'RE GUIDED BY A FORCE MUCH GREATER THAN LUCK!

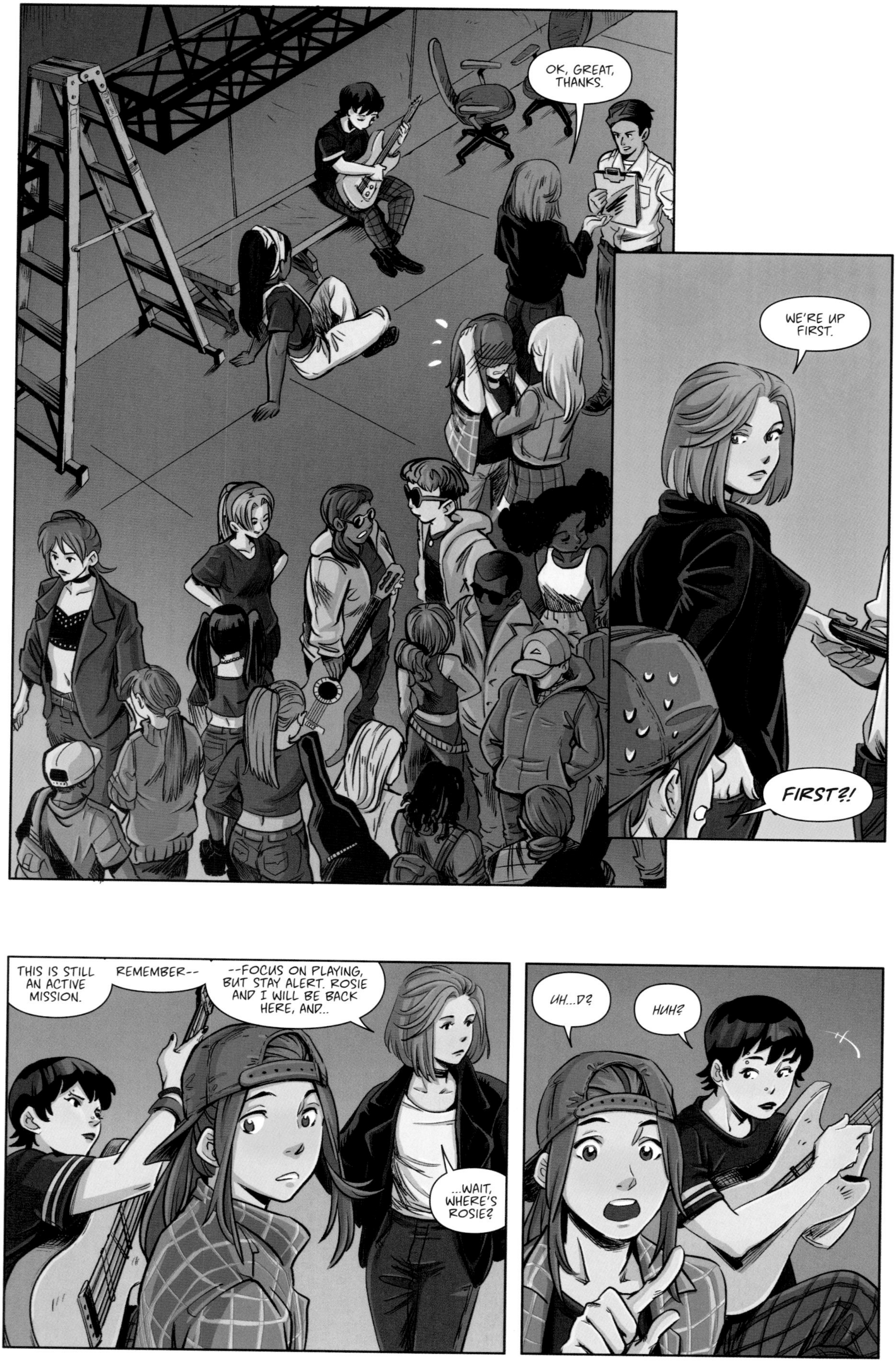

OK, GREAT, THANKS.
WE'RE UP FIRST.
FIRST?!
THIS IS STILL AN ACTIVE MISSION.
REMEMBER--
--FOCUS ON PLAYING, BUT STAY ALERT. ROSIE AND I WILL BE BACK HERE, AND...
...WAIT, WHERE'S ROSIE?
UH...D?
HUH?

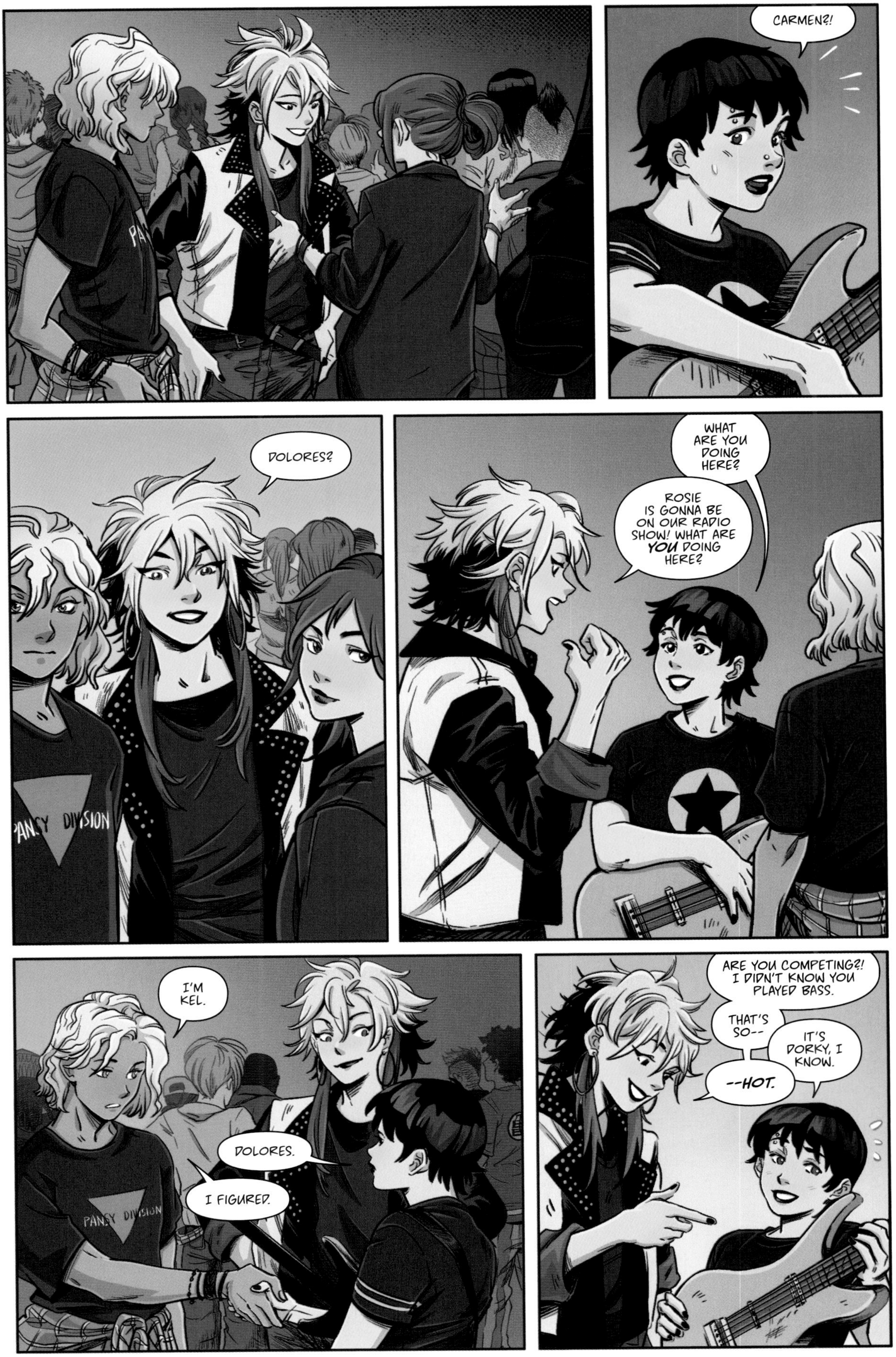
PA
CARMEN?!
DOLORES?
PANSY DIVISION
WHAT ARE YOU DOING HERE?
ROSIE IS GONNA BE ON OUR RADIO SHOW! WHAT ARE **YOU** DOING HERE?
I'M KEL.
DOLORES.
I FIGURED.
PANSY DIVISION
ARE YOU COMPETING?! I DIDN'T KNOW YOU PLAYED BASS.
THAT'S SO--
IT'S DORKY, I KNOW.
--HOT.

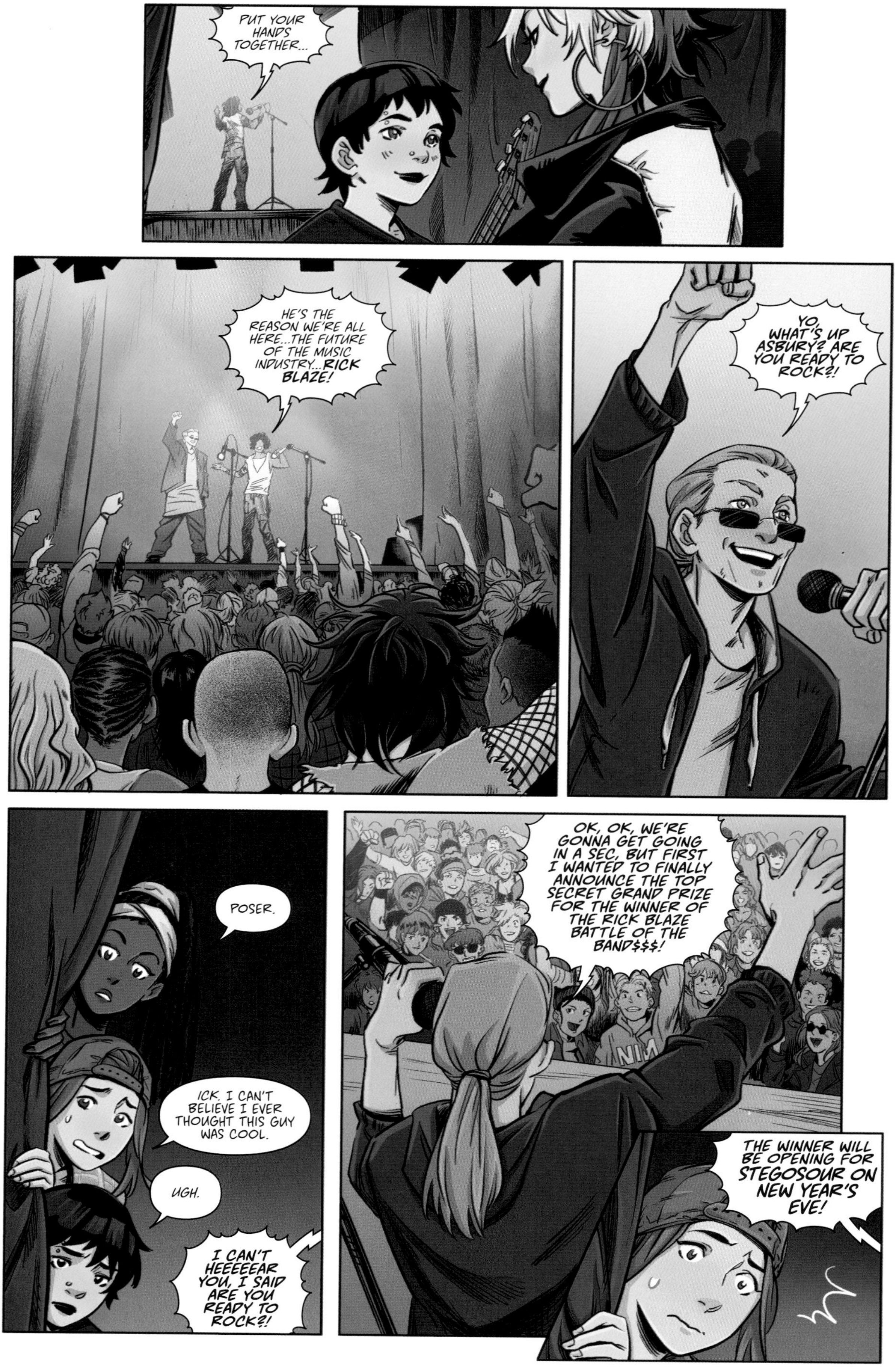
PUT YOUR HANDS TOGETHER...
HE'S THE REASON WE'RE ALL HERE...THE FUTURE OF THE MUSIC INDUSTRY...RICK BLAZE!
YO, WHAT'S UP ASBURY? ARE YOU READY TO ROCK?!
POSER.
ICK. I CAN'T BELIEVE I EVER THOUGHT THIS GUY WAS COOL.
UGH.
I CAN'T HEEEEEAR YOU, I SAID ARE YOU READY TO ROCK?!
OK, OK, WE'RE GONNA GET GOING IN A SEC, BUT FIRST I WANTED TO FINALLY ANNOUNCE THE TOP SECRET GRAND PRIZE FOR THE WINNER OF THE RICK BLAZE BATTLE OF THE BAND$$$!
THE WINNER WILL BE OPENING FOR STEGOSOUR ON NEW YEAR'S EVE!

OPENING FOR STEGOSOUR?! THAT'S MY GREATEST DREAM! BUT, BUT... NEW YEAR'S EVE?!
CHRIS...
MAYBE YOU'LL ALL START TAKING Y2K SERIOUSLY NOW.
DOUBTFUL.
OK, LADIES, STAY FOCUSED. BE ON THE LOOKOUT FOR ANYTHING SUSPICIOUS.
ALSO WANNA GIVE A BIG SHOUTOUT TO ONE OF OUR SPONSORS... SNAPSTER!
IS THAT THE SUSPICIOUS THING YOU WERE TALKING ABOUT?
UH...YES, ACTUALLY?
ARE YOU GUYS ON SNAPSTER? MAN, IT'S REALLY THE FUTURE OF MUSIC!
RICK HATES SNAPSTER...THIS DOESN'T MAKE ANY SENSE...
AND WHO DOESN'T WANT TO BE PART OF THE WAVE OF THE FUTURE, AM I RIGHT?!
UH, MAGS, YOU MIGHT WANNA CHECK ON YOUR GIRL...

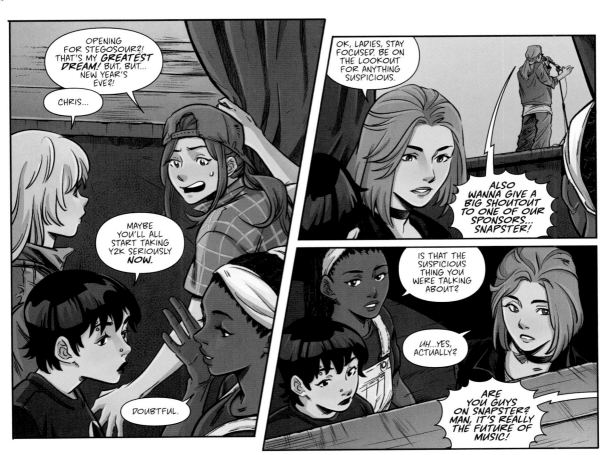

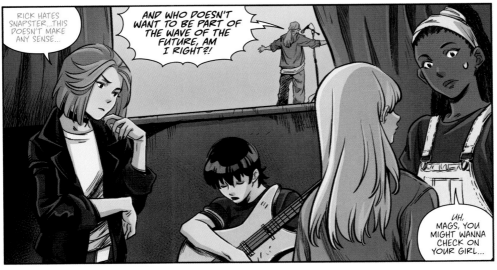

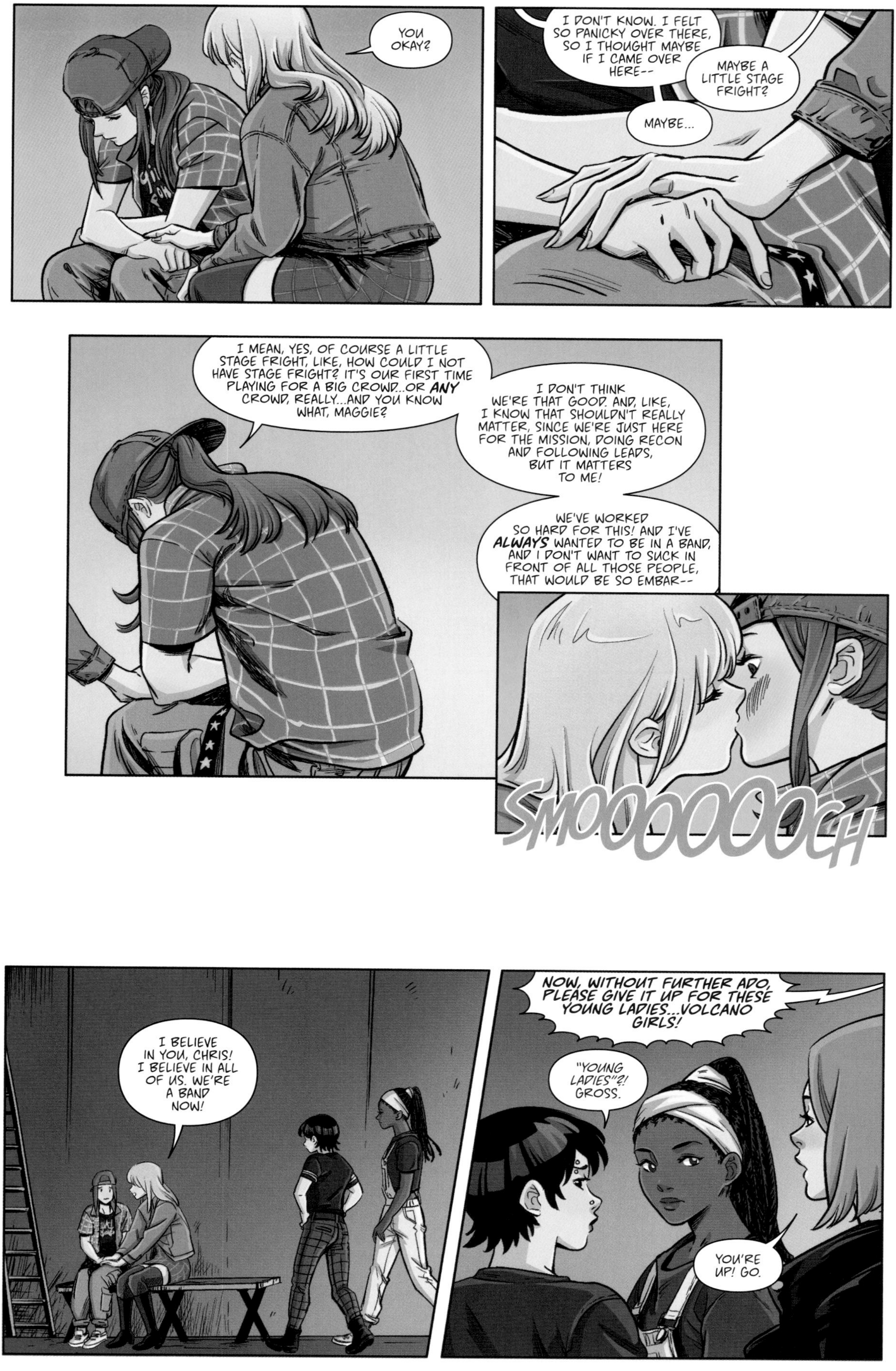
YOU OKAY?
I DON'T KNOW. I FELT SO PANICKY OVER THERE, SO I THOUGHT MAYBE IF I CAME OVER HERE--
MAYBE A LITTLE STAGE FRIGHT?
MAYBE...
I MEAN, YES, OF COURSE A LITTLE STAGE FRIGHT, LIKE, HOW COULD I NOT HAVE STAGE FRIGHT? IT'S OUR FIRST TIME PLAYING FOR A BIG CROWD...OR ANY CROWD, REALLY...AND YOU KNOW WHAT, MAGGIE?
I DON'T THINK WE'RE THAT GOOD. AND, LIKE, I KNOW THAT SHOULDN'T REALLY MATTER, SINCE WE'RE JUST HERE FOR THE MISSION, DOING RECON AND FOLLOWING LEADS, BUT IT MATTERS TO ME!
WE'VE WORKED SO HARD FOR THIS! AND I'VE ALWAYS WANTED TO BE IN A BAND, AND I DON'T WANT TO SUCK IN FRONT OF ALL THOSE PEOPLE, THAT WOULD BE SO EMBAR--
SMOOOOOOOCH
I BELIEVE IN YOU, CHRIS! I BELIEVE IN ALL OF US. WE'RE A BAND NOW!
NOW, WITHOUT FURTHER ADO, PLEASE GIVE IT UP FOR THESE YOUNG LADIES...VOLCANO GIRLS!
"YOUNG LADIES"?! GROSS.
YOU'RE UP! GO.

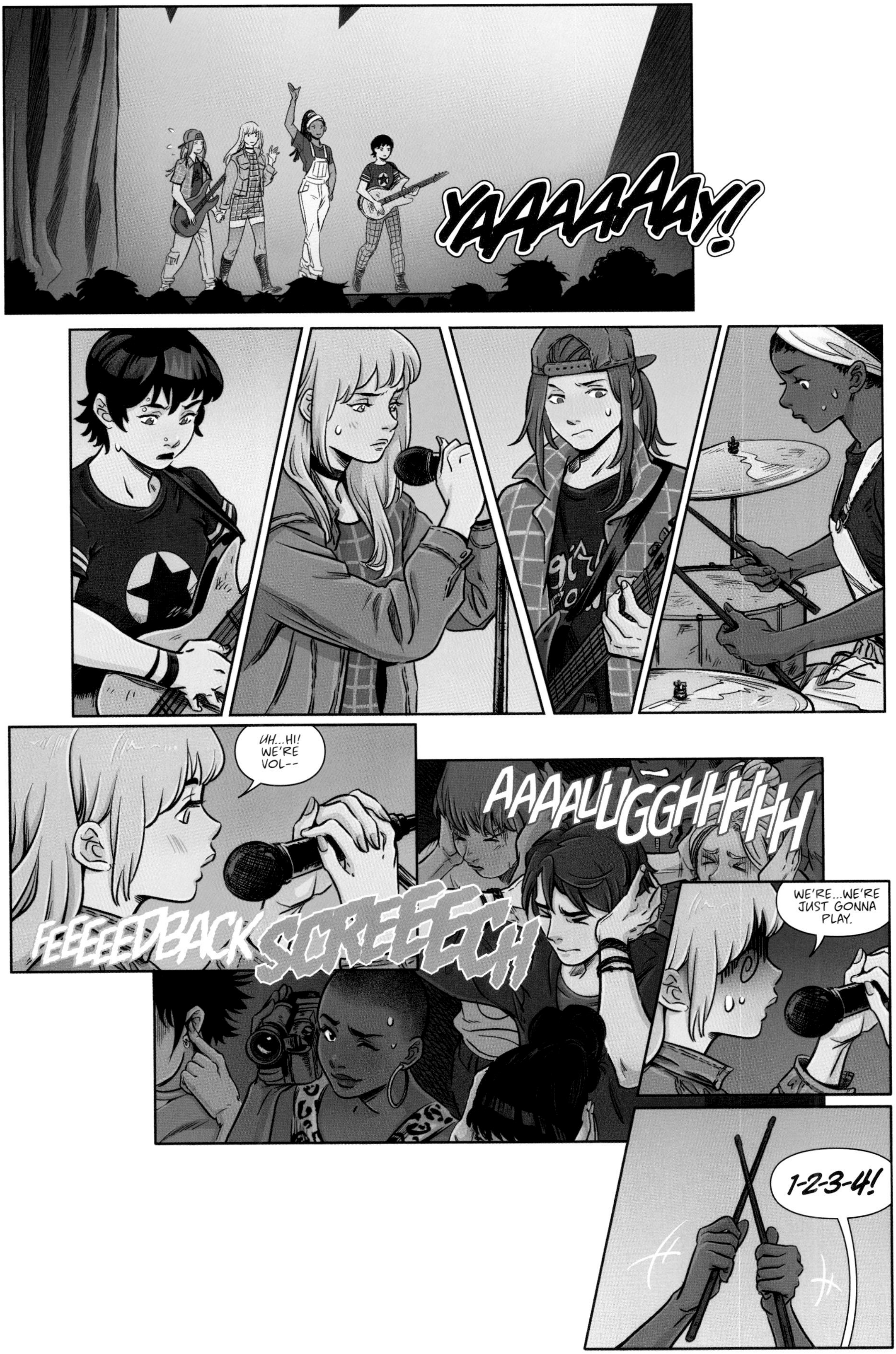
YAAAAAAY!
UH...HI! WE'RE VOL--
AAAALUGGHHHHH
FEEEEEEDBACK SCREEEECH
WE'RE...WE'RE JUST GONNA PLAY.
1-2-3-4!

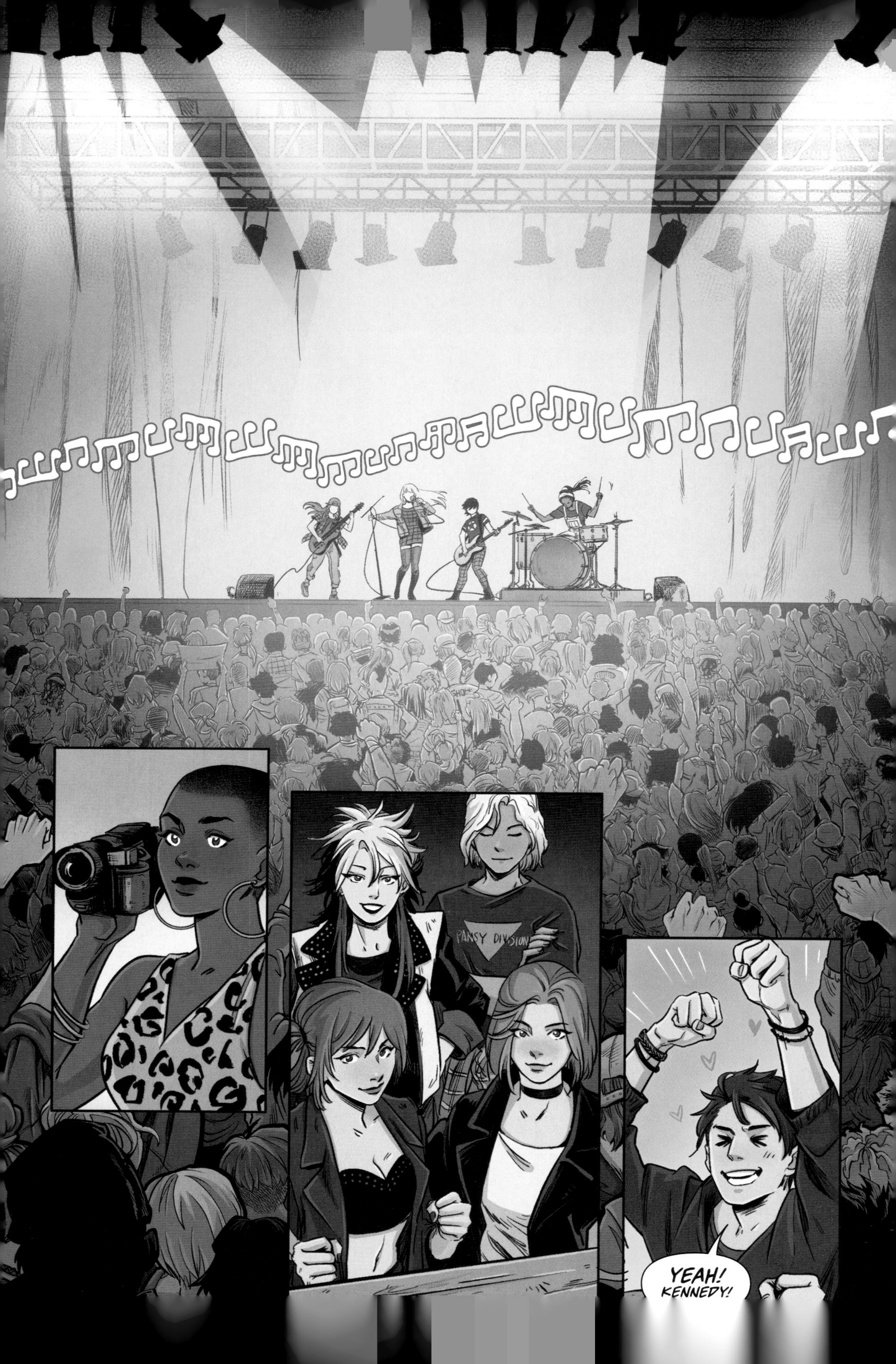
PANSY DIVISION
YEAH! KENNEDY!

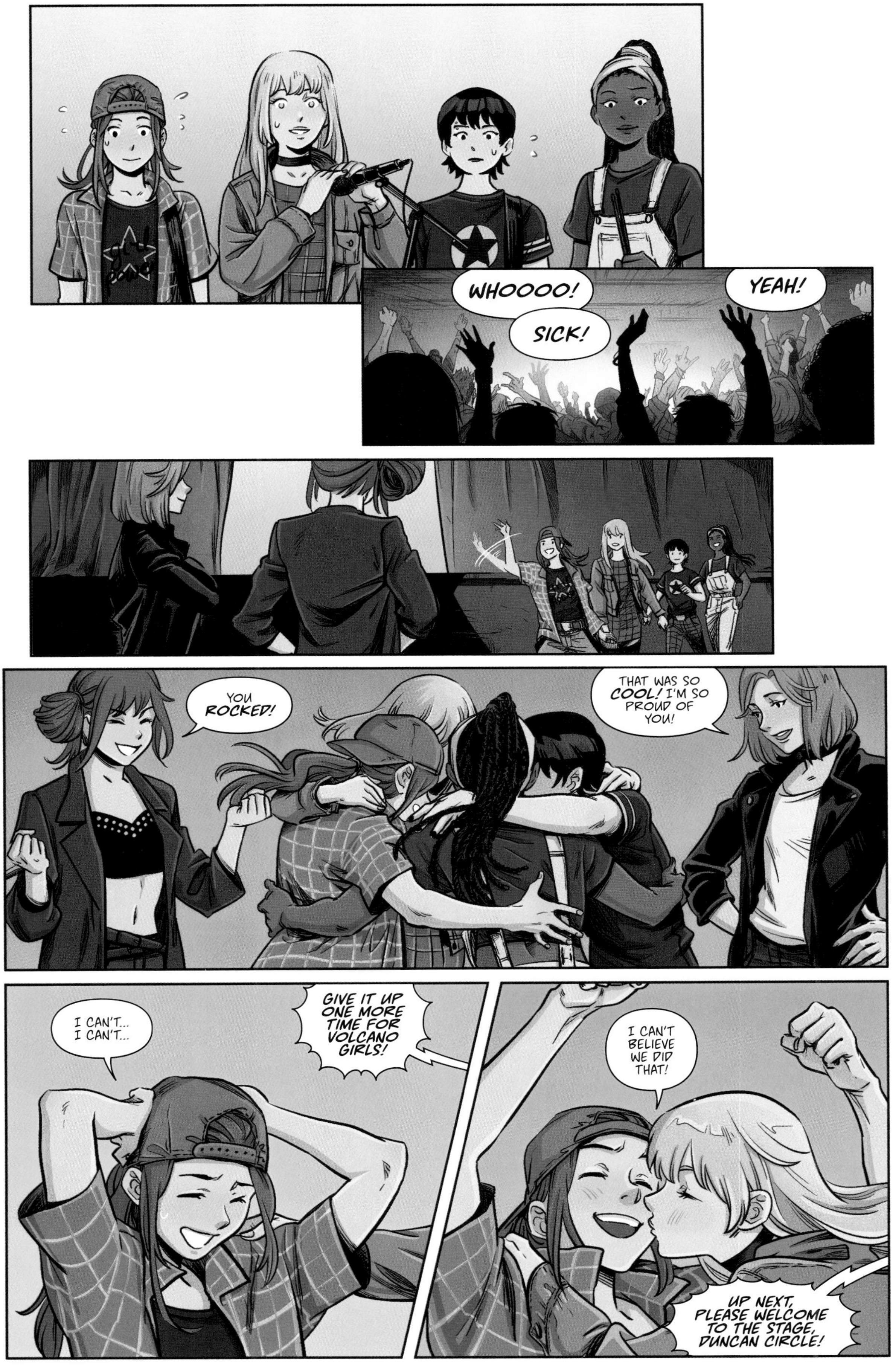
WHOOOO!
SICK!
YEAH!
YOU ROCKED!
THAT WAS SO COOL! I'M SO PROUD OF YOU!
I CAN'T... I CAN'T...
GIVE IT UP ONE MORE TIME FOR VOLCANO GIRLS!
I CAN'T BELIEVE WE DID THAT!
UP NEXT, PLEASE WELCOME TO THE STAGE, DUNCAN CIRCLE!

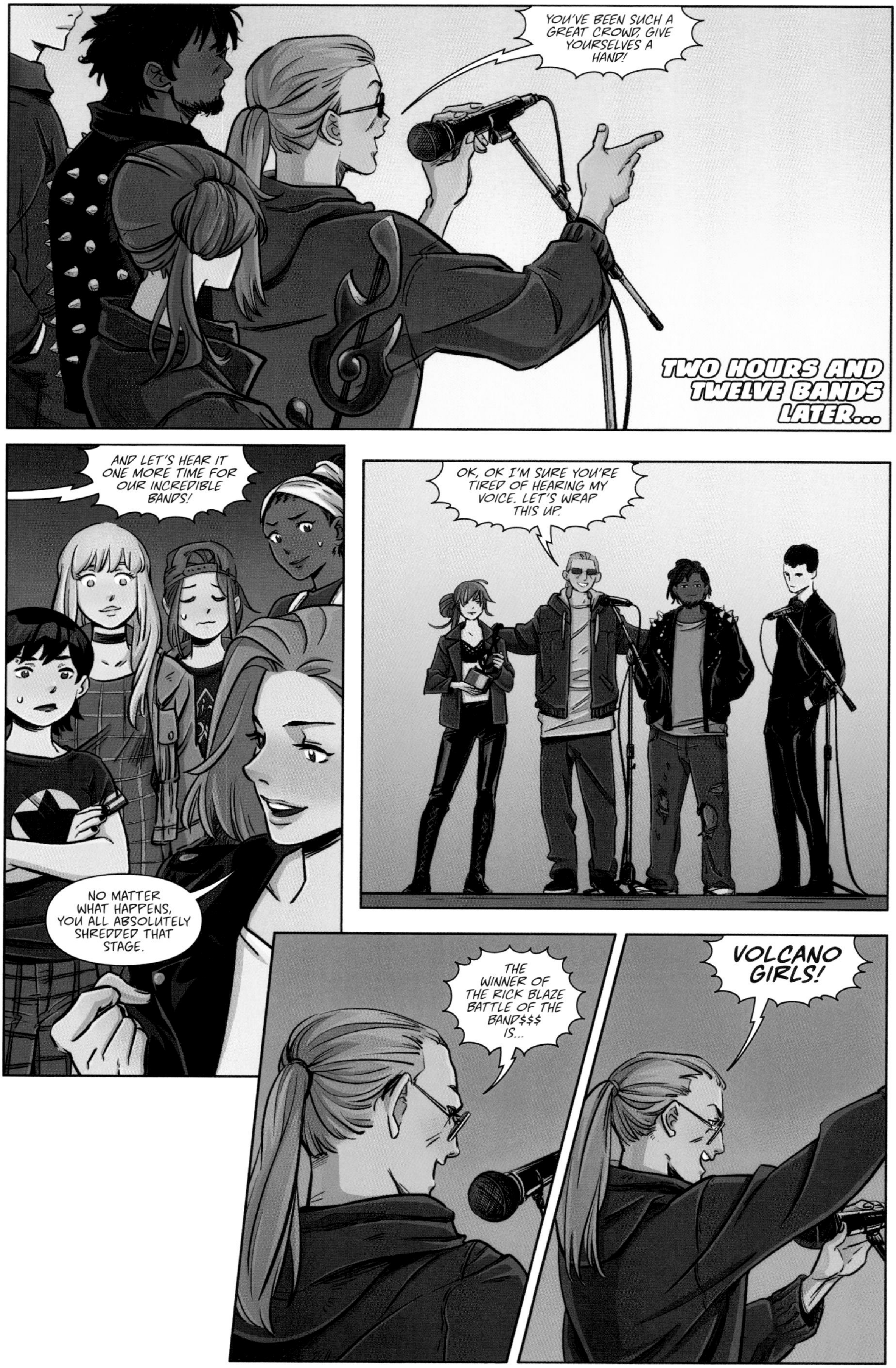
YOU'VE BEEN SUCH A GREAT CROWD, GIVE YOURSELVES A HAND!
TWO HOURS AND TWELVE BANDS LATER...
AND LET'S HEAR IT ONE MORE TIME FOR OUR INCREDIBLE BANDS!
NO MATTER WHAT HAPPENS, YOU ALL ABSOLUTELY SHREDDED THAT STAGE.
OK, OK I'M SURE YOU'RE TIRED OF HEARING MY VOICE. LET'S WRAP THIS UP.
THE WINNER OF THE RICK BLAZE BATTLE OF THE BAND$$$ IS...
VOLCANO GIRLS!

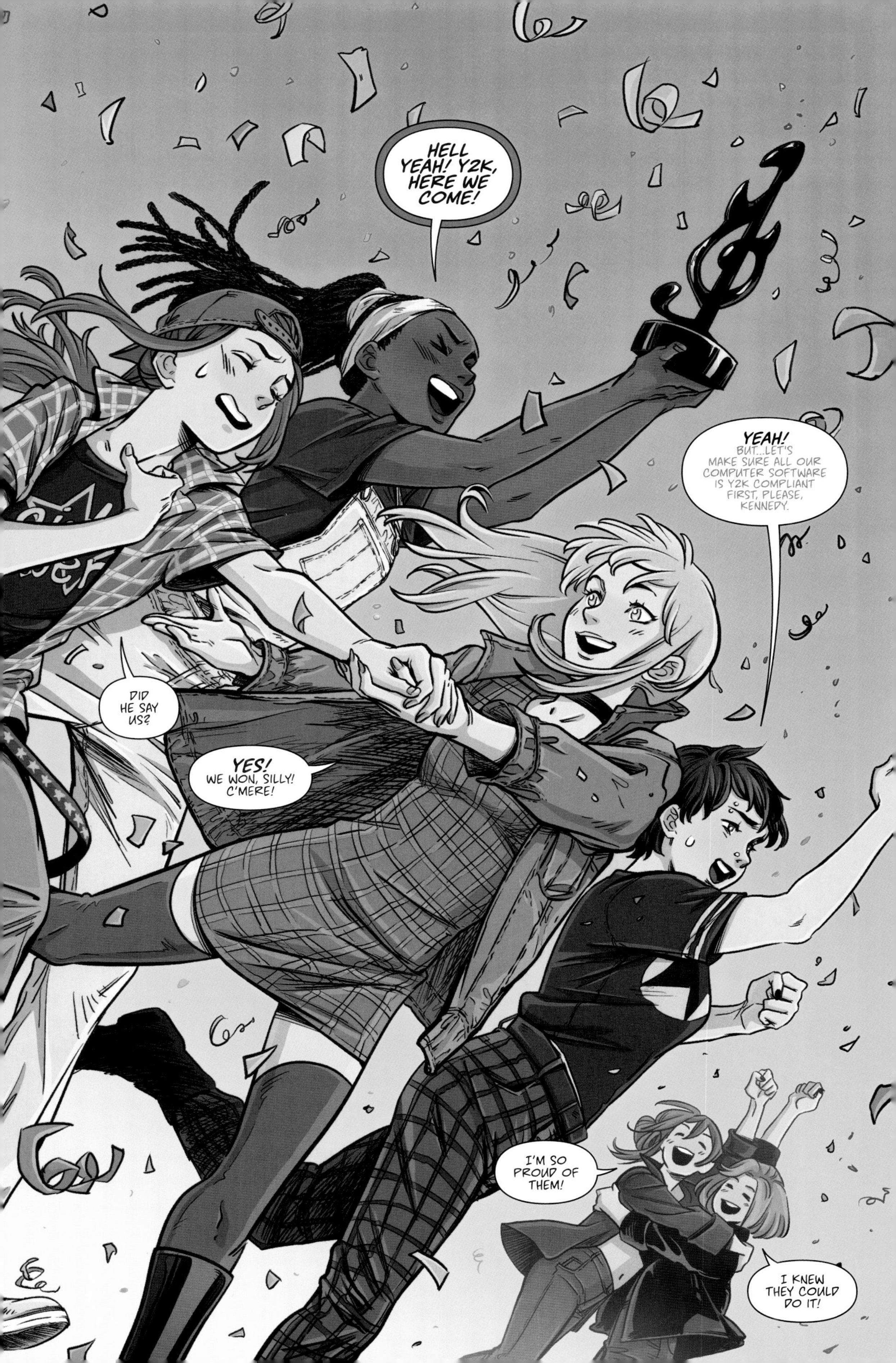
HELL YEAH! Y2K, HERE WE COME!
YEAH! BUT...LET'S MAKE SURE ALL OUR COMPUTER SOFTWARE IS Y2K COMPLIANT FIRST, PLEASE, KENNEDY.
DID HE SAY US?
YES! WE WON, SILLY! C'MERE!
I'M SO PROUD OF THEM!
I KNEW THEY COULD DO IT!

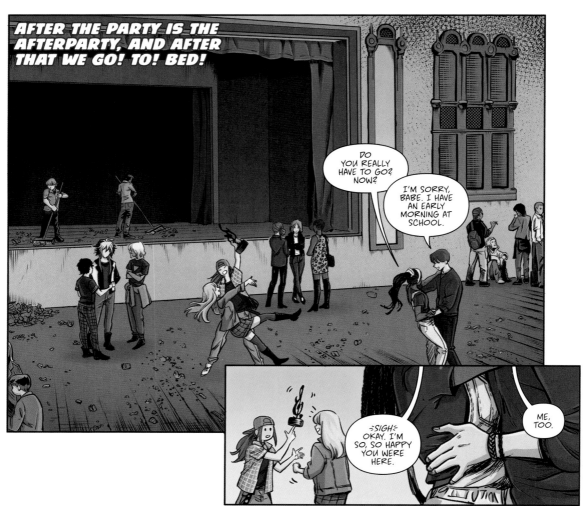

AFTER THE PARTY IS THE AFTERPARTY, AND AFTER THAT WE GO! TO! BED!

DO YOU REALLY HAVE TO GO? NOW?

I'M SORRY, BABE. I HAVE AN EARLY MORNING AT SCHOOL.

÷SIGH÷ OKAY. I'M SO, SO HAPPY YOU WERE HERE.

ME, TOO.

YOU WERE GREAT.

NOT BAD, D. NOT BAD.

IS THREE O'CLOCK STILL GOOD TOMORROW FOR YOU TO Y2K-PROOF OUR EQUIPMENT?

IT'S A DATE! I MEAN, IT'S NOT A *DATE* DATE, UNLESS YOU WANT IT TO BE I MEAN YES I'LL BE THERE.

OH, IT WAS DEFINITELY WEIRD.

THERE WAS SOMETHING ODD GOING ON. I THINK I CAUGHT IT, BUT I DON'T KNOW FOR SURE.

NO KIDDING. WE'LL REVIEW THE FOOTAGE TOMORROW.

HEY, VOLCANO GIRLS! QUICK BAND MEETING?

FIRST OF ALL, I JUST WANT TO SAY AGAIN HOW PROUD I AM OF YOU.

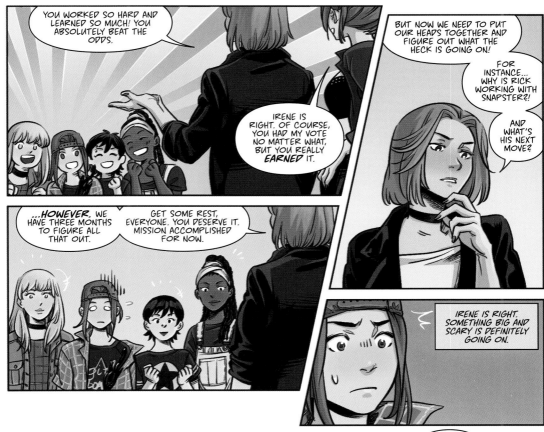

YOU WORKED SO HARD AND LEARNED SO MUCH! YOU ABSOLUTELY BEAT THE ODDS.

IRENE IS RIGHT. OF COURSE, YOU HAD MY VOTE NO MATTER WHAT, BUT YOU REALLY *EARNED* IT.

...HOWEVER, WE HAVE THREE MONTHS TO FIGURE ALL THAT OUT.

GET SOME REST, EVERYONE. YOU DESERVE IT. MISSION ACCOMPLISHED FOR NOW.

BUT NOW WE NEED TO PUT OUR HEADS TOGETHER AND FIGURE OUT WHAT THE HECK IS GOING ON!

FOR INSTANCE... WHY IS RICK WORKING WITH SNAPSTER?!

AND WHAT'S HIS NEXT MOVE?

IRENE IS RIGHT. SOMETHING BIG AND SCARY IS DEFINITELY GOING ON.

WE JUST GOTTA CONNECT THE DOTS.

HEY. YOU COMING?

OH, RIGHT. YEAH!

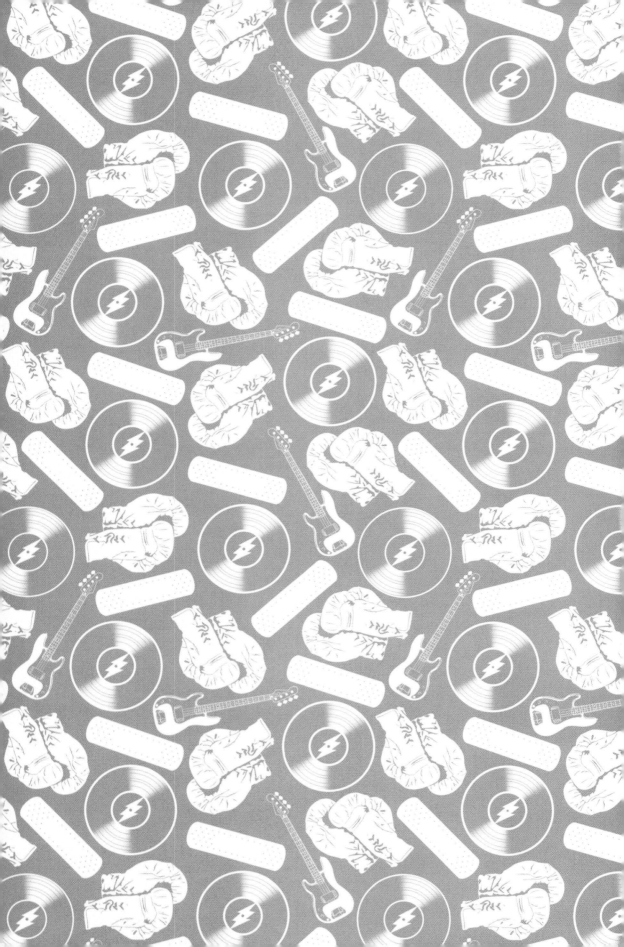

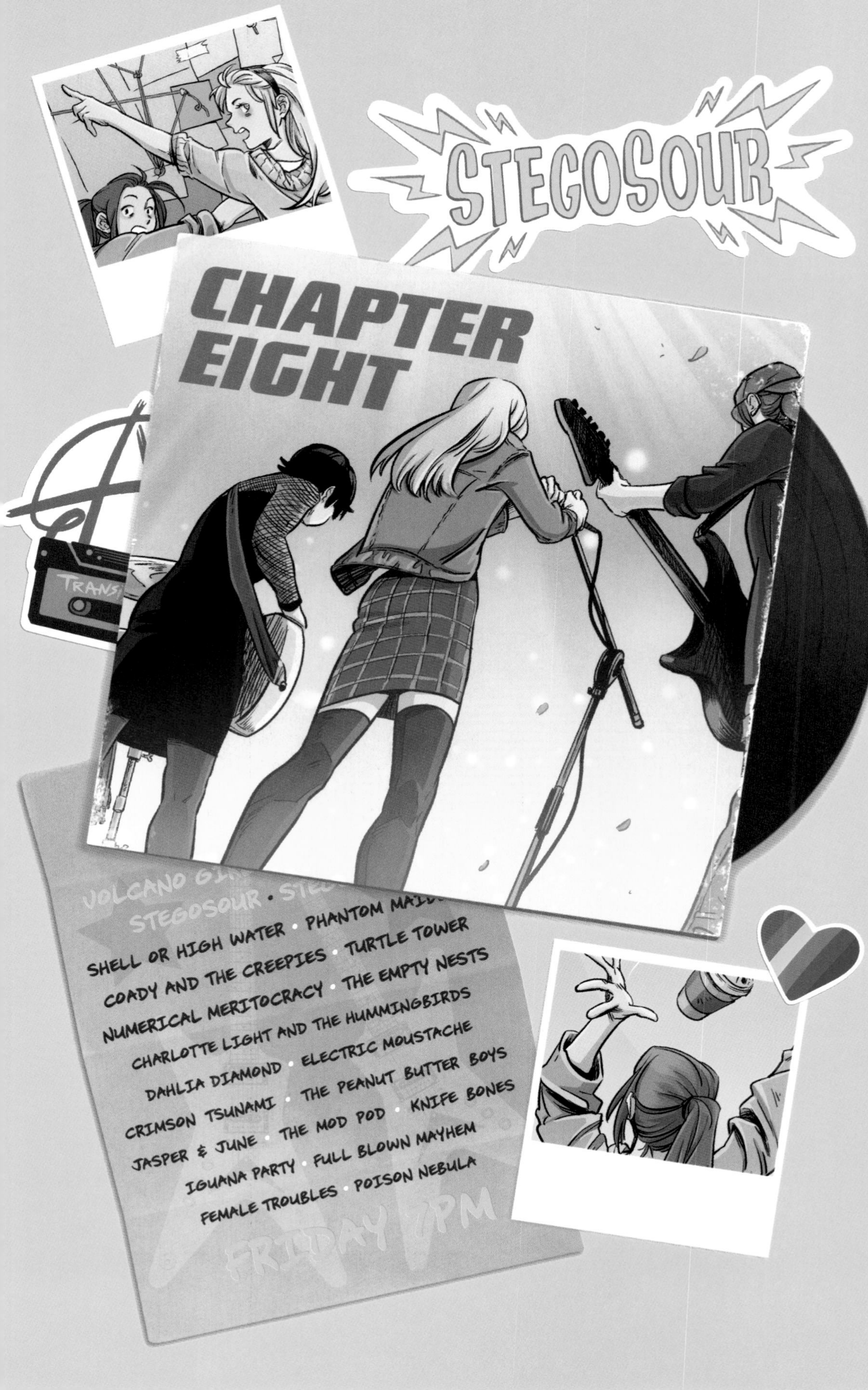
STEGOSOUR
CHAPTER EIGHT
STEGOSOUR
SHELL OR HIGH WATER
COADY AND THE CREEPIES • TURTLE TOWER
NUMERICAL MERITOCRACY • THE EMPTY NESTS
CHARLOTTE LIGHT AND THE HUMMINGBIRDS
DAHLIA DIAMOND • ELECTRIC MOUSTACHE
CRIMSON TSUNAMI • THE PEANUT BUTTER BOYS
JASPER & JUNE • THE MOD POD • KNIFE BONES
IGUANA PARTY • FULL BLOWN MAYHEM
FEMALE TROUBLES • POISON NEBULA
FRIDAY 7PM

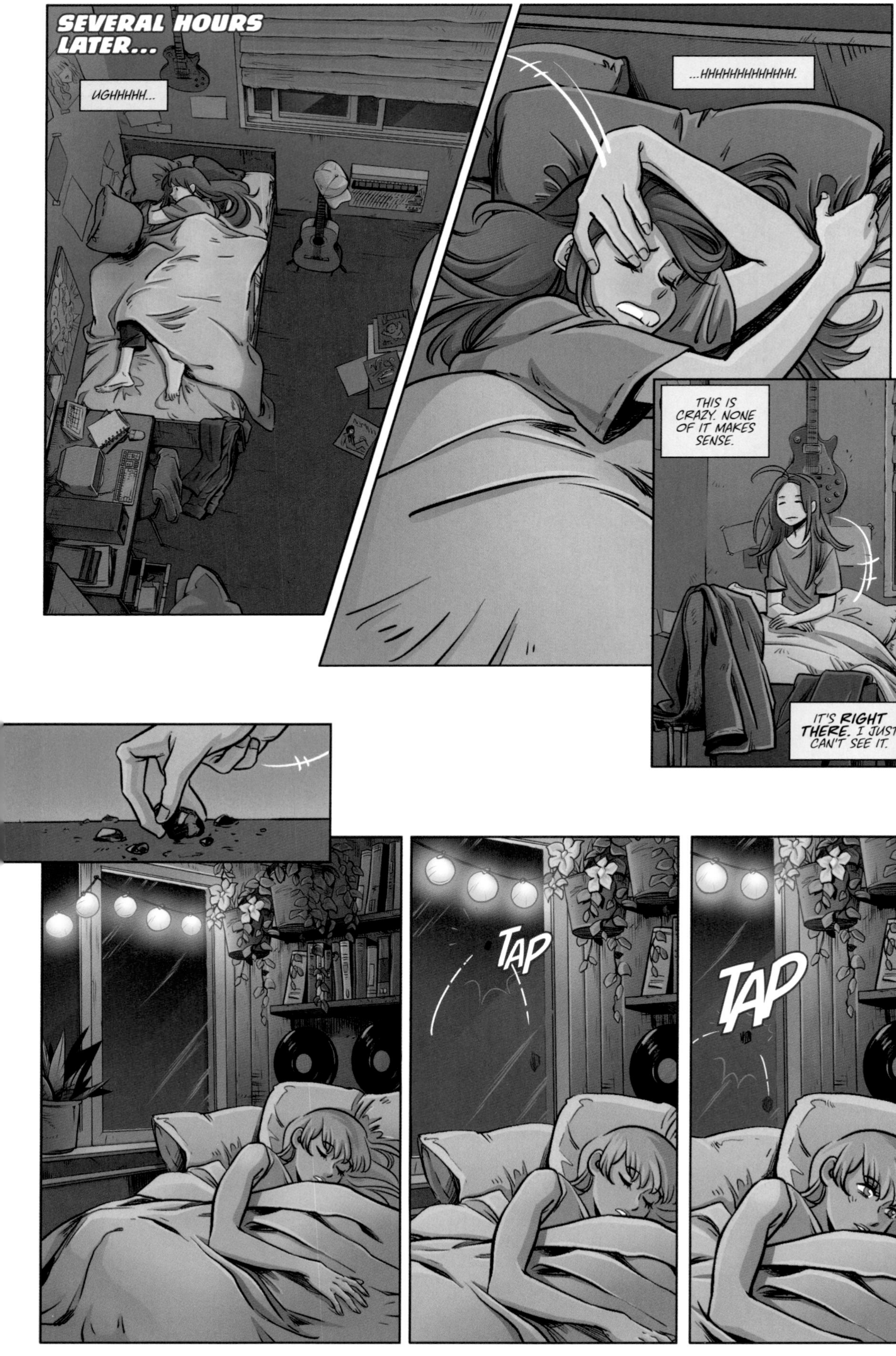

SEVERAL HOURS LATER...
UGHHHHH...
...HHHHHHHHHHHHH.
THIS IS CRAZY. NONE OF IT MAKES SENSE.
IT'S RIGHT THERE. I JUST CAN'T SEE IT.
TAP
TAP

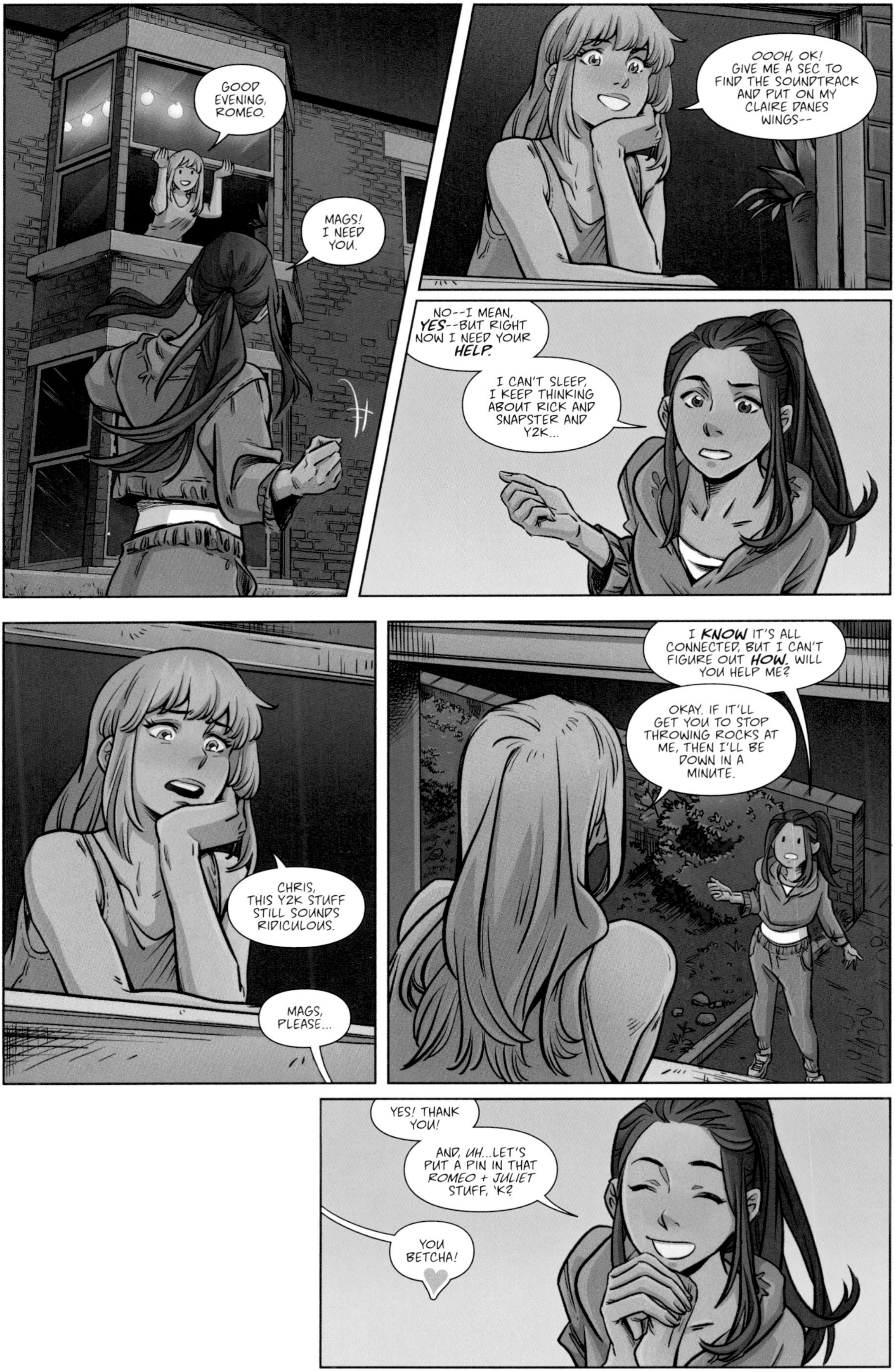
GOOD EVENING, ROMEO.
MAGS! I NEED YOU.
OOOH, OK! GIVE ME A SEC TO FIND THE SOUNDTRACK AND PUT ON MY CLAIRE DANES WINGS--
NO--I MEAN, *YES*--BUT RIGHT NOW I NEED YOUR *HELP.*
I CAN'T SLEEP, I KEEP THINKING ABOUT RICK AND SNAPSTER AND Y2K...
CHRIS, THIS Y2K STUFF STILL SOUNDS RIDICULOUS.
MAGS, PLEASE...
I *KNOW* IT'S ALL CONNECTED, BUT I CAN'T FIGURE OUT *HOW.* WILL YOU HELP ME?
OKAY. IF IT'LL GET YOU TO STOP THROWING ROCKS AT ME, THEN I'LL BE DOWN IN A MINUTE.
YES! THANK YOU!
AND, UH...LET'S PUT A PIN IN THAT *ROMEO + JULIET* STUFF, 'K?
YOU BETCHA!

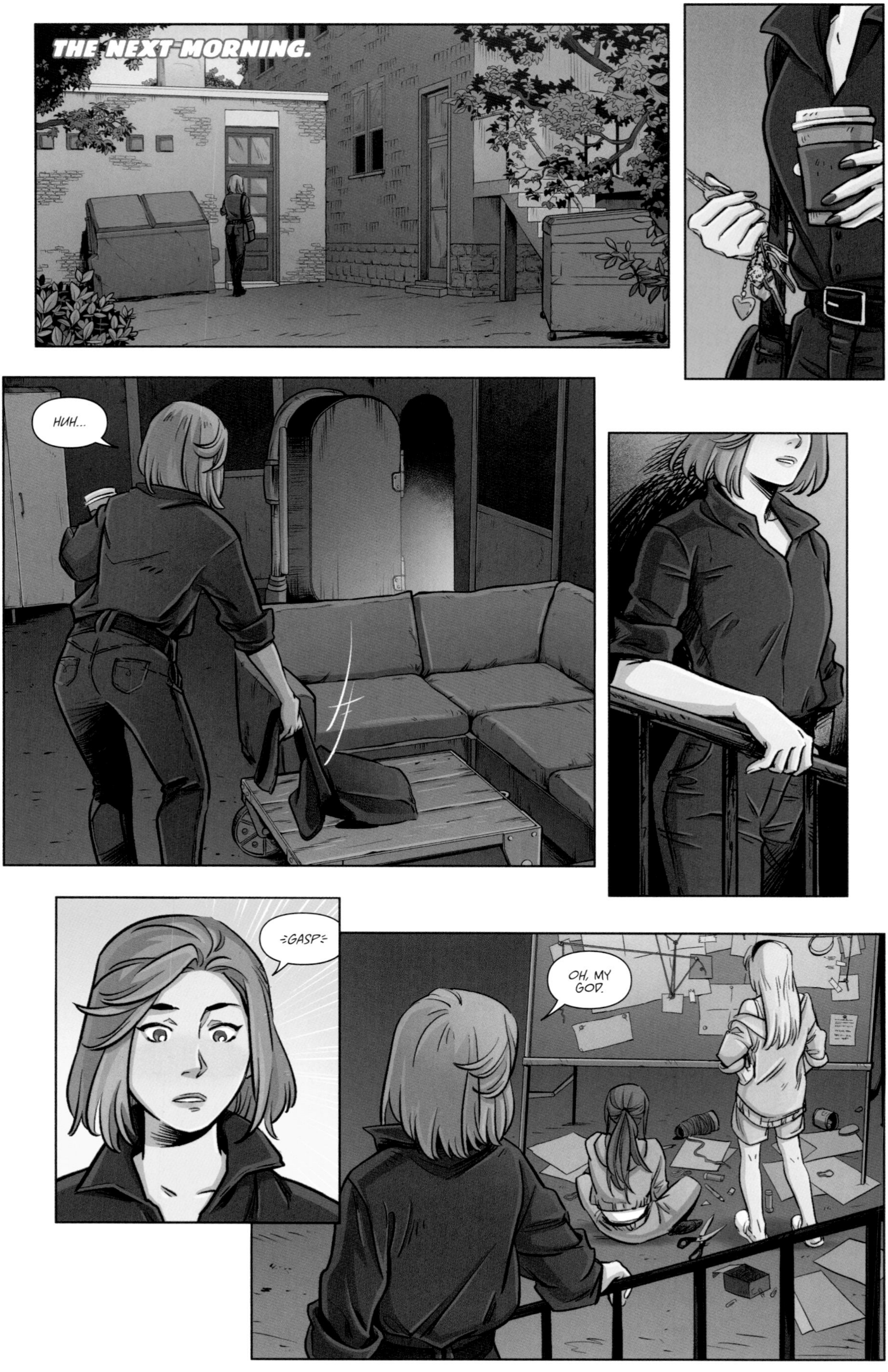
THE NEXT MORNING.
HUH...
=GASP=
OH, MY GOD.

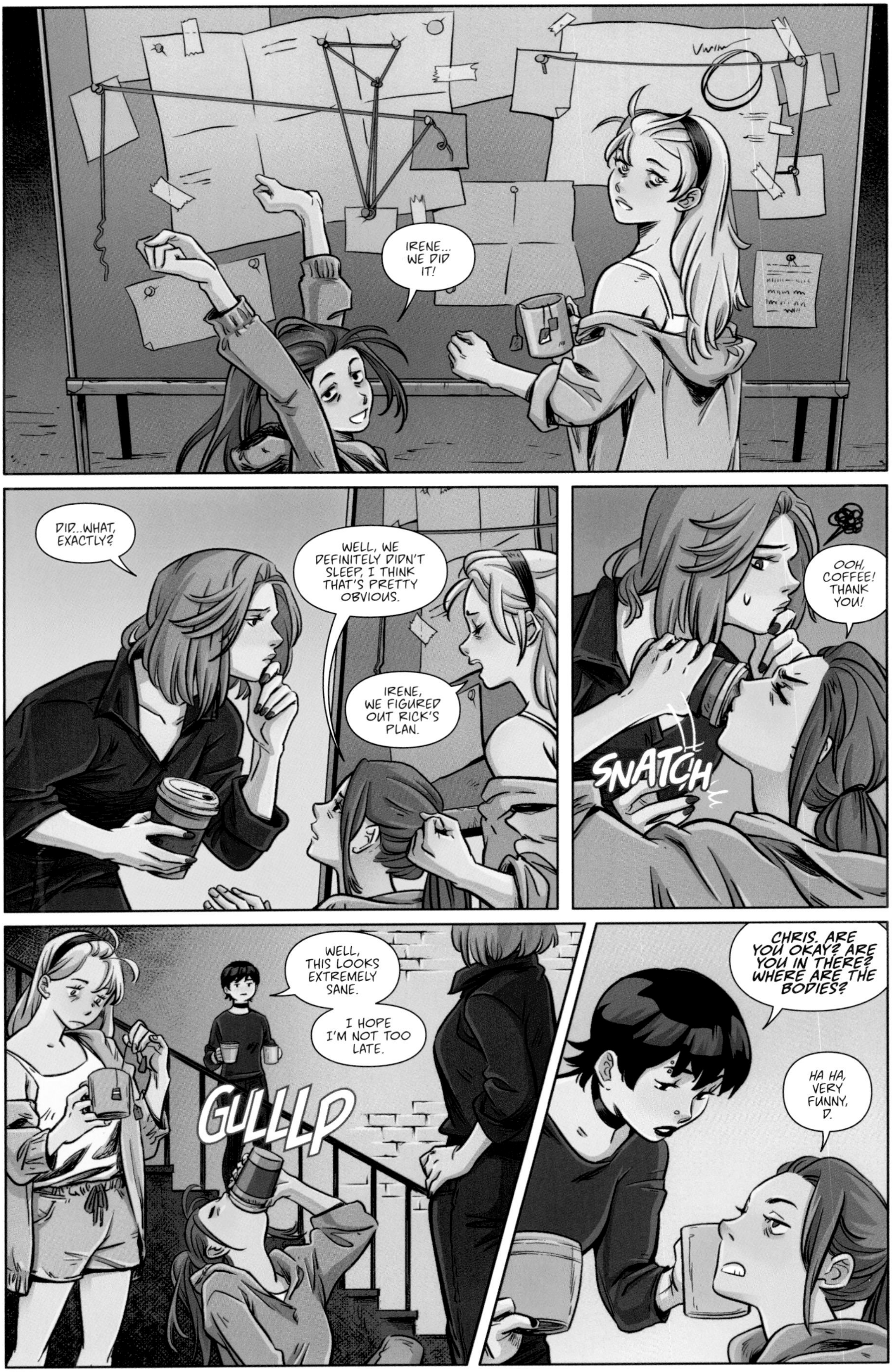
IRENE... WE DID IT!
DID...WHAT, EXACTLY?
WELL, WE DEFINITELY DIDN'T SLEEP, I THINK THAT'S PRETTY OBVIOUS.
IRENE, WE FIGURED OUT RICK'S PLAN.
OOH, COFFEE! THANK YOU!
SNATCH
WELL, THIS LOOKS EXTREMELY SANE.
I HOPE I'M NOT TOO LATE.
GULLLP
CHRIS, ARE YOU OKAY? ARE YOU IN THERE? WHERE ARE THE BODIES?
HA HA, VERY FUNNY, D.

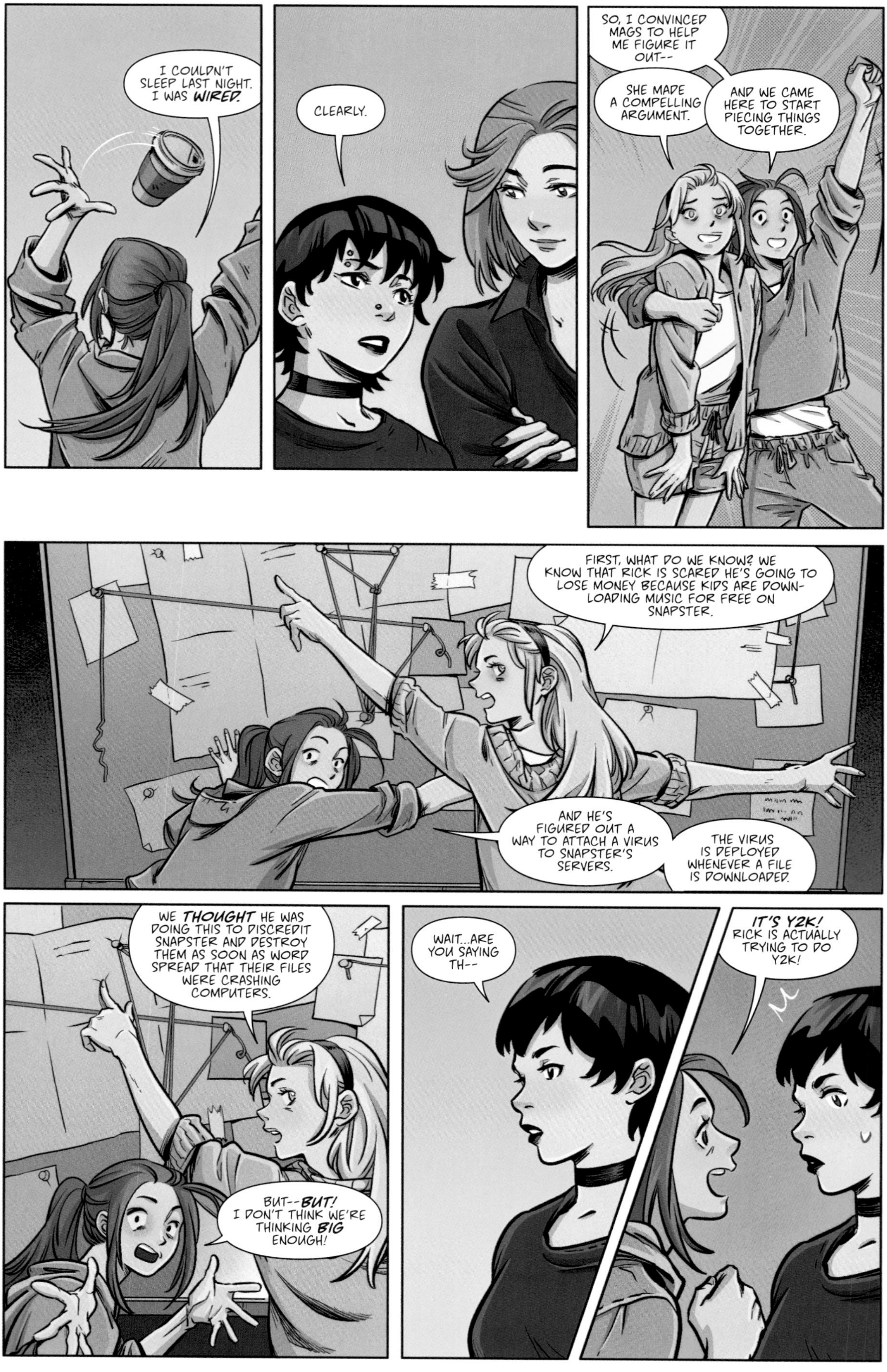
I COULDN'T SLEEP LAST NIGHT. I WAS *WIRED.*
CLEARLY.
SO, I CONVINCED MAGS TO HELP ME FIGURE IT OUT--
SHE MADE A COMPELLING ARGUMENT.
AND WE CAME HERE TO START PIECING THINGS TOGETHER.
FIRST, WHAT DO WE KNOW? WE KNOW THAT RICK IS SCARED HE'S GOING TO LOSE MONEY BECAUSE KIDS ARE DOWN-LOADING MUSIC FOR FREE ON SNAPSTER.
AND HE'S FIGURED OUT A WAY TO ATTACH A VIRUS TO SNAPSTER'S SERVERS.
THE VIRUS IS DEPLOYED WHENEVER A FILE IS DOWNLOADED.
WE *THOUGHT* HE WAS DOING THIS TO DISCREDIT SNAPSTER AND DESTROY THEM AS SOON AS WORD SPREAD THAT THEIR FILES WERE CRASHING COMPUTERS.
BUT--*BUT!* I DON'T THINK WE'RE THINKING *BIG* ENOUGH!
WAIT...ARE YOU SAYING TH--
IT'S Y2K! RICK IS ACTUALLY TRYING TO DO Y2K!

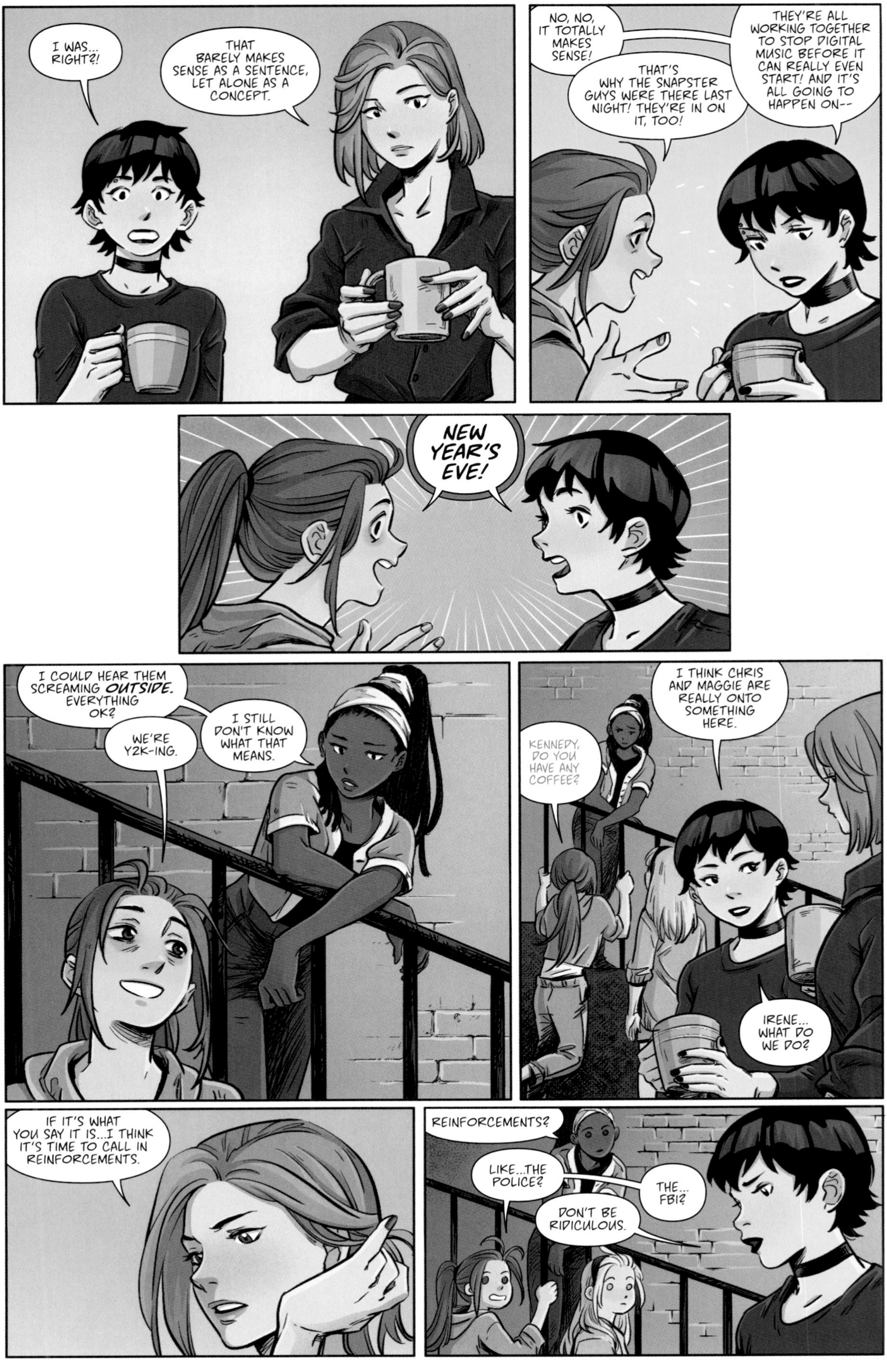
I WAS... RIGHT?!
THAT BARELY MAKES SENSE AS A SENTENCE, LET ALONE AS A CONCEPT.
NO, NO, IT TOTALLY MAKES SENSE!
THAT'S WHY THE SNAPSTER GUYS WERE THERE LAST NIGHT! THEY'RE IN ON IT, TOO!
THEY'RE ALL WORKING TOGETHER TO STOP DIGITAL MUSIC BEFORE IT CAN REALLY EVEN START! AND IT'S ALL GOING TO HAPPEN ON--
NEW YEAR'S EVE!
I COULD HEAR THEM SCREAMING OUTSIDE. EVERYTHING OK?
WE'RE Y2K-ING.
I STILL DON'T KNOW WHAT THAT MEANS.
I THINK CHRIS AND MAGGIE ARE REALLY ONTO SOMETHING HERE.
KENNEDY, DO YOU HAVE ANY COFFEE?
IRENE... WHAT DO WE DO?
IF IT'S WHAT YOU SAY IT IS...I THINK IT'S TIME TO CALL IN REINFORCEMENTS.
REINFORCEMENTS?
LIKE...THE POLICE?
THE... FBI?
DON'T BE RIDICULOUS.

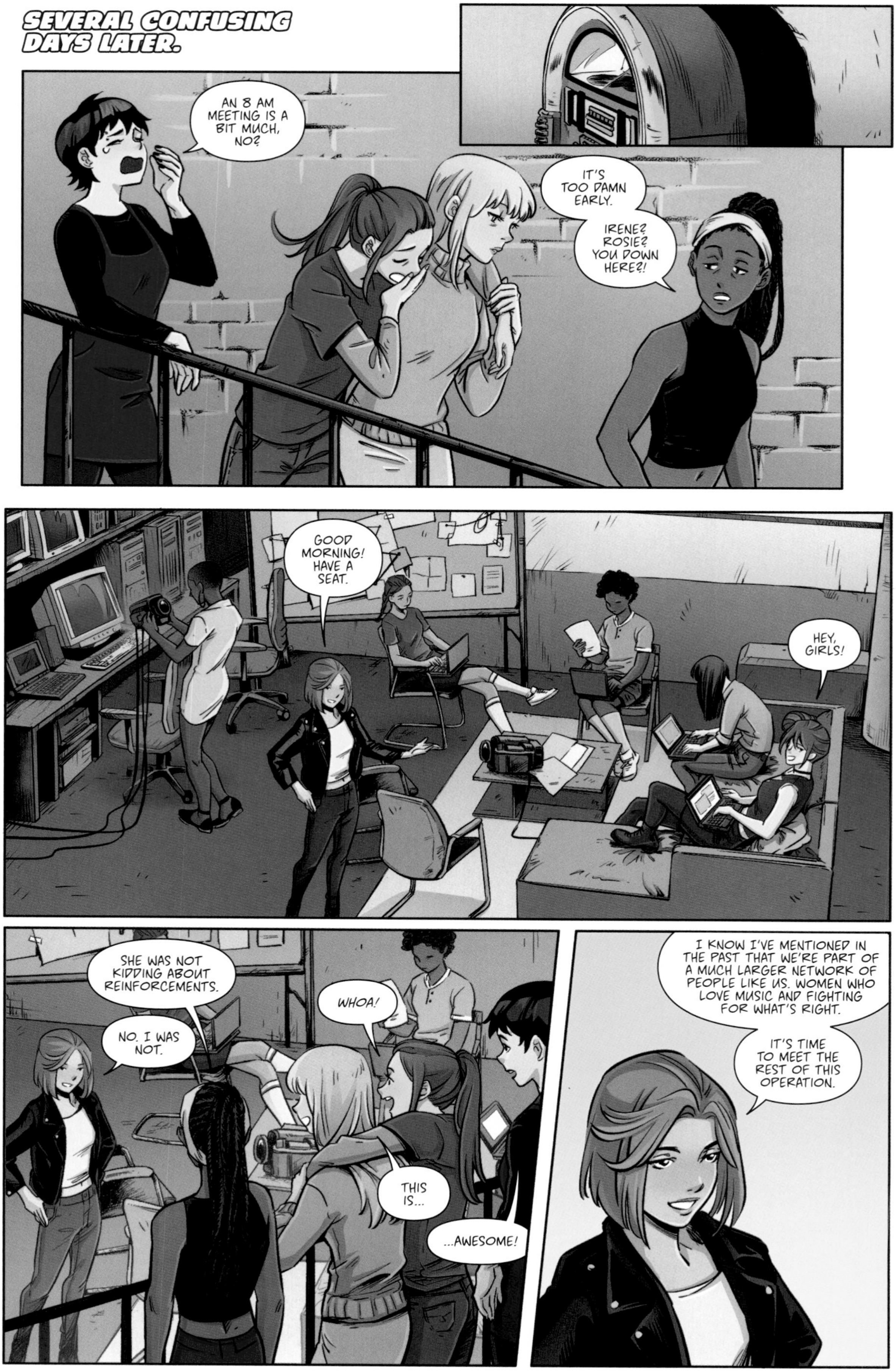
SEVERAL CONFUSING DAYS LATER.
AN 8 AM MEETING IS A BIT MUCH, NO?
IT'S TOO DAMN EARLY.
IRENE? ROSIE? YOU DOWN HERE?!
GOOD MORNING! HAVE A SEAT.
HEY, GIRLS!
SHE WAS NOT KIDDING ABOUT REINFORCEMENTS.
NO. I WAS NOT.
WHOA!
THIS IS...
...AWESOME!
I KNOW I'VE MENTIONED IN THE PAST THAT WE'RE PART OF A MUCH LARGER NETWORK OF PEOPLE LIKE US. WOMEN WHO LOVE MUSIC AND FIGHTING FOR WHAT'S RIGHT.
IT'S TIME TO MEET THE REST OF THIS OPERATION.

HELLO? IS IT WORKING?

CAN YOU HEAR ME?

LOUD AND CLEAR!

ROCK 'N' ROLL!

THIS IS IRENE AND ROSIE AT VINYL DESTINATION IN NEW JERSEY.

CODE VIOLET!

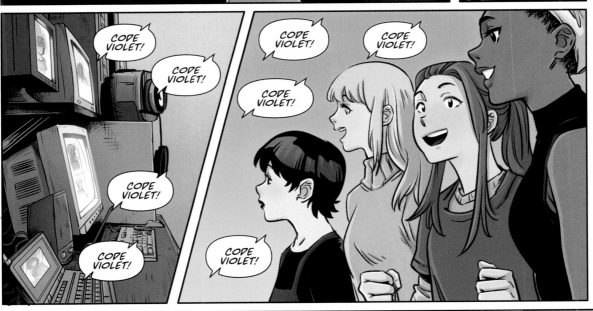

CODE VIOLET!

CODE VIOLET!

CODE VIOLET!

CODE VIOLET!

CODE VIOLET!

CODE VIOLET!

CODE VIOLET!

CODE VIOLET!

CODE VIOLET!

IT'S REALLY GOOD TO SEE YOU ALL. I WISH IT WERE UNDER BETTER CIRCUMSTANCES.

I TRUST EVERYONE GOT THE AGENDA AND READ THROUGH THE BRIEF?

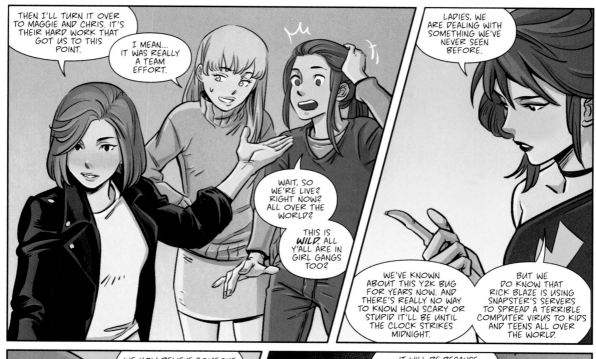

THEN I'LL TURN IT OVER TO MAGGIE AND CHRIS. IT'S THEIR HARD WORK THAT GOT US TO THIS POINT.

I MEAN... IT WAS REALLY A TEAM EFFORT.

WAIT, SO WE'RE LIVE? RIGHT NOW? ALL OVER THE WORLD?

THIS IS **WILD**. ALL Y'ALL ARE IN GIRL GANGS TOO?

LADIES, WE ARE DEALING WITH SOMETHING WE'VE NEVER SEEN BEFORE.

WE'VE KNOWN ABOUT THIS Y2K BUG FOR YEARS NOW. AND THERE'S REALLY NO WAY TO KNOW HOW SCARY OR STUPID IT'LL BE UNTIL THE CLOCK STRIKES MIDNIGHT.

BUT WE DO KNOW THAT RICK BLAZE IS USING SNAPSTER'S SERVERS TO SPREAD A TERRIBLE COMPUTER VIRUS TO KIDS AND TEENS ALL OVER THE WORLD.

WE NOW BELIEVE SOMEONE AT SNAPSTER IS IN ON IT, TOO. AND THAT THEY'RE WORKING TOGETHER TOWARDS SOMETHING BIGGER.

IF ALL COMPUTERS AND NETWORKS SHUT DOWN ON NEW YEAR'S DAY, IT PROBABLY WON'T BE BECAUSE OF A FEW LINES OF COMPUTER CODE...

...IT WILL BE BECAUSE OF A VIRUS THAT WILL BE TRACED BACK TO SNAPSTER'S SERVERS. AND THAT WILL END THE DIGITAL MUSIC REVOLUTION BEFORE IT CAN EVEN START. IT'LL PROBABLY DO A LOT WORSE THAN THAT.

RICK AND HIS BOYS CAN ONLY STAND TO PROFIT FROM THIS. SNAPSTER TOO, AS BACKWARDS AS THAT MIGHT SEEM.

WE GOTTA STOP THEM!

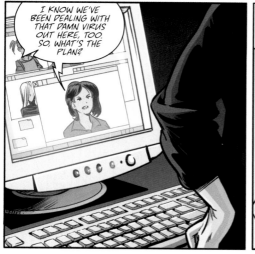

I KNOW WE'VE BEEN DEALING WITH THAT DAMN VIRUS OUT HERE, TOO. SO, WHAT'S THE PLAN?

WE'VE GOT A PLAN, BUT WE NEED EVERYONE'S HELP.

BUT WE HAVE TO KEEP IT OFFLINE. IF THEY FIGURE OUT WHAT WE'RE UP TO, THEY'LL FIND A WAY AROUND IT.

OLD SCHOOL!

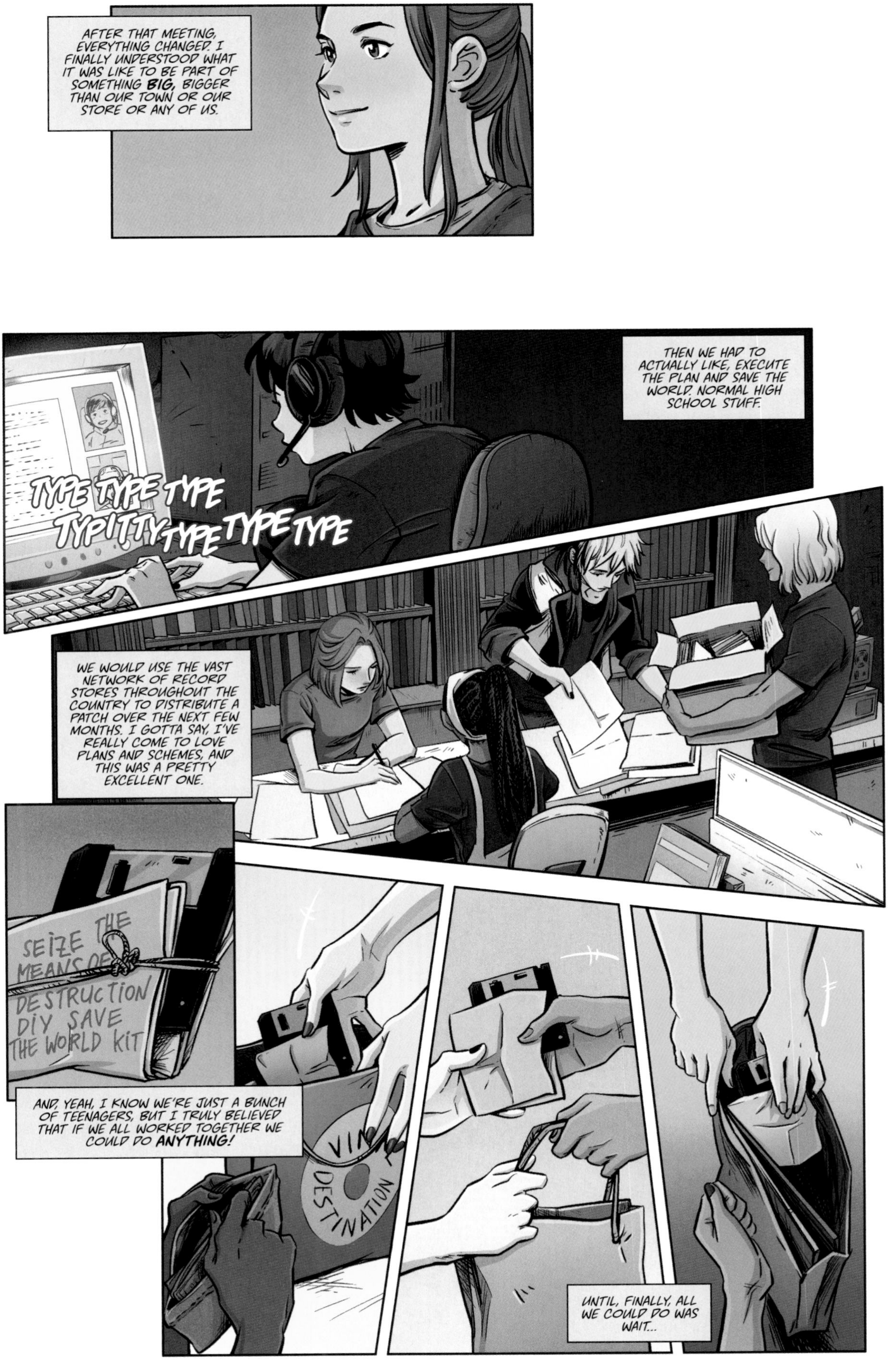
AFTER THAT MEETING, EVERYTHING CHANGED. I FINALLY UNDERSTOOD WHAT IT WAS LIKE TO BE PART OF SOMETHING BIG, BIGGER THAN OUR TOWN OR OUR STORE OR ANY OF US.
THEN WE HAD TO ACTUALLY LIKE, EXECUTE THE PLAN AND SAVE THE WORLD. NORMAL HIGH SCHOOL STUFF.
TYPE TYPE TYPE TYPITTY TYPE TYPE TYPE
WE WOULD USE THE VAST NETWORK OF RECORD STORES THROUGHOUT THE COUNTRY TO DISTRIBUTE A PATCH OVER THE NEXT FEW MONTHS. I GOTTA SAY, I'VE REALLY COME TO LOVE PLANS AND SCHEMES, AND THIS WAS A PRETTY EXCELLENT ONE.
SEIZE THE MEANS OF DESTRUCTION DIY SAVE THE WORLD KIT
AND, YEAH, I KNOW WE'RE JUST A BUNCH OF TEENAGERS, BUT I TRULY BELIEVED THAT IF WE ALL WORKED TOGETHER WE COULD DO ANYTHING!
DESTINATION
UNTIL, FINALLY, ALL WE COULD DO WAS WAIT...

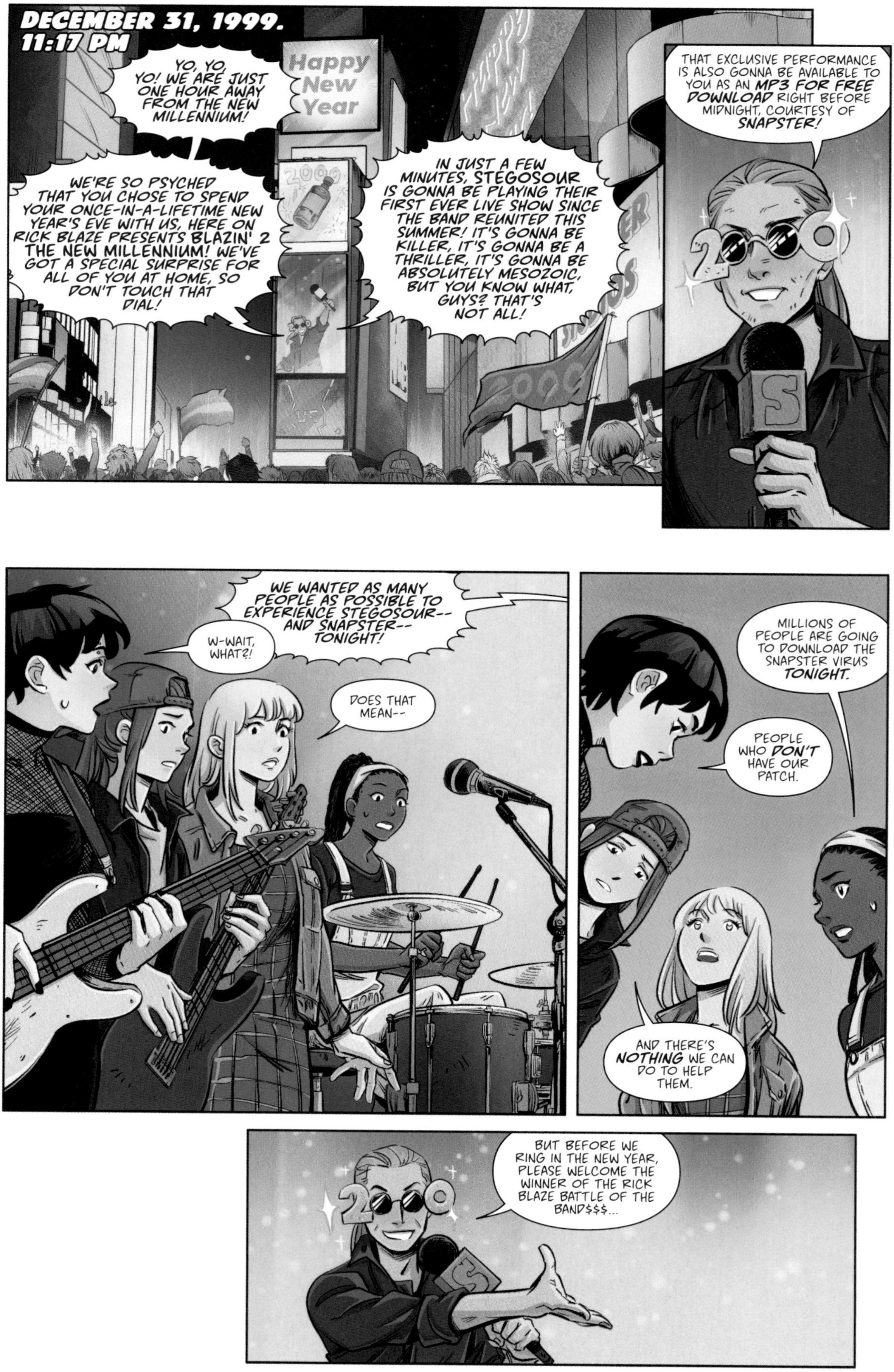
DECEMBER 31, 1999.
11:17 PM
Happy New Year
YO, YO, YO! WE ARE JUST ONE HOUR AWAY FROM THE NEW MILLENNIUM!
WE'RE SO PSYCHED THAT YOU CHOSE TO SPEND YOUR ONCE-IN-A-LIFETIME NEW YEAR'S EVE WITH US, HERE ON RICK BLAZE PRESENTS BLAZIN' 2 THE NEW MILLENNIUM! WE'VE GOT A SPECIAL SURPRISE FOR ALL OF YOU AT HOME, SO DON'T TOUCH THAT DIAL!
IN JUST A FEW MINUTES, STEGOSOUR IS GONNA BE PLAYING THEIR FIRST EVER LIVE SHOW SINCE THE BAND REUNITED THIS SUMMER! IT'S GONNA BE KILLER, IT'S GONNA BE A THRILLER, IT'S GONNA BE ABSOLUTELY MESOZOIC, BUT YOU KNOW WHAT, GUYS? THAT'S NOT ALL!
THAT EXCLUSIVE PERFORMANCE IS ALSO GONNA BE AVAILABLE TO YOU AS AN MP3 FOR FREE DOWNLOAD RIGHT BEFORE MIDNIGHT, COURTESY OF SNAPSTER!
WE WANTED AS MANY PEOPLE AS POSSIBLE TO EXPERIENCE STEGOSOUR-- AND SNAPSTER-- TONIGHT!
W-WAIT, WHAT?!
DOES THAT MEAN--
MILLIONS OF PEOPLE ARE GOING TO DOWNLOAD THE SNAPSTER VIRUS TONIGHT.
PEOPLE WHO DON'T HAVE OUR PATCH.
AND THERE'S NOTHING WE CAN DO TO HELP THEM.
BUT BEFORE WE RING IN THE NEW YEAR, PLEASE WELCOME THE WINNER OF THE RICK BLAZE BATTLE OF THE BAND$$$...

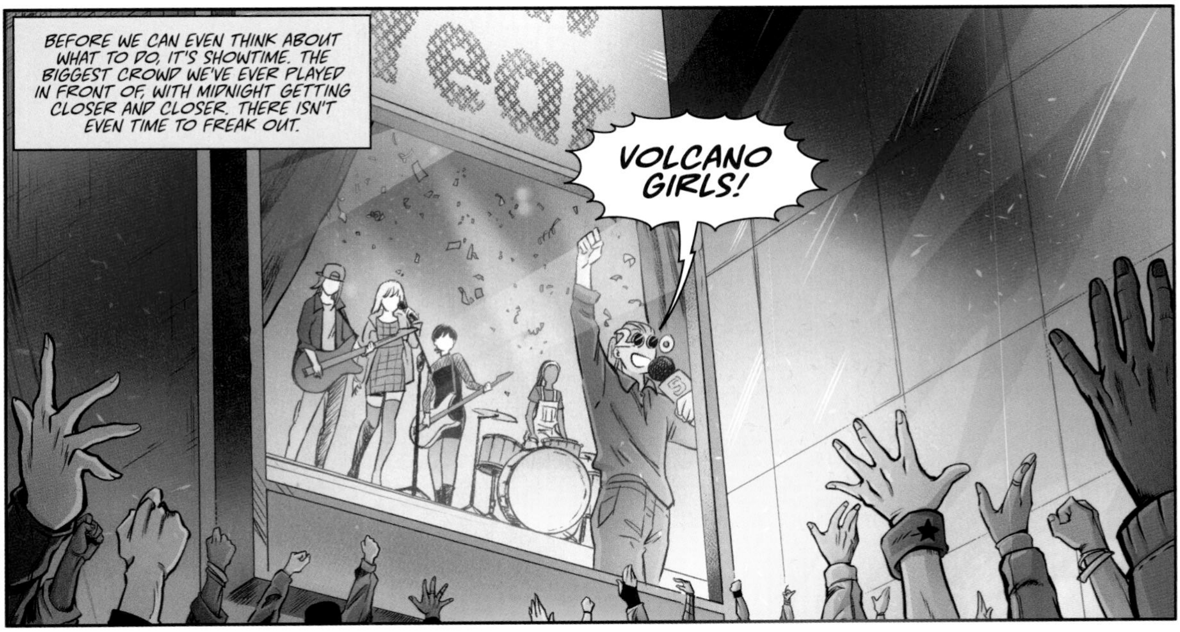
BEFORE WE CAN EVEN THINK ABOUT WHAT TO DO, IT'S SHOWTIME. THE BIGGEST CROWD WE'VE EVER PLAYED IN FRONT OF, WITH MIDNIGHT GETTING CLOSER AND CLOSER. THERE ISN'T EVEN TIME TO FREAK OUT.
VOLCANO GIRLS!

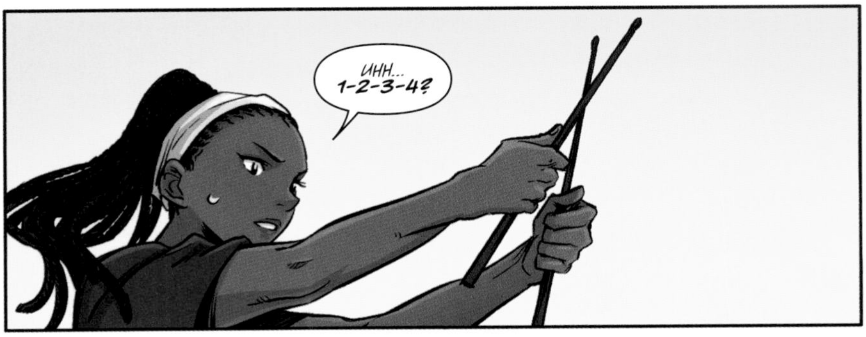
UHH... 1-2-3-4?

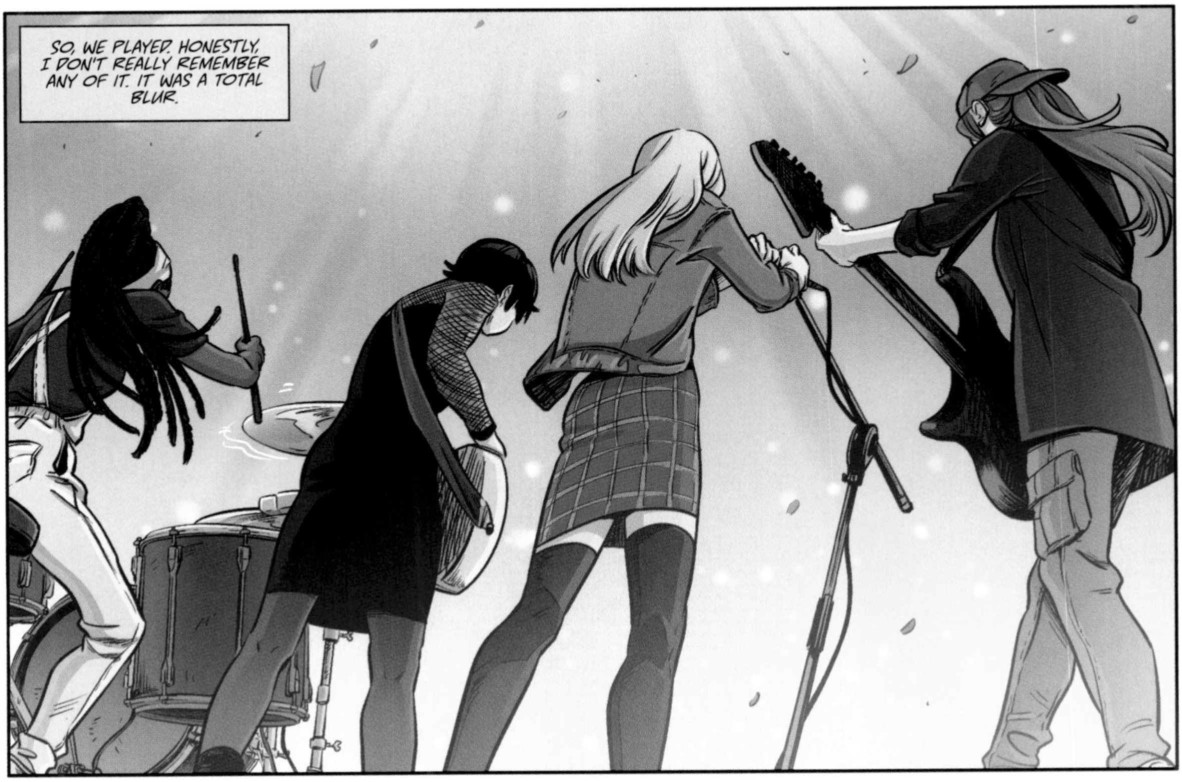
SO, WE PLAYED. HONESTLY, I DON'T REALLY REMEMBER ANY OF IT. IT WAS A TOTAL BLUR.

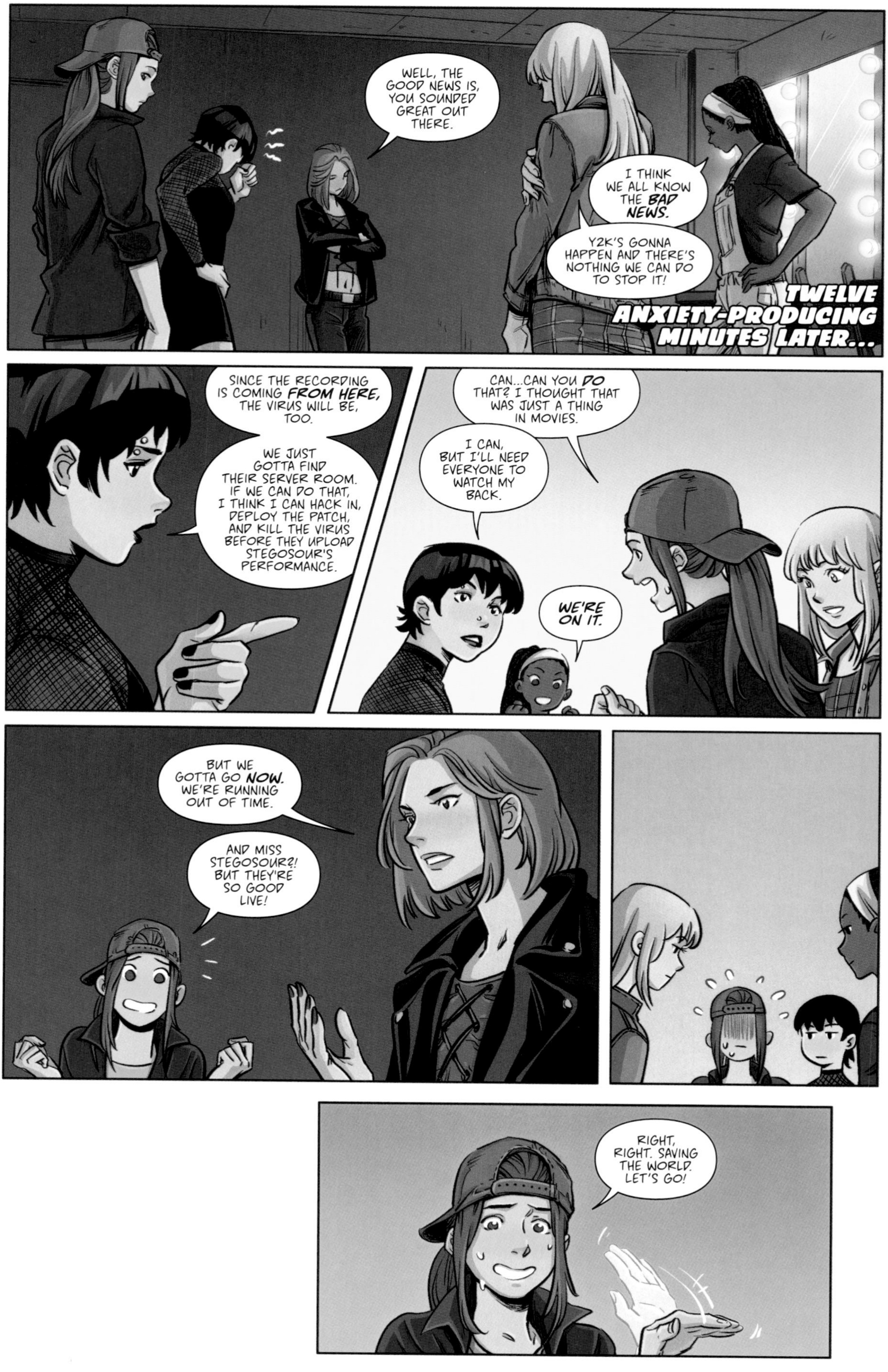
WELL, THE GOOD NEWS IS, YOU SOUNDED GREAT OUT THERE.
I THINK WE ALL KNOW THE BAD NEWS.
Y2K'S GONNA HAPPEN AND THERE'S NOTHING WE CAN DO TO STOP IT!
TWELVE ANXIETY-PRODUCING MINUTES LATER...
SINCE THE RECORDING IS COMING FROM HERE, THE VIRUS WILL BE, TOO.
WE JUST GOTTA FIND THEIR SERVER ROOM. IF WE CAN DO THAT, I THINK I CAN HACK IN, DEPLOY THE PATCH, AND KILL THE VIRUS BEFORE THEY UPLOAD STEGOSOUR'S PERFORMANCE.
CAN...CAN YOU DO THAT? I THOUGHT THAT WAS JUST A THING IN MOVIES.
I CAN, BUT I'LL NEED EVERYONE TO WATCH MY BACK.
WE'RE ON IT.
BUT WE GOTTA GO NOW. WE'RE RUNNING OUT OF TIME.
AND MISS STEGOSOUR?! BUT THEY'RE SO GOOD LIVE!
RIGHT, RIGHT. SAVING THE WORLD. LET'S GO!

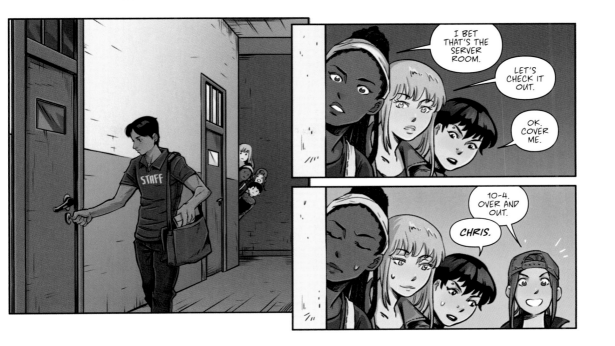

I BET THAT'S THE SERVER ROOM.

LET'S CHECK IT OUT.

OK. COVER ME.

10-4. OVER AND OUT.

CHRIS.

CRAP, IT'S LOCKED!

ch–ch–ch

HERE, I GOT IT.

CLICK

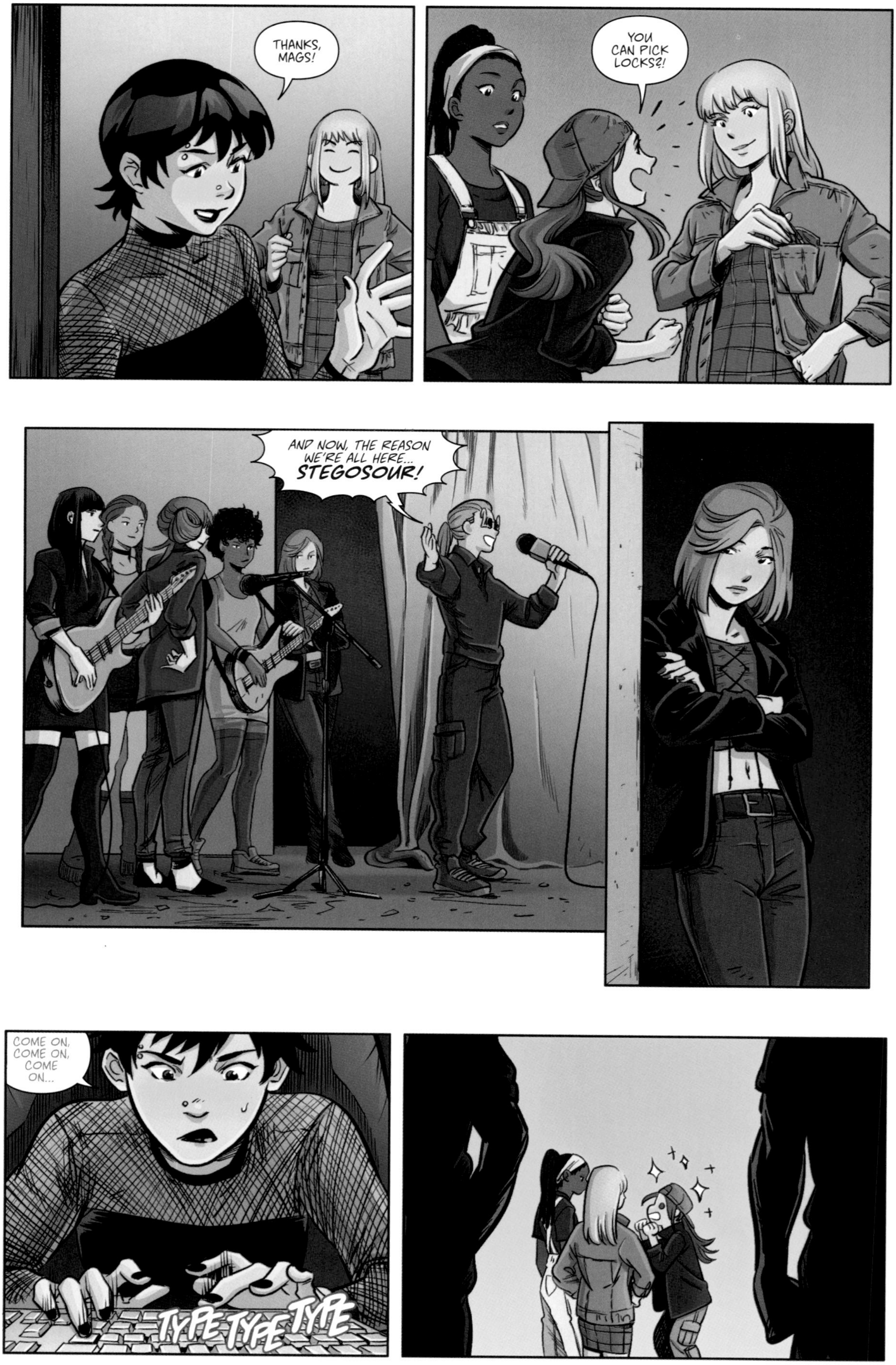
THANKS, MAGS!
YOU CAN PICK LOCKS?!
AND NOW, THE REASON WE'RE ALL HERE... STEGOSOUR!
COME ON, COME ON, COME ON...
TYPE TYPE TYPE

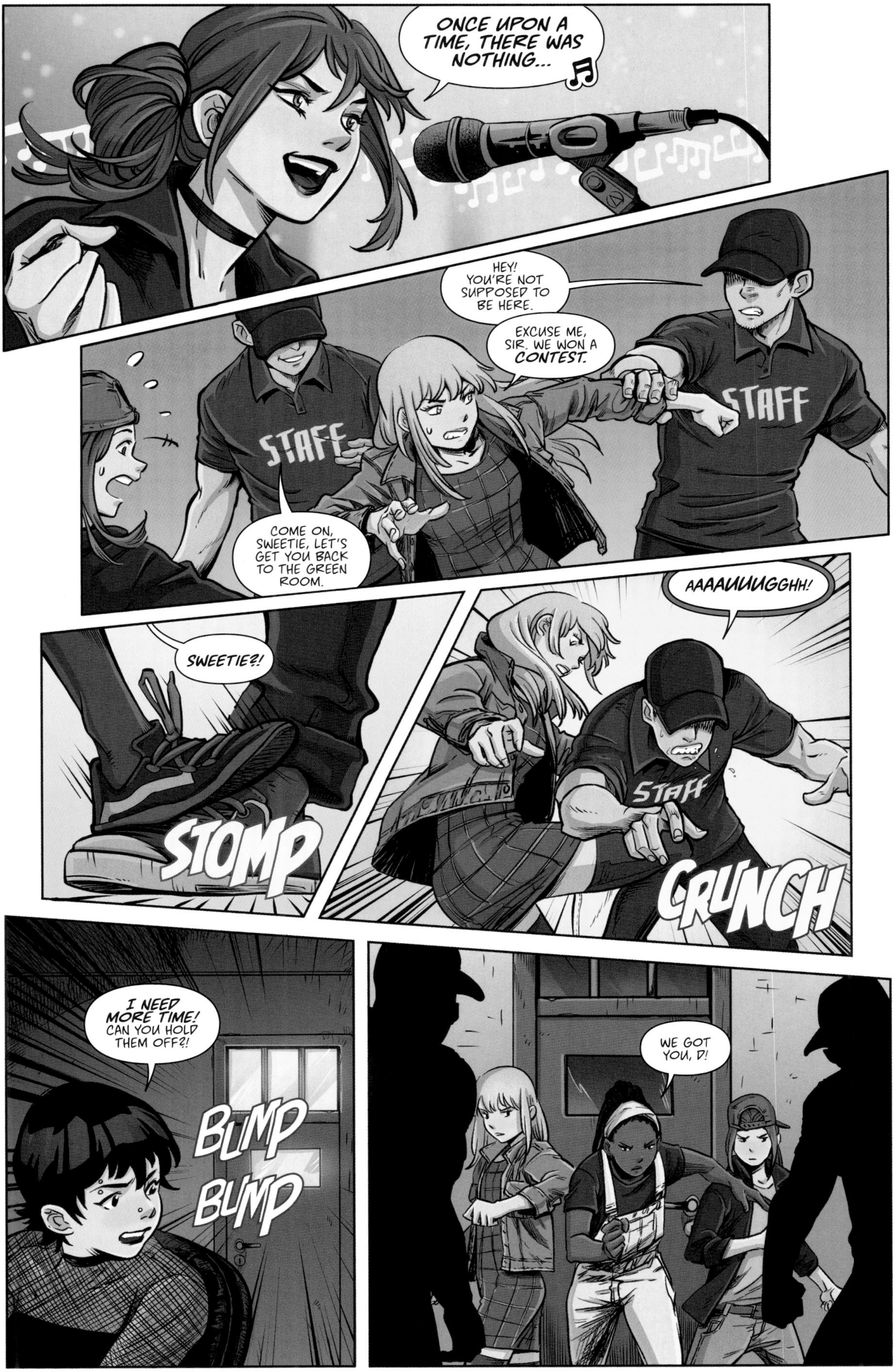
ONCE UPON A TIME, THERE WAS NOTHING...
HEY! YOU'RE NOT SUPPOSED TO BE HERE.
EXCUSE ME, SIR. WE WON A CONTEST.
COME ON, SWEETIE, LET'S GET YOU BACK TO THE GREEN ROOM.
STAFF
STAFF
SWEETIE?!
STOMP
AAAAUUUGGHH!
STAFF
CRUNCH
I NEED MORE TIME! CAN YOU HOLD THEM OFF?!
BUMP
BUMP
WE GOT YOU, D!

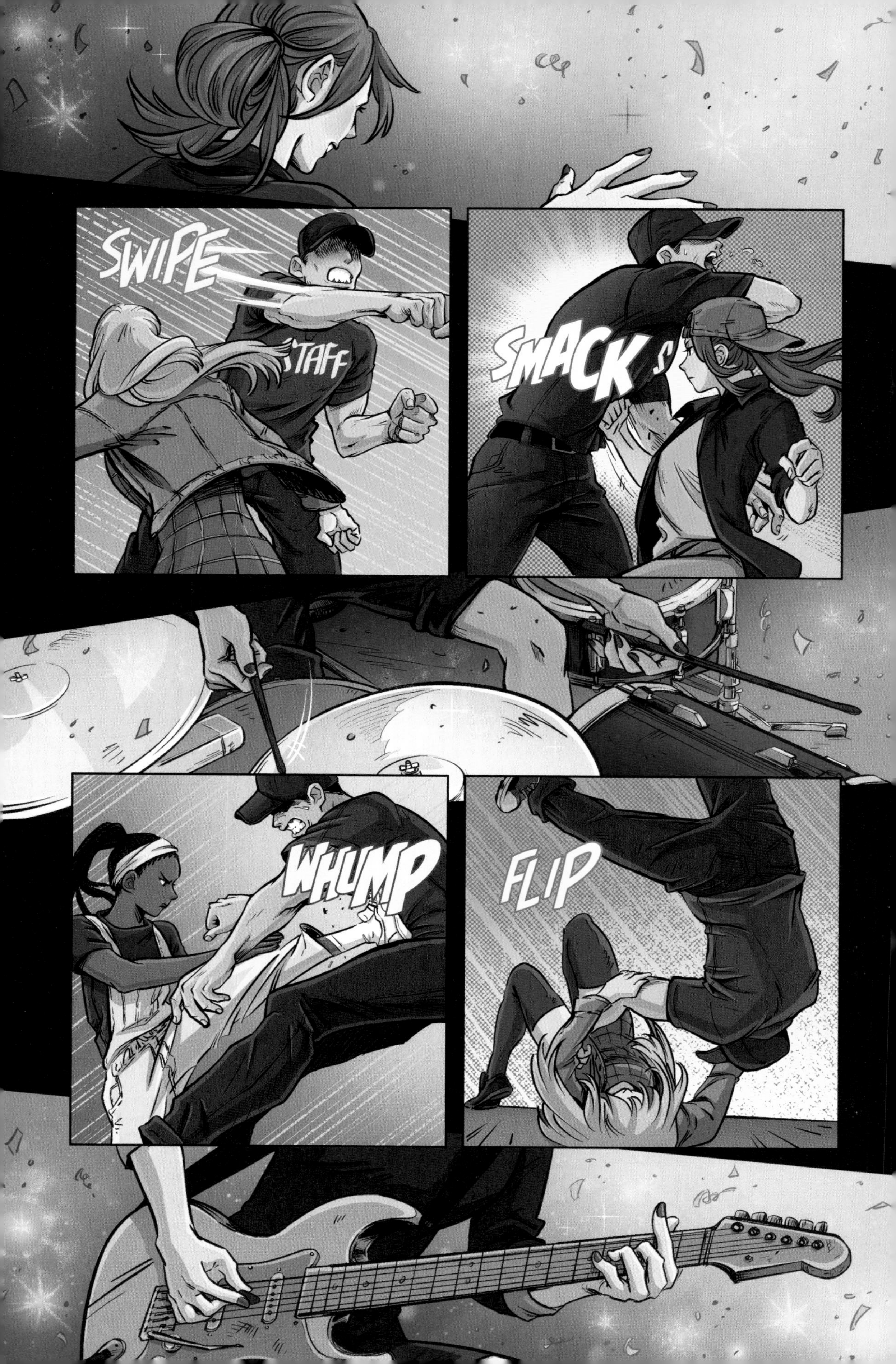
SWIPE
STAFF
SMACK
WHUMP
FLIP

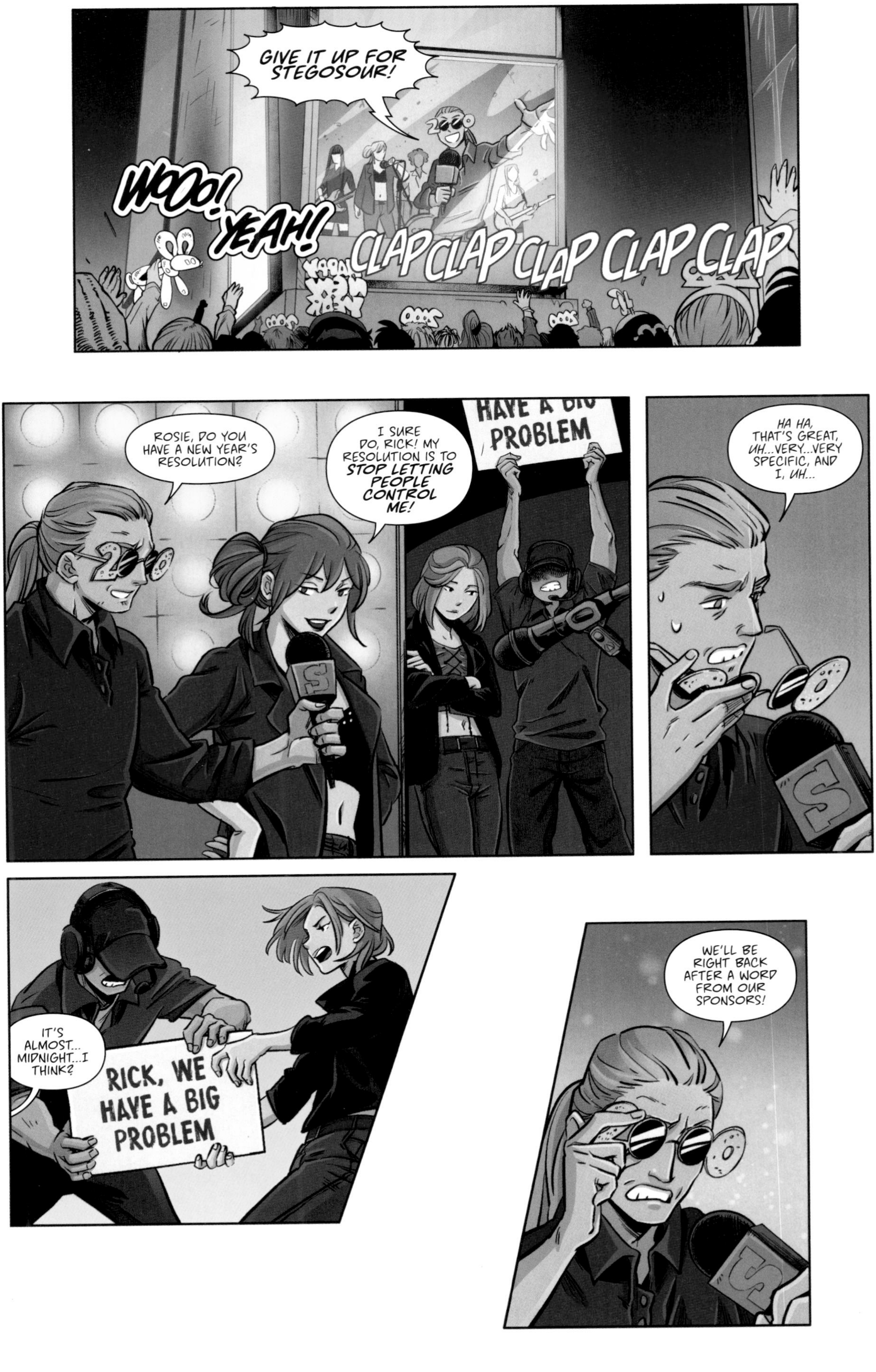
GIVE IT UP FOR STEGOSOUR!
WOOO!
YEAH!
CLAP CLAP CLAP CLAP CLAP
ROSIE, DO YOU HAVE A NEW YEAR'S RESOLUTION?
I SURE DO, RICK! MY RESOLUTION IS TO STOP LETTING PEOPLE CONTROL ME!
HAVE A BIG PROBLEM
HA HA, THAT'S GREAT, UH...VERY...VERY SPECIFIC, AND I, UH...
IT'S ALMOST... MIDNIGHT...I THINK?
RICK, WE HAVE A BIG PROBLEM
WE'LL BE RIGHT BACK AFTER A WORD FROM OUR SPONSORS!

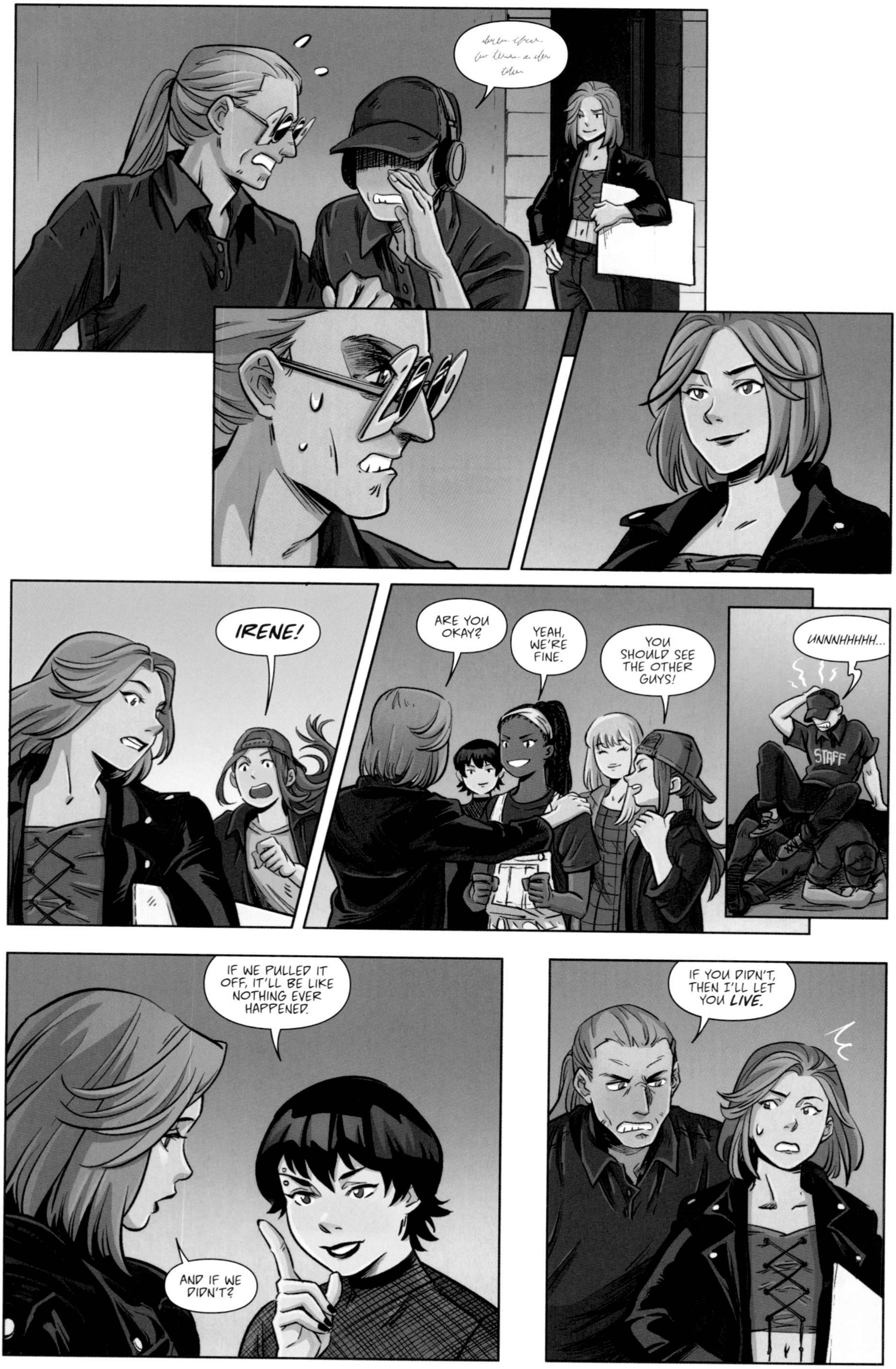
IRENE!
ARE YOU OKAY?
YEAH, WE'RE FINE.
YOU SHOULD SEE THE OTHER GUYS!
UNNNHHHHH...
STAFF
IF WE PULLED IT OFF, IT'LL BE LIKE NOTHING EVER HAPPENED.
AND IF WE DIDN'T?
IF YOU DIDN'T, THEN I'LL LET YOU LIVE.

AND WE'RE LIVE IN 5, 4, 3...

...2, 1...

AAAAAAAAND WE'RE BACK, AND JUST MOMENTS AWAY FROM MIDNIGHT!

LIVE COUNTDOWN NEW YEAR

PUT YOUR HANDS TOGETHER ONE MORE TIME FOR OUR OPENING ACT, THE RICK BLAZE BATTLE OF THE BAND$$$ WINNERS, VOLCANO GIRLS!

AND OUR SNAPSTER REP HAS JUST INFORMED ME THAT MILLIONS OF YOU HAVE ALREADY DOWNLOADED STEGOSOUR'S ICONIC PERFORMANCE!

OKAY, HERE WE GO!

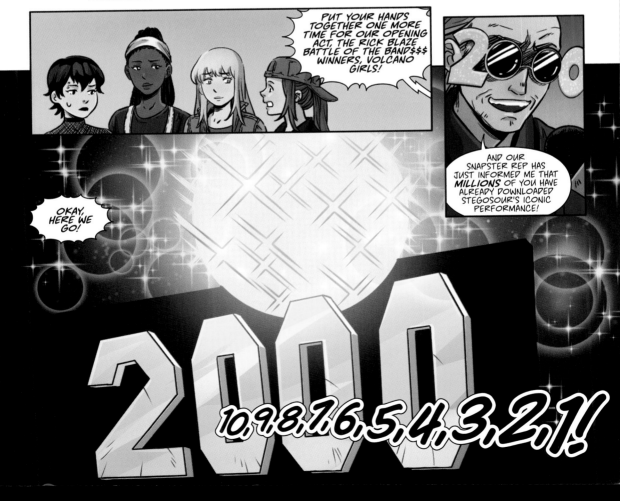

10, 9, 8, 7, 6, 5, 4, 3, 2, 1!

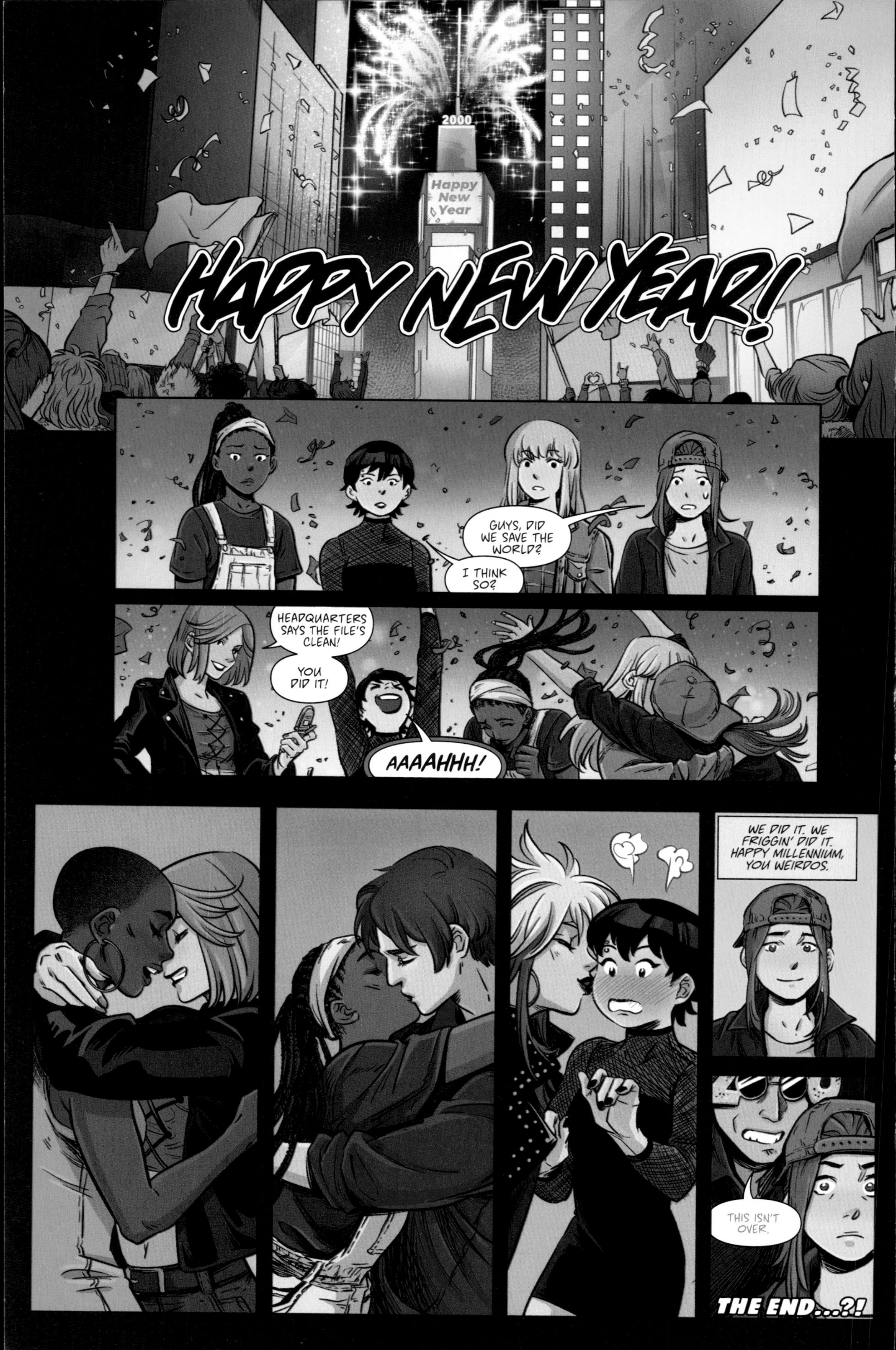
2000
Happy New Year
HAPPY NEW YEAR!
GUYS, DID WE SAVE THE WORLD?
I THINK SO?
HEADQUARTERS SAYS THE FILE'S CLEAN!
YOU DID IT!
AAAAHHH!
WE DID IT. WE FRIGGIN' DID IT. HAPPY MILLENNIUM, YOU WEIRDOS.
THIS ISN'T OVER.
THE END...?!

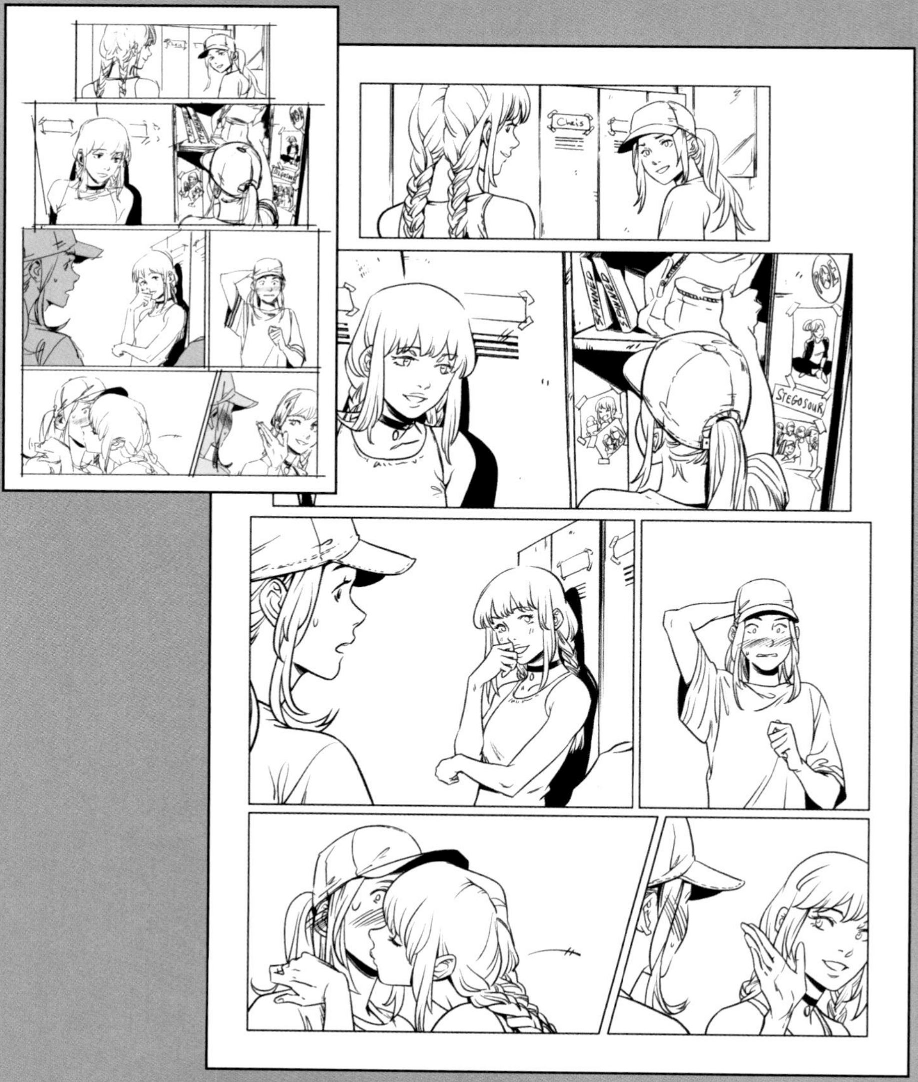
Chris
STEGOSOUR

PAGE 20

PANEL 1: Maggie and Chris are at the lockers after work. Scene should feel reminiscent to the scene in issue 1 when Maggie gives Chris the magazine with Rosie on the cover. The girls are being very affectionate whilst trying to unlock their respective lockers.

CAPTION: A hard day's work later…
CHRIS: Did I already tell you you look cute today?
MAGGIE: It might've come up once or twice.

PANEL 2: Lockers open now. Chris' locker isn't sad anymore, it's lived in, covered in photos of her and Maggie, a group photo of the whole staff, Stegosour stuff, etc. Would love to see a Poe star sticker. Chris is busy with her bag and stuff, Maggie faces her.

CHRIS: What are you doing this weekend? I was thinking of going to see "American Pie"…
MAGGIE: Actually I wanted to talk to you about that. My dads are out of town this weekend…

PANEL 3: They face each other. Chris' eyes are wide. Maggie smiles, a hint of shyness.

MAGGIE: So I was thinking maybe we could hang out at my place?
CHRIS: All weekend?

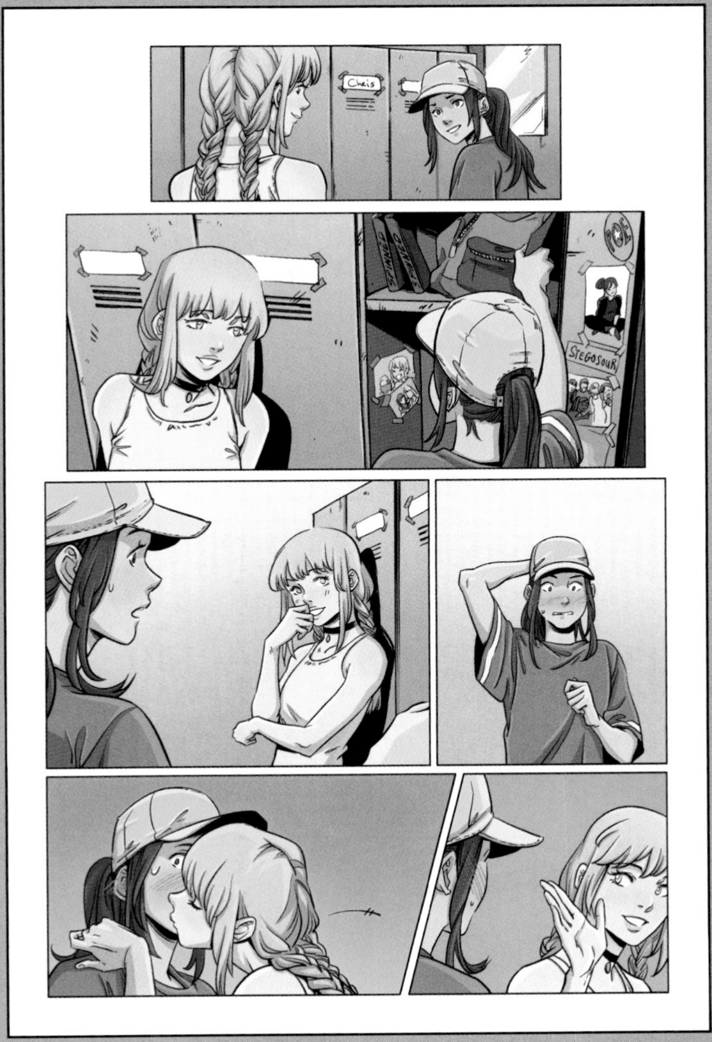
Chris
STEGOSOUR

MAGGIE: All weekend.
CHRIS: Alone?
MAGGIE: Alone.

PANEL 4: Chris is a sentient ball of flame, but manages to sorta keep it together.

CHRIS: Uh…yeah. Cool. I mean, I gotta ask my folks but…
CHRIS: That sounds…good.
MAGGIE: Good?
CHRIS: Great! Sounds great.

PANEL 5: Maggie leans in and gives Chris a kiss.

PANEL 6: Maggie leans back. Chris blushes.

MAGGIE: Ok. I'm outie. See you tomorrow.

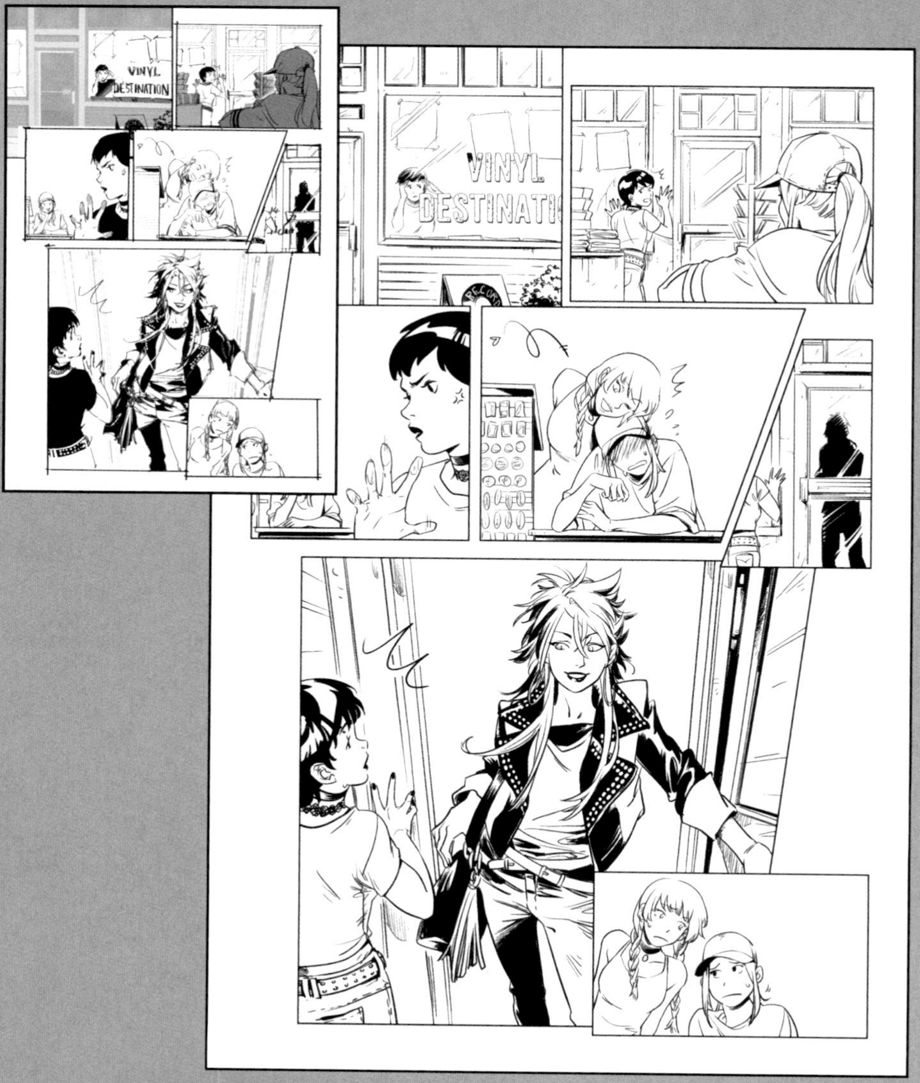
VINYL
DESTINATION

PAGE 23

PANEL 1: Evening exterior shot of Vinyl Destination. D is anxiously peering through the glass doors, waiting for someone.

CAPTION: The next night…

PANEL 2: Inside the store, it's almost closing time and pretty quiet. D is still at the door. Chris is at the registers, watching her.

CHRIS: A watched door never opens.
D: Ugh.

PANEL 3: D turns to Chris, who is being a pain in the ass.

CHRIS: Waiting for your girrrrrrlfriend?
D: She's not my GIRLFRIEND, she is a highly-respected radio DJ.
CHRIS: You loveeeee her.
D: I am not having this conversation with YOU, of all people, right now. Or ever.

PANEL 4: Maggie flirtatiously pops behind the registers next to Chris, leaning in close. Chris is all hot & bothered.

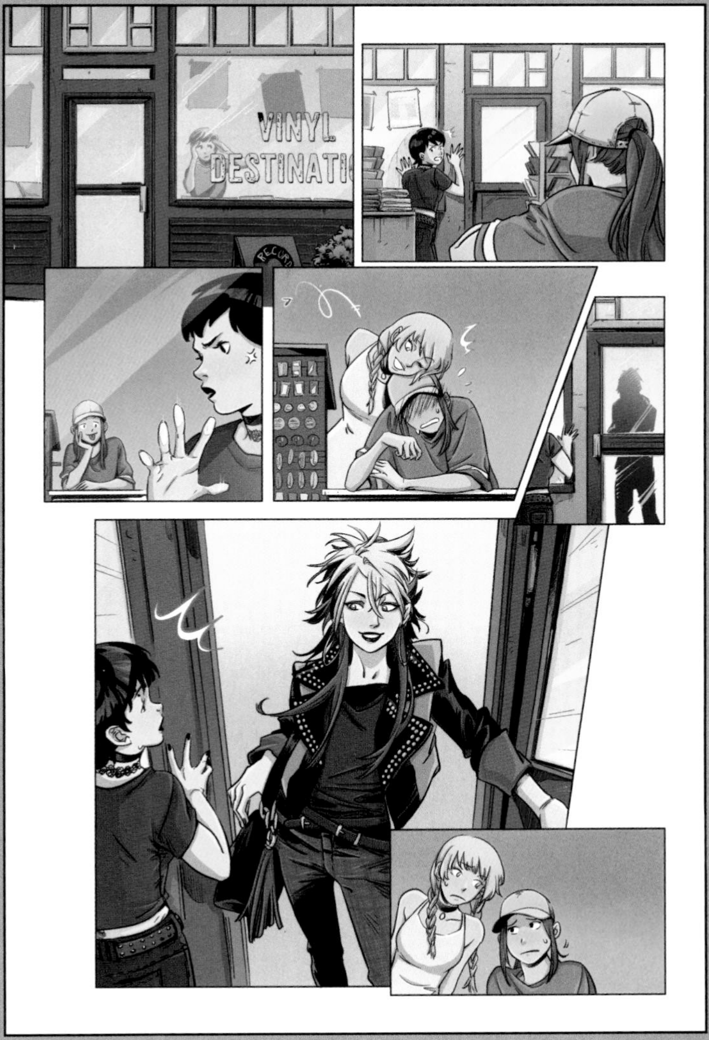
VINYL

MAGGIE: Aw, Chris. Be nice. D has a crush. You know what THAT'S like.
CHRIS: I…uh…what? Is it hot in here?
D: (possibly off-panel) I do NOT have a crush!

NOTE: the gag in this scene and actually EVERY scene leading up to this is that anytime Chris is in the background she should be continuing to lose her mind about her impending weekend with Maggie.

PANEL 5: Suddenly the door opens. In walks an extremely cool punk rock trans woman named Carmen. She's probably closer to Irene and Rosie's age, but not much older than college-kid D. Did I mention she's cool? She's the coolest. D absolutely loses her cool, sounding more like Chris than the D we know.

CARMEN: Hey! I'm looking for Dolores? I'm from Transister Radio.
D: Hi! Hey. Yeah. It's me. Uh, I mean. I'm Dolores. From Vinyl Destination. Which you already knew, because you're here. Right. Uh.

PANEL 6: Maggie and Chris exchange a look. This is painful.

Carmen: (possibly off-panel) I'm Carmen.
D: (possibly off-panel) My friends call me D. And you! You can call me D.

PAGE 25

PANEL 1: Back room of the store. Kennedy sits on the couch, writing in a notebook. It's quiet and she's alone, unaware of the comedy of errors that was just happening out on the floor.

      CAPTION: Meanwhile…

PANEL 2: Suddenly, Logan drops down beside her with a Johnny Waffles bag. She's happy to see him.

      LOGAN: Dinnertime!

PANEL 3: He gives her a kiss as she closes her notebook.

      LOGAN: Whatcha writing?
      KENNEDY: Oh just some angsty teen journaling.
      LOGAN: Good time to take a break?
      KENNEDY: Always.

PANEL 4: Kennedy puts the notebook aside as Logan sets out their food: burgers, fries and shakes. The usual. He's excited, full of energy.

      LOGAN: How was your day?

KENEDY: It was good. Unremarkable. How was yours?
LOGAN: Good. Busy. Some calls with school. Lots of shopping with my mom.

PANEL 5: Kennedy looks sad as Logan bites into his burger.

KENNEDY: I can't believe you're leaving so soon.

PANEL 6: Logan puts his burger down and faces Kennedy. She stares down blankly, messing with her hands.

LOGAN: I can't either.
LOGAN: I'm gonna miss you so much, babe.

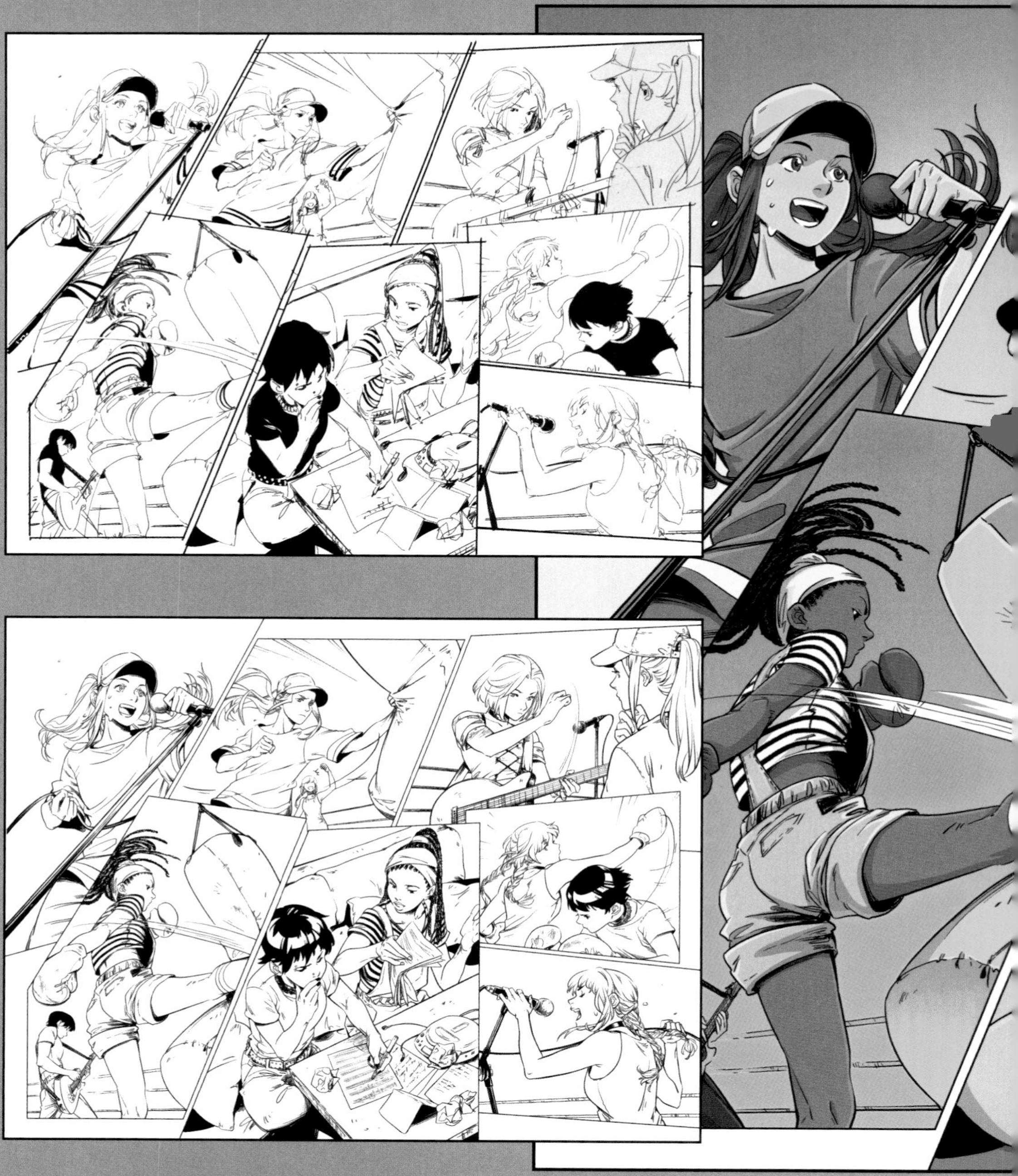

PAGES 28-29

An awesome band practice and fighting spread. Chris is singing into a microphone in one panel, punching a punching bag in another. Kennedy is kicking a martial arts dummy in one panel, giving sheet music pointers to a thoughtful D in the next. Maggie and D are sparring in one panel, Maggie is playing music in another panel. Irene is showing Chris something on the guitar. It is a FIGHTING/ MUSIC BONANZA!

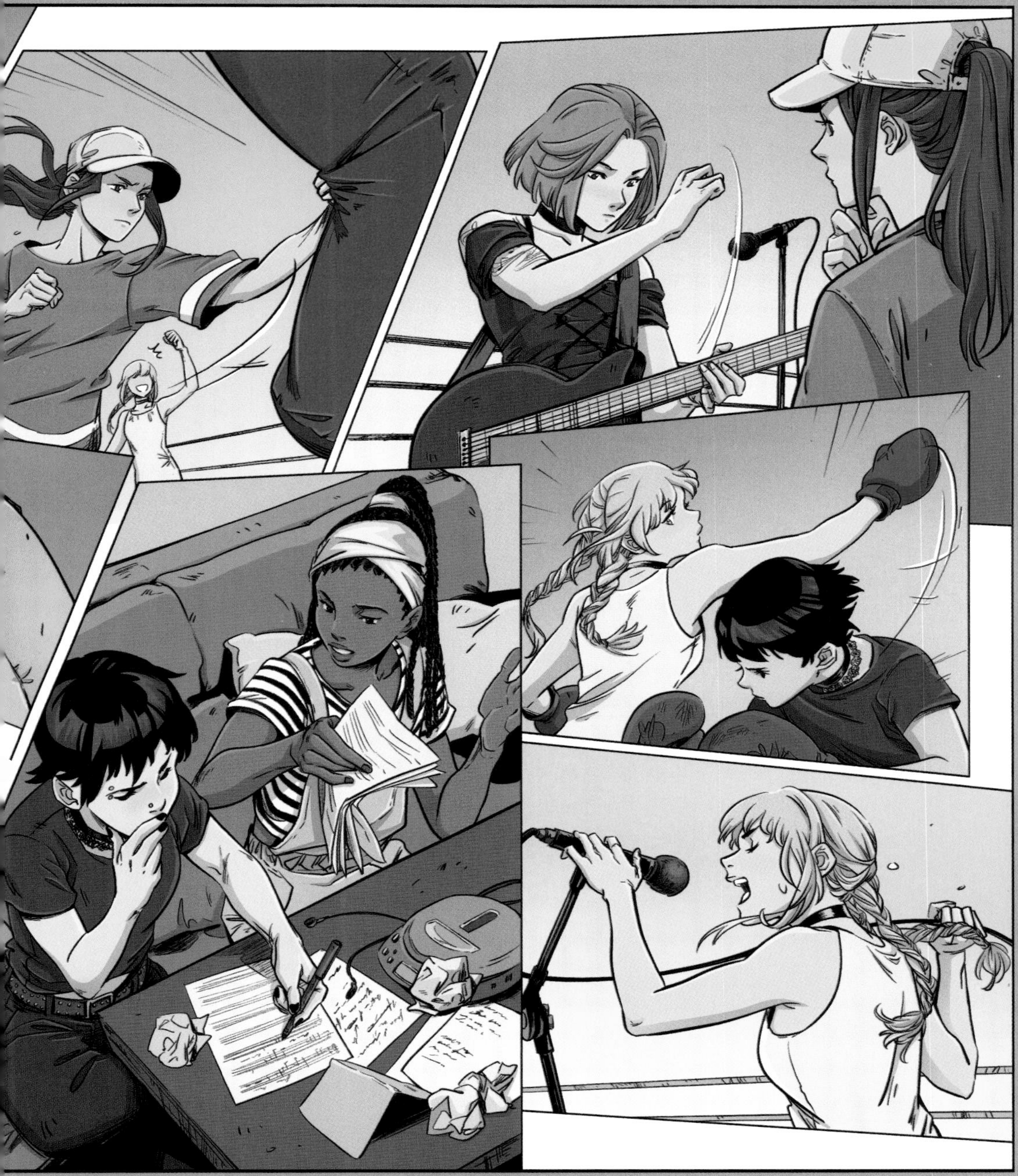

PAGE 76

PANEL 1: It's much later, everyone is exhausted and happy from partying as they stand in the middle of the room, most of the crowd has gone and Convention Hall staff are starting to clean up the mess. There's glitter and confetti and streamers all over everyone and the trophy. D is talking to Carmen and Kel. Kennedy and Logan are slow-dancing for no reason. Rosie, Simone and Irene are huddled together around a bar table. Maggie and Chris are being dorks with the trophy.

> CAPTION: After the party is the afterparty, and after that we go! to! bed!
> KENNEDY: Do you really have to go? Now??

PANEL 2: Close on Logan and Kennedy embracing (kissing?). *Behind them, Chris is trying to balance the trophy on one finger as Maggie eggs her on.*

> LOGAN: I'm sorry, babe. I have an early morning at school.
> KENNEDY: *sigh* Okay. I'm so, so happy you were here.
> LOGAN: Me, too.

PANEL 3/4 (IF NECESSARY?): Close on D, Carmen and Kel. Kel seems maybe slightly impressed by D?? *Behind them, Chris drops the trophy and she and Maggie both panic. We can also see Logan exiting in the background.*

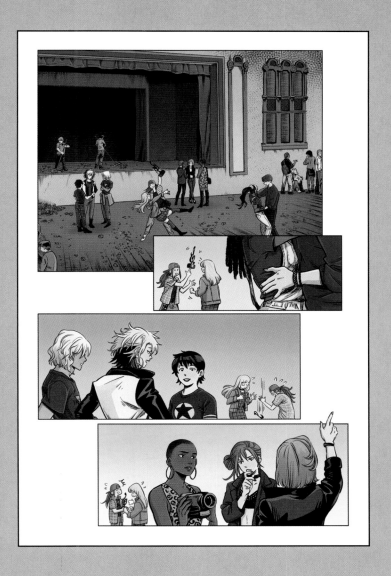

CARMEN: You were great.

KEL: Not bad, D. Not bad.

CARMEN: Is 3 o'clock still good tomorrow?

D: Yeah. I'll make sure all of your gear is Y2K compliant.

KEL: Is that a euphemism for something?

PANEL 5: On Rosie, Irene and Simone, huddled together, conspiratorially. *Behind them, Chris and Maggie examine the trophy and it is ok!!! Phew! Kel and Carmen can be seen exiting now as well.*

ROSIE: Oh, it was definitely weird.

SIMONE: I'll review the footage tomorrow.

IRENE: (to the girls) Hey, Volcano Girls! Quick band meeting?

DISCOVER
ALL THE HITS

STEVENSON • ELLIS • WATTERS • ALLEN
LUMBERJANES
BEWARE THE KITTEN HOLY
NEW YORK TIMES BESTSELLING SERIES

Allison + Treiman + Cogar
GIANT DAYS
VOLUME ONE

RIBON • FISH • PEER
SLAM!
VOLUME ONE

Hope Larson • Brittney Williams • Sarah Stern
GOLDIE VANCE
"Scoot over Nancy Drew..."
—Los Angeles Times
Volume One

THE BACKSTAGERS

TYSON HESSE'S
DIESEL
IGNITION

Lumberjanes
Noelle Stevenson, Shannon Watters, Grace Ellis, Brooklyn Allen, and Others
Volume 1: Beware the Kitten Holy
ISBN: 978-1-60886-687-8 | $14.99 US
Volume 2: Friendship to the Max
ISBN: 978-1-60886-737-0 | $14.99 US
Volume 3: A Terrible Plan
ISBN: 978-1-60886-803-2 | $14.99 US
Volume 4: Out of Time
ISBN: 978-1-60886-860-5 | $14.99 US
Volume 5: Band Together
ISBN: 978-1-60886-919-0 | $14.99 US

Giant Days
John Allison, Lissa Treiman, Max Sarin
Volume 1
ISBN: 978-1-60886-789-9 | $9.99 US
Volume 2
ISBN: 978-1-60886-804-9 | $14.99 US
Volume 3
ISBN: 978-1-60886-851-3 | $14.99 US

Jonesy
Sam Humphries, Caitlin Rose Boyle
Volume 1
ISBN: 978-1-60886-883-4 | $9.99 US
Volume 2
ISBN: 978-1-60886-999-2 | $14.99 US

Slam!
Pamela Ribon, Veronica Fish, Brittany Peer
Volume 1
ISBN: 978-1-68415-004-5 | $14.99 US

Goldie Vance
Hope Larson, Brittney Williams
Volume 1
ISBN: 978-1-60886-898-8 | $9.99 US
Volume 2
ISBN: 978-1-60886-974-9 | $14.99 US

The Backstagers
James Tynion IV, Rian Sygh
Volume 1
ISBN: 978-1-60886-993-0 | $14.99 US

Tyson Hesse's Diesel: Ignition
Tyson Hesse
ISBN: 978-1-60886-907-7 | $14.99 US

Coady & The Creepies
Liz Prince, Amanda Kirk, Hannah Fisher
ISBN: 978-1-68415-029-8 | $14.99 US

BOOM! BOX

AVAILABLE AT YOUR LOCAL COMICS SHOP AND BOOKSTORE
To find a comics shop in your area, visit www.comicshoplocator.com
WWW.**BOOM-STUDIOS**.COM

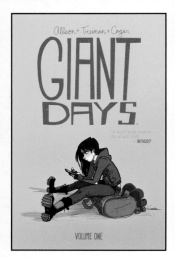